Warmonger President

World War Three

John Barnes

John Barnes

First Edition Published in the United Kingdom
in 2024 by aSys Publishing

eBook Edition First Published in the United Kingdom
in 2024 by aSys Publishing

Copyright © John Barnes 2024

John Barnes has asserted his rights under 'the Copyright
Designs and Patents Act 1988' to be identified as
the author of this work.

All rights reserved.

No part of this book may be reproduced or transmitted in any
form or by any means, electronic, mechanical, photocopying,
recording, or otherwise, without prior written permission
from the Author.

Cover Image: Stock Photo Secrets

Disclaimer

This is a work of fiction. Names, characters, businesses, places,
events and incidents are either the products of the author's
imagination or used in a fictitious manner. Any resemblance to
actual persons, living or dead, or actual
events is purely coincidental.

ISBN: 978-1-913438-84-5
aSys Publishing 2024

Chapter 1

She was placed in the conifers and when Darya Kam's eyes opened, she saw branches agitating rapidly above her. She felt the cold air hit her face—icy winds coming straight from the Arctic, whistling and howling. The whole Washington D.C. area succumbed to the storm's brutal, vice-like grip.

Kam's first thought was that an error had occurred during the transfer. It wasn't Archaia 7, the winter planet. Earth was a galaxy distant. *A wormhole malfunction,* she pondered. The logical conclusion. She was saddened by her misfortune, but the sights and sounds of the storm were a pleasant distraction. She loved stormy weather. The sounds of the winds through the branches lulled her to sleep and her heat pack and exhaustion did the rest.

Two hours passed, and Darya's eyes flickered and opened again. She tried to make sense of what she was seeing, and then she remembered. The powerful shock during transportation. A system malfunction. She remembered a quiet, warm place on a platform deep in space, and her male colleague for the flight, Lieutenant Commander John Bowerstk. His physique; his smile; his aftershave. There were visions of him watching her pre-flight. When she walked in, she thought he looked impressed by her looks, which of course wasn't rocket science. Purely human nature. Recollections of what now seemed a distant past.

The heat suit failed, and she sat up, and checked her flight suit for what had passed with her. She found equipment placed about her person. Tied on. There was money, weapons and means for survival. She felt better.

Across on a different galaxy and in a different sector of the universe, on Archaia 7, her co-pilot, Bowerstk, was facing other problems. The transfer placed him next to the entrance of a metro station in Archosk. It was the biggest city on the planet, and for hundreds of years it had an underground system. People thought it a refuge against nuclear war, such as the one which had affected the planet of Mysteron. For now, Bowerstk hoped it would provide protection against the cold.

For hours he must have been unconscious; at the mercy of anyone who had dared to check him and his flight suit for items of value. The city dwellers left him alone in the place where he sat. He was on a sidewalk next to the entrance to a metro station called Paveletskaya.

Two local stray dogs noticed him. Their barking and snarling woke Bowerstk, but also brought attention from the authorities. The distant sound of a police siren hung in the cold air.

As the sirens intensified, echoing around Paveletskaya, Archosk resident Paul Srour's attention was also brought to the man. He had been passing on the opposite side of the street. Paveletskaya was on the way to Srour's office, near the church whose spires and parapets grace the banks of the Moskva River running through Archosk.

Srour stopped in his tracks, because he could see that the man being attacked by the dogs was not from Archaia 7. Unbelievably, Bowerstk looked at Srour; the look was dark and menacing, as if he had singled Srour out from the crowds. What was strange, was that Bowerstk was the alien, and Srour was only reacting to his presence.

The local dogs catapulted events. There was a neighbourhood commotion, and the inevitable flight of the alien, pursued by the policeman.

The images of that fateful day remained with Srour. They were etched into the fabric of Srour's brain, like the inscriptions on the graves of his ancestors or of the words printed on this page. Srour couldn't delete the memories of those events, and neither would he care to. Why? Because the day Lieutenant Bowerstk arrived on Archaia 7, and into Srour's life, was the day when he saw for the first time tears in Helen's eyes.

Helen Moskva. To Paul Srour, she was "Lena" or "Anella" depending on the day and his mood. The morning of the day of Bowerstk's arrival on Archaia 7 was when he watched tears welling up in Helen's eyes, tinged and magnified with blue and green reflections. He saw her dark head buried in his tight embrace. He wondered, did she feel, as he did, that something would happen that day to change their lives forever? Had that been the reason for her tears?

He remembered how, the previous day, he said something which broke the spell of the two week long relationship. But that couldn't have been the reason. There had been no tears! How weak the unbalancing thread that holds together human lives! Helen had been pulling too hard, straining the thread, and now it seemed inevitable that the bond would break. But women have power over men as storms have power over the sea. Like storms, they change the surface, producing something temporary. The depths remain fixed and unchanging.

Without words and in an instant, Helen pulled him back into her orbit. Her smiling face and blue eyes had greeted him that night from the rain drenched streets. She kissed his wet face and ran her fingers through his dark, sodden hair. But still they did not make love. Theirs was a platonic love. They held each other that night, as every night, and for now at least, they glided each other's hands over the contours of their young, athletic bodies.

When Srour awoke, his eyes focussed on the rays of the Blue Star entering the window of the ground floor room Lena shared with her sister. The window had no curtains and the wooden slats of the blind hung pitiful, and broken.

On the morning transport to Lena's nearest metro, Temonia, Lena surprised him. She took Srour's hand, squeezed it, and looked long and deep into his face. It was obvious that she was searching. She was looking for answers to her questions, which, not coming, only weighed on her more heavily. As the transport pulled into Temonia, the Metro link, Srour noticed tears rolling down Lena's lily white cheeks. There were barely seconds for Srour to dry those tears before they had to get off the transport.

The metro arrived, and they pushed their way deep within a carriage. Lena pressed her body against Srour's, burying her head in his chest. Srour felt her trembling; crying still. The whole morning he had detected a change. A deep sadness is impossible to hide, especially from those upon whom one's life depends. But how could such a woman, who as far as he was aware, had grown up in Archaia 7, become moved to tears in such a short time? He wanted to know more. To question her. He pulled her head from his body so that he could focus on her. Again, he dried her eyes.

'Your stop is next,' she said.

'Meet me tonight, downtown,' said Srour. 'We need to talk.'

'About what?' she said, her fine features stretched into a look of concern.

The train was coming to Paveletskaya. Srour's stop.

Srour kissed her on her cheek and left, joining the moving masses leaving the carriage.

At the top of the escalators at Paveletskaya was one of Archosk's most crowded avenues. A huge, rude man in a hurry pushed Srour into a wall as he hesitated at the top of an escalator. Srour spun round, but the assailant was gone, lost in the crowd. Srour didn't know why he had hesitated, but for whatever reason he now wasted even more time in the tiny corner of the street where he found himself. It was there that he became aware of the alien being attacked by dogs on the other side of the avenue.

A cold shiver spread down the length of his spine. *What is he doing here? And why was no one taking any notice of him?* His initial fright turned to excitement. They had locked looks. It seemed to Srour there was a bond, and a reason for contact. Srour crossed the avenue.

His name was Lieutenant Commander John Bowerstk, and Srour tried everything to help him. Srour and he toured the length and breadth of the city in the search for a job for him. The alien was a big man and his occupation and provenance from Archaia 9 restricted the type of work he was able to find. Srour decided his best hope lay in the security industry. Srour was familiar with many of the city's nightspots. He even knew some nightclub managers. They began a more or less happy preamble through Srour's favourite haunts.

Srour noticed Bowerstk's attitude toward him change over the course of the days that they knew each other. First he was relaxed, happy even. Each day they began a new search. There was hope. Then, as it became more and more clear that the job search was going to be fruitless, the darker side of Bowerstk's character came to the fore.

The daily rigor was to drop Helen off by at her work stop, then to continue to Archosk Church and get the latest job offers. Each day brought fresh hope to Srour's new friend. He talked a lot those long, carefree, mid-winter days and Srour came to understand him. He was lost, not only in space, but also within himself. He did not, at that time, have a clear understanding of who he was or of his past. He told Srour he was a commander of a star ship, and it seemed to make sense. He was in great shape, and he showed a keen interest in the politics of Archaia 7, and in his surroundings. He appeared ready to fight or flight at a moment's notice.

After a week of searches something happened. It was the first in a series of events which led Srour to re-evaluate the wisdom of helping Bowerstk. They had encamped for the night in one of Archosk's busiest night-clubs. It was a place, Srour thought, which would employ Bowerstk on a cash in hand, no questions asked, basis. They had spoken to and made the acquaintance of the doorman. In turn, the doorman helped them to find the manager, a man who Srour already knew. The manager told them they were welcome to stay in his club all night, where the venue's tall, blonde waitresses plied Srour and Bowerstk with whisky. But no job.

In the early morning, they left and faced the bright, blue starlight. They were looking for their bearings on the empty street. Their bodies were weak from lack of sleep; but energized by a mixture of alcohol and energy drinks. The buzz carried them to a café on the corner of the street.

Taking seats at the wooden tables they ordered a couple of vodka red bulls and hot, burning, espresso coffees. There were several groups of rowdy drunkards who took turns to pester the lone waiter. As for Srour and Bowerstk, they chose to remain silent. They made short work of tall drinks before addressing the waiter for more.

'What's the matter?' Srour asked his new friend on seeing a troubled taint on the usual serene lines of his face.

Bowerstk leaned his huge body across the table, almost upsetting it and its deck of drinks.

'Do you notice something strange about this venue?' he uttered in low tones.

Srour looked around. Everything seemed normal.

Srour said, 'We are sitting in a café in the centre of the club district on an early Saturday morning. What could be more normal than the friendly drunken decadence which surrounds us?'

'Don't look now, but when you can, take a look at the barman.'

Srour resisted the temptation to turn his head.

'What is it?' Srour asked, doing his best with his peripheral vision. Nothing seemed less normal.

'Listen,' the flight lieutenant said. 'We are being followed.'

Srour's ears pricked up with his words and he fixed the flight lieutenant with interest.

'What makes you think so?' Srour asked, studying him.

The waiter passed the table and Bowerstk ordered a new round of drinks. Srour looked at the barman. Whether by luck or purpose the barman was staring at Srour. When Srour noticed his interest, he looked away, carrying on with his various bar duties.

'That's strange.'

'What is?' answered Bowerstk.

'We are of some interest to the barman.

'Haven't you considered that you may not be the only one with roving, observant eyes? He noticed you are different. Like me, he can see that you're from Archaia 9. Of course. You would not be the only one arrived from Archaia 9. But you have changed since your arrival. If I was to see you now, for the first time, I would not recognize you as different.'

'Then what made you recognize me the first day?'

'Many things. Dress, attitude towards your environment, the look in your eyes.'

'Do you notice something else about the barman?' Bowerstk asked.

Srour cast a glance in the direction of the bar. The barman noticed the look. But the barman appeared just to be working. He was washing glasses and serving the few couples at the bar, talking and joking with his colleagues.

'He's whistling!' said Bowerstk.

'So what?' said Srour.

'Well. That's just the point. Ever since I arrived on Archaia 9, people have been whistling.'

'It's not a forbidden activity!' said Srour.

'Maybe not, but that's how they let me know that they are here, watching me, following me. They're creating an environment of stress for me here in Archaia 7, that's all.'

'It's possible that you're reading too much into it. It's called coincidence,' said Srour.

'No. They're watching us, and following us. And now they know who you are now. You'd better watch yourself too.'

'What do you mean?' said Srour.

'Maybe you're one of them too. That means our "meeting" at Pavaletskaya was not so random. Maybe you were sent to get close, and make sure that I don't complete my mission.'

Which Srour found difficult to accept. After everything he had done, Bowerstk was thinking he was an enemy, not a friend.

That evening they met Lena after her work. They dined on fish, rice and dry white wine in a chic restaurant in the heart of the city pleasure district. It was Saturday night and the streets were full of people looking for a night out. They were looking to relieve the stresses of the working week through alcohol, dance and sex. The streets were lined by bars and lounges, and the type of clientele sought was evident by the beautiful girl photographs displayed on advertisements.

Not surprisingly they found themselves in a club whose underground rooms vibrated to Archaia 9's modern beats. There was a retro dance floor and they stayed there till the early hours, consuming copious amounts of Archaia 9's finest whisky. They didn't care about money. What they spent today, they could earn tomorrow.

Had Srour not left Bowerstk alone with Lena that night, in that club, things would have worked out differently not only for Srour, but for the whole of humanity. But Srour did leave Bowerstk with Lena. Talk about the butterfly effect! For him that night's events snowballed in a few months to disaster. For humanity, it led to strange salvation.

'Where are you going?' Lena asked Srour in the heart of the action.

'Just outside for some air.'

'Okay. Don't be long.'

Srour placed a kiss on Lena's lips, motioning to Bowerstk a gesture which escaped him. Perhaps it was the whisky, but Srour felt safe to leave her with him. He was big, strong and Srour knew he could handle himself in a fight. Anyway, Srour was only going out for a few seconds.

When Srour got back everything had changed. Not the music or the atmosphere. Heavens no. As if Srour could care less!

'What happened?' Srour asked, sitting down at the low table. Theirs was a dark recess of the club, and the table was replete with whisky, ice and mixers. Waitresses plied the areas between the recess and the dancefloor.

Lena looked sad. A look had crept over her face from God knows which quarter, and covered the happiness which had been there when Srour had gone out. She shrugged her shoulders. And though the dancing and the drinking continued, a change had occurred.

Srour didn't return with Lena to her room with the sister and the broken blind, instead taking a transport back to his home in Fryazino, on the outskirts of Archosk. Bowerstk had no job, and no home, so he took Bowerstk with him.

Soon after their arrival in Fryazino, Bowerstk began to talk more and more about himself. It was as if the atmosphere of the peaceful, laid back provincial town had succeeded in jump-starting his memory. His childhood memories came first. Just after the major star had set, while walking in the evening light which at that time of year took hours to fade, something out of the blue dropped from his lips.

'Paul, are all people bad?'

'What?' said Srour, hardly able to answer. If he did not know what had prompted it, any response would have sounded stupid. The potential to confuse his sensitive mind would have been too great.

'You know, I was when I was younger.'

'What? *You* were bad? I thought you were asking me about *people*.'

'I was. You have been kind to me. Others have not.'

They came to a small bridge over a turbulent river which ran beside a tiny forest of trees, and found a path leading down to it.

Bowerstk's words aroused empathy in Srour. He pondered as he walked. What had the flight lieutenant gone through before he came across him at the metro? 'John,' he asked. 'Tell me everything you can about your life, before I met you I mean.'

Bowerstk gave Srour a dark look, and Srour's first thought was to wonder whether it had been wise to ask him.

'I don't remember anything,' he replied. 'Only waking up on the crowded avenue with dogs snarling in my face where you first saw me.'

'Then how can you be sure that all humans are bad. Isn't that what you think? You have had too little experience.'

'Human experience? I've had my fair share. Although I am from Archaia 9, we're both human. Convergent evolution. You may see me as an "alien," at least you did once, we share human DNA.'

About the flight lieutenant's professed amnesia, Srour did not know whether or not to believe him. Bowerstk said he remembered nothing about his life immediately before the day they met. But could he trust him? He would never know, Srour realised, and accepted his words. He had his own reasons if he did not want to tell Srour the truth.

There was a wooden bench on the banks of the swift flowing river, and they sat and rested a while. Behind them lay the pine forest, and then came the start of the mountains from where the river tumbled. The evening air was cool, though the breeze had strengthened. It was setting the pine branches above and behind them into constant motion. The noise of the wind as it passed through thick branches transported Bowerstk to a place his conscious mind had long forgotten.

'I remember a life far from here,' the Lieutenant pronounced. 'The place where I was born.'

'Where?' Asked Srour.

'Mystis.'

'Mystis?'

'A city on Mysteron. A planet and a world where man lives in harmony. Harmony is the only ruler of his interactions with nature, with himself, with the mysterious, mystical spiritual realm. People of other planets merely dream of such interaction; such insight. To the men and women of Mystis, it is nature itself. We are born with it. Each has the 'gift'; the ability to see a dimension hidden to the inhabitants of other worlds.'

'And here on Archaia 7? Do you still have this ability?' asked Srour. 'You can see into the spirit world?'

The flight lieutenant looked at Srour with eyes which seemed to bore into his inner being. If one did not know that they were already friends, they would say the look was one of suspicion.

'I had lost it, but then it came back. The imperfections of the teleportation process brought it back to me.'

'So now you *do* remember? You know that you arrived through a teleportation channel? Tell me the truth.'

'No. I don't *know* it.'

A wave of new doubts assailed Srour. Why had he accepted the version of his teleportation arrival?

'I only remember two time frames,' Bowerstk continued. 'One is now. In the other, I have images and recollections of Mystis. I know I grow up there, and I remember its name. In the middle there is only void.'

Srour wanted to push him. Through pressure by whatever means if needed. To see if his story held up. Or whether he would present further indications of holes or knowing emissions. In the end he said simply, 'Tell me about your home, its people, its customs.'

'I remember ...'

He hesitated, and Srour could see that the flight lieutenant was crying. His lips and voice trembled like leaves caught in the evening wind on the branches above them. Unlike people from Archaia 7, Bowerstk's emotions were given free reign.

'My father and mother. My brothers and sisters.'

'What happened to them?'

'The nuclear war. That stupid, destructive war which the political leaders of Mysteron didn't know how to, or did not want to avoid.'

'Didn't? You mean they could have avoided it?'

The flight lieutenant looked caught up in thought at the question. Then he said with seeming conviction, 'Yes. Mysteron had received the wisdom. Our leaders knew exactly what they were doing. They were warmongering. Seeking conflict, not peace. You see, Mysteron comprised three political blocks. They vied for control of resources. Water. Food. They knew the danger of warmongering. Push hard for conflict, and you get conflict in return. For every action a reaction.'

'Like a cat,' said Srour.

'A cat?'

'I like analogies. They help understand complexities. If you stroke a cat, it reacts in a nice way. It returns good vibes.'

'Ah,' said Bowerstk. 'But if you poke it, watch out! Stroke a cat, and you get something in return. Exactly that! States are similar. Treat your fellow states in a respectful way, and you can work together. Liberalism, of course. Which is not what happened to the political blocks on Mysteron. They kept pushing for war. Realism ruled the warmongers, and they played out their zero sum games without seeming to care where the limits were. In the end they exceeded red lines, and a nuclear conflict initiated. They should have known better. After all, they had received the wisdom.'

Words ripped from his throat, against his will. What pain, Srour wondered, had caused such a transformation? Srour wanted to continue, to question his new friend. He was hungry for more insights into the mysteries of the universe to which he felt he was now party to. He said, 'The wisdom come from Archaia 1?'

'Yes. The nuclear war on Archaia 1 happened first, and in the same way. Political blocks. Imperialism. Hegemony. Warmongering by political blocks seeking to extend their reach.'

They got up, and walked back to Fryazino centre through the increasing winds and gathering gloom. The light was fading, and

Archaia 9's only moon rose in the east, illuminating their path in its silver, ghostly light.

Srour returned to Lena that evening. Early the next morning, when the starlight paled the eastern sky outside the broken window, a subtle ringing tone of Lena's telephone stirred him. He opened his eyes. Lena had chosen to sleep in her sister's bed, as she did when she was angry with Srour. They had fought earlier in the night. She had fallen asleep only after promising Srour that she did not want to know him anymore. Srour added it to the rest of his experiences with Lena. He knew her well. Tomorrow it would have been already forgotten.

Lena answered the call. Srour listened through feigned sleep. He listened as she told the caller the code to the front door. Then she hung up.

Sasha. Srour knew that name. The admirer. The rival. That much Lena had told him the evening before at the height of their argument. But Srour could not get his head around the fact that was staring him in his face. Why had Lena invited him to the small apartment? For what? Srour felt a cold shiver run down his spine. There was a hot, sweaty sensation seizing his body. There was one free room in the apartment, and it was already furnished with a bed. What was she planning?

Lena's sister came back to the room. She woke Srour up, asking him for one of the two pillows which his bed sported. He handed it to her and fixed his puffy eyes on Lena. She had gone back to her sister's single bed. She was sleeping already, but was it a real sleep, or one feigned like Srour's a few minutes earlier?

Hours later, at 7.30, Srour got up, made coffee for Lena, leaving it on the floor next to her, resisting the impulse to awaken her. He showered, his head swirling with the night's events. On the way back from the shower room, he pushed the handle of the free room, and found it locked.

Srour finished his preparations to leave, and Lena came to the door to say goodbye. He held her slim body close to his, and kissed her. Then he was gone.

That evening, after the office, Srour went back to Fryazino. Images and thoughts had been racing around his head the whole day. He felt tired and irritable. To stay again in the city that night would have only made matters worse. He needed a break. He needed to think, to figure out exactly what had happened during the fateful night.

Srour sent Bowerstk a text message whilst on the transporter and he was waiting for him when it arrived. He told Bowerstk about Lena, but that did not help him. He missed her.

Three days passed, and Srour thought again and again of that night. He read the signs, and they told him that Lena had a lover. He felt betrayed, and angry. Further proof of her betrayal came three days later, in the shape of a text.

'How are you? Where have you disappeared? Why didn't you call me?'

'In Fryazino. I thought that you have Sasha. And we are only friends. I love you this way.'

'Paul. To me so bad in my heart. I am tired of everything.'

Those words stabbed, like a knife, Srour's heart. He knew himself, and knew what they meant. For him now there could be no going back. Not even could he see her again. Why?

He would lose too much. The only way he could win was to keep the memory of her alive in his heart. A light remained, distant, at the end of a long tunnel. A hope that the circumstances of their break up, her fault against him, would mean that Srour would remain forever in her heart. If he was to see her again, that memory would change. It was a risk he could not take.

The loss of Helen "Lena" Moskva seized Paul Srour in his soul. He talked to his new friend to help bear it. To understand a different point of view; a spiritual one, not only what had happened, but her. To him, his new friend's description of the spiritual, mystical planet suggested a way to contact her, to see her again.

Srour longed also to see her again not only in the world of spirits, but in the physical realm too. Lena contacted him many times asking to meet, but he rejected those requests. She was better off without him, he thought. He would never know for sure to what point she had betrayed him, even if she did at all, but it didn't matter. He was and would always be a loner. She needed a man and a family. Sooner or later it would have broken, and this way she would not waste any more time.

Bowerstk was becoming more and more open during the weeks after the break-up. He and Srour talked a lot about his home planet and their hopes for the future. A welcome distraction to the pain of missing Lena, which weighed on Srour more than ever.

'What if we were to travel to your home city?' Srour asked, early one morning while they were still lying on their sleeping mats in the Fryzino apartment.

'To Mystis?' Bowerstk answered. 'Why not?'

Srour had thought he would have been hostile to the idea. 'You would like to?'

'Of course. It's my home. But how? Is it possible?'

'Leave that to me.'

Mysteron was a forbidden planet. Destroyed by nuclear war, it was in full rebirth mode. Rain had been seeded there by the scientists from Archaia 1. There needed to be a lot of it.

The radiation and the fallout had to be reduced to zero.

Journalists were needed to spread the word of the difference the galactic agencies were making to life there. Though not the most difficult to get to in terms of distance and cost, it was impossible to land without permission. Permission came usually in the form of a 16 digit landing code, which was hard to get. It was a code which changed daily. Transmission of the code prior to landing was needed. Then, the name of the captain and the ship had to correspond to that pre-arranged and logged into galactic agencies. Though approaching and landing on Mysteron was difficult, impossible it was not. Soon they succeeded in exchanging their sleeping mats on Archaia 9 for double beds in a galactic agency palace on Mysteron.

***

At the end of the first day Mysteron, Bowerstk told Srour, 'Lena has gone.'

They were relaxing at the Blue Bar in central Mystis. Bowerstk told Srour he would have to leave him alone on Mysteron, if Srour's intention was to stay there a while. The flight lieutenant's unit needed him back. They had messed up the transportation of him and Darya Kam, and it was not known where Kam had ended up.

'Gone?' Srour shrieked. 'Gone where?'

'Back to Archaia 9.'

'Why?'

'To cure a broken heart,' said Bowerstk. 'Science Centrale on Archaia 9 hired her. You know the work they do right? She has a new life and a new boss, her brother Colonel Richard Kemp.'

'You're saying she came from Archaia 9?' Srour's head was full of apprehension and sadness.

'Sorry. I knew it would hurt you. If you had made love to her, you would have known it.'

Only one thing weighed more on Srour than his pain at hearing that Lena had needed to mend a broken heart. A broken heart that he had caused. He needed to know what work she was involved with. He fixated the flight lieutenant's dark eyes across a table replete with Mysteron's best whisky and mixers, and said, 'Tell me this. What work does Lena do for her brother, this Colonel Kemp?'

'That, my friend, is classified. But I can tell you what everyone knows. Archaia 9's Science Centrale is engaged in one field. A singular activity. Deterministic prediction. In other words, the ability to influence events on other human inhabited planets in the near galaxies.'

'And for what purpose?' asked Srour.

'To prevent other planets going the same way as Archaia 1.'

Chapter 2

The chill bit deep in the hollow between the snow drifts in the conifer strand. Darya Kam was wide awake. She was deliberate and attentive, and watching the Potomac at the foot of the slope. She noted its slow waters half visible through gaps in the conifers.

Kam twisted around, looking in the opposite direction, or tried to. She felt something snag. A piece of the heat pack, she thought. The building across the field was more mansion than house. It had a classic façade. *French Renaissance*, thought Kam. It reminded her of the Louvre, Paris. She had seen images in the training.

Time to make a move, and she made to get up, and again felt the object in her clothing snag. She unzipped the panel, and extracted the object.

It was a radio-transmitter, and she remembered it from the training. There was a headset, and she recalled that there would be a recorded message. She felt stupid for not having checked her clothing earlier, but then remembered. The transportation was playing games with her memory. It was normal not to remember the first thing to do on awakening. That was why they designed it to snag.

She extracted the radio-transmitter, and plugged in the headset, placing the earphones on. She flicked the switch, and recognised the voice of her trainer, a man who had grown up on Mysteron. She listened to his instructions, unable to withhold a gasp of surprise. *How could they know that I would be here, under conifers between a field, a house and the Potomac?* So the transport to Earth was not a mistake after all. She terminated the message, and as instructed, she threw the radio-transmitter into the snow. She heard it explode. A muffled thud.

The conifers near the mansion formed a grove. They were large, and they had big, strong branches. The wind had eddied around the mansion, and the largest conifer of the grove had very little snow adhering to its thick branches. Kam realised the branches would make climbing it easy, and felt fate had smiled on her. Or was it all known? Predetermined?

She climbed when the gusts of the hurricane, the snow and the cold allowed her to. There was also the lights which swept the vast garden, and every now and then she flattened herself to the tree to prevent anyone seeing her. Finally, she arrived in position, wedged in the upper branches. With her hands free, she scanned the house her big, dark eyes glued to powerful binoculars. First the façade, and then the river to the right. Then the fields of the park which extended down to it. Nothing.

Which made sense, she thought. There were still some minutes to go.

She had purchased the Omega in the morning. After listening to the message. She had discovered money, and figured she needed essentials. Omega watch. Binoculars. A warm black leather jacket. All pre-determined, she figured.

She had moved back to the conifer by 10 am. McClean had been good for splashing her cash. The watch, because she needed a precise timekeeper. The jacket, because she had been cold in the conifers. The oversized garment looked large, but she liked it. The Omega had a red, sweep second hand and now she was watching as it ticked down the seconds to the zero hour. 10.44 am.

The final seconds ticked away, and a movement caught her eye. It came from down on the right; where the Potomac ran through Eucalyptus trees. She focused the binoculars on the spot, and saw a tall man.

Six foot, she thought. Or 6 foot 2. He looked warm, despite the blizzard, He had black pants and jacket, and he was moving towards the mansion. She caught her breath; *the exact time and location!*

The man used a red-bricked wall for cover. It plunged a part of the lawn into shadow from the river. He was checking his bases. Then he advanced to the façade, and went to each window. One at a time, trying each before moving onto the next. Then one of the windows opened. He climbed in and disappeared.

Kam climbed down from her vantage point and approached the house. Slow and assured. Confident. There was a line of low bushes and small trees which plunged the lawn into shadows. Their boughs were waving up and down and they were full of snow. She was aware that the sound of the wind was filling her with pleasure. Then it happened.

Four shots in quick succession. She looked down at her wrist. The time was spot on.

Chapter 3

Colonel Richard Kemp accelerated the proton sports car to near the speed limit of the steepening straight. Archaia 9 City was in his rear view mirror. Ahead were the White Mountains, and their snows had receded. It was the height of summer on the planet of Archaia 9.

The road curved left, and then became a two in one gradient. Ahead was the mountain palace, his childhood home. He had left Science Central in the early evening, and now he had thirty five minutes left to get to the palace. He wasn't going to miss a single second. All three triplets would be there, Captain Zena, Helen "Lena" Moskva, recently returned from Archaia 7, and him

Their connection went further than blood. The people of Archaia 9 knew of their "powers." He, Zena and Lena did not conceal their abilities when the story first broke. Lena had returned from Archaia 7, and she was back working at Science Central on the deterministic predictor.

Kemp skidded to a halt in the parking lot. Above the parking, for two hundred meters, the iron ladders soared. Soon his hands clung like vices to the steel rungs. Around him, the mountain air was warm and clean.

On the last section of the ladders, he felt exhilarated. Soon, Zena, him and Lena would be all together for the first time in years. He wasn't going to let anyone or anything come between him and his sisters. Soon enough, he was striding onto the cool grass of the terrace, the viewing platform, between the palace and the cliff above the ladders.

'You made it!'

Zena jumped up from her towel. She ran barefoot across the grass, to the strand of conifers which clung to the cliff at the point where the ladder ended, and swung into the arms of her triplet. The bear hug lasted longer than usual.

'With a meeting like this at stake, was that ever in doubt?'

Back down in Archia 9 City, and in a laboratory of Science Central, a feeling of helplessness gnawed at Helen "Lena" Moskva. From the window of the second floor office, she watched as the minor star set behind the mountains. A thin veil of cirrus cloud formed above its jagged, snowy peaks. They seemed close at hand. The humidity, a giant lens. The dark 32 year old with lily white skin and fine features was used to interpreting the signs through which nature routinely indicates its immediate future. To her it was second nature. Since her return from Archia 7, she had re-joined the research effort, and her gift was more obvious than ever. She had no doubt that she had been helped in no small way by the theoretical and physical research effort her brother had completed. But at that moment, her determinist sense was telling her only one thing: if the professor failed to come in the next 10 seconds, she would be late. It wasn't every day that a text was sent to the other side. She was ready for the follow up.

The other side, thought Lena. What a joke. For us, its opposite in every way. Anti-matter. Anti-neutrons. Name it. For them, it's us who are "exotic".

The office door swung open and her boss, Professor Etruich, a man who seemed to be in a constant hurry, breezed into his office, so she put her thoughts on hold.

'Lena, thanks for waiting. Sorry to keep you. Oh, no! Please! Don't get up.'

Lena hid her frustration. She allowed her face to blossom into a smile as he drew close. She said, 'I was told to come to see you before leaving today.'

'Yes. That's right,' replied the professor. 'You know, these are heady times.' His hair, a massive expanse of white, blew across his face in the growing breeze which entered the room from an open window. 'We will be famous,' he pronounced.

'Professor,' replied Lena, 'The machine is far from fully tested. The fact that we sent a text to Earth does not mean we will succeed in preventing what they will term their Third World War.'

'You forget, I have ultimate hope, Ms Moskva.'

'But ...'

'Please ...!' The professor was holding a finger in the air. It succeeded in freezing Lena mid-sentence.

'Ask yourself. Has your ability, your gift, call it what you want, ever failed you?'

'Well ..., No,' replied Lena.

'Precisely! So neither will our machine. We will prove empirically what generations of theoretical professors both here, on Earth, on Polaris, and Archaia 1 have failed to prove experimentally.'

'Which is?'

'That in any completely closed system, if one can measure completely the mass and velocities of every atom, one can predict the future. Free will is dead. Long live determinism!'

Lena had not taken her eyes off the professor since he had started ranting, and regarded him still. She considered with care what he had said. Was he, she wondered, as crazy as the other researchers in the secret Deterministic Research Institute made out?

Two hours later, Lena was approaching the top of the ladders. She was soaked. Her white knuckled fists clung to the cold steel of the ladder, the only access route to the mountain lodge owned for generations by her family. She had made good time to that point thanks mainly to the nimble hydrogen sports car she had left on the mountain road now two hundred meters below her.

She had profited from the thrilling combination of dangerous roads and engine power to drive her blood adrenaline as high as she could in preparation for the climb up the cliff. There was no way the crazy professor was going to make her even a second late for her meeting with her brother and sister.

She wanted to savour every moment of that meeting, caught up in the feeling that her very life was reaching some climax. Things were fast moving. First, the development of the Deterministic Predictor Machine. Now an Earth text, and her brother selected for the mission to test it. Fear too. And not the physical fear of clinging to a ladder hundreds of meters above a road. Every cell in her body was telling her that it would be the last meeting with her triplet brother.

The last fifty meters of the ladder were the hardest. There was no need now for any hydrogen powered sports car for blood adrenaline production. She needed only to look down. There were powerful up-draughts, and she felt an adrenaline surge. She clung ever tighter to the ladder with fists that seemed to want to crush it.

She heard strong wind in conifer trees, and knew she was close to the top. She felt back in her childhood when she had spent whole summers there. But then, she thought she heard another noise, becoming audible—the heavy chattering of helicopter rotors, and knew it only mean one thing. Her father. She jumped off the ladder onto the bare rock at the top of the cliff, and sprinted to the landing pad. Nothing. She had been fooled again by the "chatter" in her mind.

Instead, her brother, Lt. Colonel Richard Kemp, greeted her.

'These are dangerous times. We need to be fit.'

They walked, under the light of a gathering storm towards the grassy terrace where Zena was relaxing. It was the open, grassy land which separated the landing pad from the familiar stones of the mountain palace.

Lena said, 'Congratulations on your appointment. Not that there was any real choice for them. I mean, you understand more about deterministic theory than anyone alive.'

'Except you,' corrected her brother.

'Yeah, maybe.' She laughed. All three triplets had "The Gift" as others had called it. That ability to predict the close future. Everyone on their planet hoped it would put an end to the nuclear wars which threatened their survival.

That night the deep, contented sleep of the triplets was broken by the rasping roar of jet engines.

Their father, Commander Peter Ursella brought the helicopter in low over the peaks behind the mountain palace, the retreat that he and his children still used.

The storm had passed, and it had left a hot summer night in the mountains to the far to the west of Archaia 9. The charismatic Commander Ursella felt happy for his role of stopping the nuclear war. He was in the Special Forces. Thanks to him and his children, the Deterministic Predictor was operational. And now that project was finally entering the final stage.

Zena jumped out of her bed, and watched the helicopter approach from high on the rocky peak behind the lodge. She threw on a dressing gown, and met her siblings in the Great Hall, and hastened down to meet their father. They were happy. In the year since they had seen him last, Zena and Kemp had missed their father. Now that Lena was back from Archaia 7, Commander Ursella knew he had to make a trip to the mountain palace. He shut down the engines, and scrambled over to his children.

Long embraces followed and then they walked to the grassy terrace with its fine views of the valley. The city lights were twinkling in the distance, and above them, the eastern sky was brightening with the approaching dawn.

'You will never guess where I have been today,' said Commander Ursella, laying on the grass.

'To the Desert Planet!' hazarded Kemp, stretching out beside his father. Zena and Lena sat crossed legged.

'No. Not the Desert Planet; the Water Planet!'

'I never knew we could send people to Earth,' said Zena, her eyes wide with amazement.

'Well. The technology has been around for ages.'

'So why are we doing it now?'

'In a word, necessity,' answered her father. 'We need to test the Deterministic Predictor on a planetary scale before anyone in the West will believe it is truly capable of making 100% accurate predictions.'

'Ok, I understand the need, but not the technology. I must be out of touch,' said Zena.

'Well, we have been using what we call "Individual Projection Substitution," IPS, as a weapon for years, mainly to create key agents in the West which then work for us without knowing it. But it was always a one way transfer. The agents were created, and worked for us, but they were gone forever. Now the guys in Archaia 1 have broken into the technology of bringing back those IPS agents...'

'And you were their Guinea Pig,' cut in Lena, a look of anger spreading across the fine lines of her face. 'I can't believe you let them use you!'

'Oh, come on!' replied her brother. He turned onto his back and cast his eyes to the sharp outline of the granite towers on the ridge thousands of meters above them. 'That's what we have been living for, you and me. To honour our parents and put our lives on the line to save the planet, and our people. If you and I can't do it, who can?'

Lena looked at her father with eyes that were fiercely jealous and protective. She would give her life for her father, and could never control herself when his life came under threat. Finally, she smiled, and said, 'So tell us about it.'

'Well, yes. As I said, I was the first IPS agent who was ever brought back from a mission. The test itself was pretty simple, and made on Earth because of all the inhabited planets, Earth is the one which best lends itself to such a deterministic experiment. You see, apart from a few continents, Earth is water covered, but there are islands too. Events in sea areas surrounding small islands will not generate catastrophic shifts of futures. Dramatic shifts require a continental location.'

Kemp said, 'I get it. You identified an event on Earth which you and your team considered would produce only a small, un-catastrophic change in world events. Let me guess. The event occurred on the edge of an island.'

'You're right, Richard. By changing a small, traceable "island-ocean" event, and comparing the actual shift in Earth futures produced with the one which would have occurred had we not intervened, we can test the Deterministic Predictor Machine.'

'And did it work?'

'Well, the guys in Archaia 7 are at present running the Deterministic Predictor on the new Earth system. We should have the results sometime tomorrow.'

'And what Earth event did you change?'

'An event off Koh Tao, a small island in the Gulf of Thailand, surrounded by wild, deep waters. Perfect for such a test. We used a preliminary version of "Planetary Radar Technology." PRT for short. Part of the Planetary Deterministic Project, PDT. Together the PRT-PDT. We identified an event in Space-Time whose outcome would have limited repercussions for Earth's future. In the identified event, an American adventurer will drown in a kayak accident on November 1, 2024. He will try to take a three person kayak around a wild section of the Koh Tao coast in huge seas. He will be capsized by huge waves, and the mountainous seas will drive him onto sharp granite rocks of a rocky cape. There, the seas will pound him till he dies. I was sent to the same space-time coordinate and, during the storm before his fated attempt to kayak around the coast, substitute Ross. The substitution process is complicated to explain, but … Well, there are two parts to the process. In the first, I basically use the energy of a bolt of fork lightning. But that's only half of it. There has also to be a local "agent" working the system on Earth. In this case, it's a lady named Alexandra Kirilenka. She will invent the Earth's first prediction machine. That allows us to link to Earth's destination fabric. Kirilenka hasn't figured out yet that she is only acting because she has linked to our system. But that doesn't matter. The system works nevertheless. Right now, we're waiting for Kirilenka to figure out the capabilities the new technology brings.'

'So you become this American guy on Earth in 2024. That's hard to believe,' said Lena.

'I know. Bear with me,' continued Ursella. 'You see, we know from PRD that the reason Lee Ross will die is because he keeps too close to the shore. The waters are deep off Koh Tao, but the huge waves are less likely to capsize a large three person kayak if the kayaker keeps way from shore.'

'I get it,' said Zena. 'You substitute Ross, right? I've heard about this.'

'Yes. During the storm when a bolt of lightning strikes the place where he is sheltering in the small, wooden "Pirate's Bar" built above the rocks of San Maung Bay. Ross will be sheltering, drinking beers in the bar with his two friends, a couple. The three person kayak is below the bar, on the coarse, golden sand of the beach. I take the three person kayak and, picking what seems like a lull in storm, paddle like crazy into the teeth of the wind. The waves are huge; full ten meters. I manage to prevent the kayak capsizing. Unlike Ross, I take it way out to sea before starting to turn towards the home bay. I continue paddling like a madman. Only by maintaining a good forward speed is the capsizing tendency of the kayak reduced. And the seas do not succeed in capsizing me. I power the kayak past the second headland of granite rocks and into the calmer sea of the home bay . . . '

'So you save Ross?'

'Ross is saved, yes. None the worst for his adventure. What's more, that actually will happen in the future. He will not drown that day, and goes on to live a simple life with minimal interaction to world events.'

'And now what? Your team is evaluating the shift in the determined world future that your action will have?' asked Zena.

'Exactly. And the preliminary report is that we will avert Earth's first nuclear war in 2024.'

'How is that possible?' asked Kemp.

'Simple. We checked the fate of Earth on the PRT-PDT. As things stand, on 7 November 2024 at 18.30 Russia will explode a thermonuclear device on Berlin, setting off a general thermonuclear war between the US and Russia. But that will only happen if Ross dies on Koh Tao on November 1, 2024.'

'But how is that possible? Why does Lee Ross surviving matter?' asked Richard.

'Everyone's life actions echo in eternity. Ross's actions as a CIA agent, and a director of CIA operations matter more than most. Without him, the world events extrapolate to nuclear Armageddon.'

Chapter 4

Virginia Cortez sat at her work station at Fairfax County Police Department. The phone rang and she took the call and got busy with the details. An eyewitness by the name of Darya Kam had heard gunshots at a mansion on the far end of Boyle Lane. The last mansion before the Potomac. Cortez knew enough to know that the particular mansion was the biggest, and most expensive of the Boyle Lane mansions due to the proximity to the Potomac.

She thought her name was fitting because she lived in downtown McLean, Virginia, USA. But her quick-thinking intellect was the product of her birthplace, Mexico City, Mexico. Those skills came in now, because there was stress in the voice of the eyewitness, and she analysed it. She triaged the call, and moved on to the name and location of the closest asset.

Lieutenant Victor McGovern was cruising between Langley Ridge and Boyle Lane. The Ford Explorer was bowling along with a low roar. The streets were clear. Late in Fairfax County, on a cold night, thought McGovern, and then he heard the call. McGovern repeated the details and heard Cortez double check his read-back.

McGovern's Explorer u-turned and doubled back, and then swung into Boyle Lane, and he saw the eyewitness, who was waiting because that is what Virginia Cortez had told her to do. The patrol car squeaked to a stop two feet from the kerb. McGovern motioned the woman to approach.

Getting a head start on the details came easy to McGovern. He liked small talk. One statement led to another, and so on. Like it was software. In the first thirty seconds he found out the eyewitness's name was Darya Kam. She said she wasn't used to taking orders from females. After a minute talking, McGovern found out the suspect was Russian.

'How do you know that?' McGovern asked.

'Because of this.' Kam passed him a passport.

'Where did he drop it?'

'Who said he dropped it?'

'Okay. Where did *you* get it?'

'I stole it from him because he left it in his vehicle, in the shadows. As soon as he was out of earshot, I moved in and shook it down.'

'Well. We're going to take a ride now, down to that vehicle. But aren't you afraid I will arrest you?'

'What for?'

'Breaking and entering?'

'I didn't break anything, and the only thing I took was this passport.'

'Why?'

'Because there was nothing else to take.'

'You're a hardened criminal.'

'No,' said Kam. 'But I am sharing this with you. And there is another reason.'

'Which is?'

'He's Russian.'

'That's not a crime.'

'Russia invaded a sovereign country. I am being honest.'

'What's the war in Ukraine got to do with it?'

'Just thinking aloud. That's not a crime either.'

'Sounds to me like you're a Robin Hood type. Like you were doing the right thing. Good Karma traded against bad.'

'Something like that.'

McGovern felt a twang. Being honest was part of his territory. But who is honest one hundred percent of the time? No one. Last time he checked would have been when he printed some documents. It was a case for a friend. She was in a tight spot, which meant she had not a dime to spend on printing of her court documents. Four copies needed. The Appeal was 53 pages, so there were 212 pages in total. There was no possibility for printing in the morning because she was in court next day. For contempt. So he went ahead and printed them at work. Which was a dishonest act. He was using his position for self-advantage. Fraud. He was stealing. Theft. Felonies. Caught, and he would lose his job. Push or jump. He did neither and the matter slipped.

He checked his watch. Five minutes since the call, which meant the suspect had either returned to the car and was gone, or he wasn't. It was a two way thing. A simple binomial. Time to see for himself.

He turned to Kam, and said they were wasting time, and that that they were going to continue in the Explorer, and then he called up support. Support got back to him when he and the eyewitness were tearing down the track beside the Potomac.

'Over there!' said Kam, pointing to a black sports car. Someone parked it on a no-end driveway. It ran east-west and split the fields between the mansions and the Potomac.

'The black Mustang?' asked McGovern.

'That's it.'

McGovern drew alongside. It was a Mustang with out of state plates. He read them to Virginia Cortez, who confirmed it had been stolen. Cortez added, 'And the victim is Victoria Feodor. She is the owner of the mansion and a Moldovan lawyer with links to Russia. She's licenced to practice here in Washington.'

McGovern sighed and got busy figuring out what it all meant. A lawyer linked to Russia in Washington D.C. The US State Department territory, he thought. Virginia Cortez was still on the end of the line. She said, 'The file has been sent to the US Marshal Service.'

McGovern told the eyewitness to stay where she was.

'Am I under arrest?' asked Kam.

'If it makes you feel any better.'

He locked Kam in the patrol car, and then he inspected the Mustang.

He could feel the heat rising from the bonnet. There were ticking noises. Cooling metal. The vehicle had been driven fast. The tyres were still warm, as were the wheel hubs. He went back the patrol car and called up control, and gave them his co-ordinates.

Virginia Cortez came back to him, saying there was a US Marshal en-route.

'Why?' asked McGovern.

'Standard practice,' said Cortez. 'He'll be there in a matter of minutes.'

A distant chattering of helicopter rotors became audible. McGovern went back to his patrol car.

'Am I free to go?' said Kam.

'If the US Marshal says so,' said McGovern.

The helicopter was a Huey. It touched down hard and fast on the expansive lawn of the mansion. The pilot wasn't taking prisoners, thought McGovern. That or a death wish. Either way, it was obvious that the guy in the thick brown leather jacket and long black hair who jumped down from the open door was the US Marshal, and the one to be calling the shots.

McGovern strode out to meet him. The guy was short, and he had a moustache and a full head of coarse, black hair, streaked grey. He had green dress uniform. There was a name badge on his chest with "Conor Firestone" written on it.

McGovern saluted.

The US Marshal said, 'I'm Captain Conor Firestone. McGovern, here's what we have. The video of the intruder. Slavic. Blonde. Six foot two. Around 25 years old.'

Firestone listened and McGovern laid out the situation. He looked at his watch. 32 minutes since the killing. His team surrounded him; they had done this before. They were erecting a makeshift tent with a wooden table and two chairs. But everyone was standing around. McGovern guessed it was standard US Marshal Service in Washington D.C., on a busy unit. The weather was about to turn bad. The wind was increasing, blowing the snow off the trees. Big snowflakes were hitting.

Firestone shouted out to the women and men surrounding him through the snow and the wind and the thunder. He said, 'Listen up. The target is Slavic. Blonde. Six foot two. He has a 33 minute head start from here, Potomac Fall Road. Activate your teams. I want a 30 mile cordon radius with officers on each road. I want best options in fifteen minutes. Get on it!'

One of Firestone's team, a young lady, short and blonde, ran up to him. She was carrying a down jacket. The jacket did not have the name-badge. Not that anyone noticed. She passed it to Firestone and he put it on, and then Firestone and McGovern ran straight to the patrol car. When they got there, the snow was blowing as a blizzard.

'Am I free to go now,' shouted Kam as McGovern opened the door.

'I told you, lady. That's up to the US Marshal.'

McGovern got behind the wheel and Firestone got into the back, next to Kam, saying, 'Okay Ms Kam. What can you tell me?'

Kam said, 'Are you Conor Firestone?'

Firestone looked down at his jacket, and then he stared at her. He wasn't one to surprise easily, but the name was not visible. He said, 'How do you know my name?'

Kam said, 'You need to know something. The President is a warmonger and a traitor. He is out of control. His actions against Russia are pushing the planet to the brink of destruction. He's a narcissist who only cares about himself. You need to replace him.'

'And who are you?'

'My name is Darya Kam, and what I am about to tell you will not be easy for you to come to terms with.'

'Try me!'

'I come from a different world. A different planet. Even a different galaxy. But there are things I know which you will be able to confirm. At the least, you will think I am a psychic. Your Lee Ross's actions will determine Earth's destiny. And why? Because otherwise, there will be the Third World War. The others are Victoria Feodor, Helen "Lena" Moskva and Alexandra Kirilenka.'

Firestone's mind was on autopilot. Subconscious wheels were turning. He saw Kam's eyes say she was telling the truth. Or thought she was. Then he saw them fall onto his sidearm. It was a standard Glock 18, and he had never fired it in anger. But he had left it exposed. If he had thought about it, he would have been reassured that he always left it secure. The retainer strap was on. But something told him this time he had made a mistake. Perhaps the look in Kam's eyes as she stared. He glanced down and Kam grabbed it, pulled it up, and shot a bullet straight and true into her forehead. What was left of her slumped back against the door. Blood pooled in the foot well.

McGovern and Firestone overcame their shock at what just happened, covered her and then they drove around to the scene of the shooting. McGovern parked next to the pool and locked the Explorer. The rear windows were tinted. And besides, there were other things to take care of. What happened to Darya Kam would have to wait.

He and Firestone raced to the front of the building, to two uniformed officers one on each side of the pillared doorway. Blue strobe lights flickered all around the crime scene, strobing, penetrating. The whole area was cordoned off with police no-entry tape.

The officers on the door waved McGovern and Firestone through, and they sprinted up the spiral staircase, two steps at a time. 36 minutes since the shooting, they breezed into the room of the shooting and then a call buzzed in Firestone's pocket. Firestone took the call, and after several seconds he hung up and said, 'There's a man running west along Georgetown Pike towards Difficult Run.'

'What's his description?' said McGovern. His look was stony faced and serious. Had the assassin broke cover? Possible, but unlikely in his view. More probable was that the assassin was in some thicket on the banks of the Potomac. Hunkered down. That's what McGovern would do. It didn't fit that he would be running in plain sight on a highway.

'The description fits.'

'He's probably heading for Difficult Run Trail, then,' said McGovern. 'There's no cameras on the trail. It's just a hiking path through the national reserve. I'd say there's a good chance that's our man.'

'It leads back to the Potomac,' said Firestone.

'Right. Which means he knows the terrain. He's leading us to the dead cover areas in Virginia and Maryland.'

Firestone turned to McGovern, and said, 'You're coming with me. The chopper will pick us up out front. We have a five minute window before we lose him on Difficult Run.'

Which turned out to be not far from the truth. They scrambled out into the cold of the storm, climbed into the Huey, and flew the sector for ten minutes, back and forth between the intersection and the Potomac. Without a sign. Not even that of any animals which inhabited the area; and there were boatloads. Rabbits. Foxes. Deer. The problem wasn't the technology. It was the equipment itself. The helicopter's thermal imaging was wanting, and other choppers would be the same. Time to shorten the odds. Firestone took out his mobile, and speed-dialled a number he thought he would never need.

CIA Director of Operations Lee Ross sat at the expansive bar in the unbridled luxury of his boss's mansion in the heart of Virginia's back country. The bar was well stocked. There was a selection of the finest whiskies from Scotland and Ireland, and there were a selection of red and white wines from France and Italy. Expensive. It looked not unlike the bars in downtown Washington D.C. But this was a private affair.

He had grown closer to Zak Hoffman over the months since recruited, but they were not old buddies. Despite all of that, some weekends he chose to be at Hoffman's mansion.

It was late, and Hoffman had long retired to the arms of his latest sweetheart. The large patio windows were open to the lawn despite the wind and the snow. He got up and poured himself a drink. Jack on coke and ice. The second one. It would help him relax. The territory required it, he thought, and felt better.

Glass in hand, swirling the ice three times in a circular motion, he walked over to the double glass patio doors and looked across the wintry landscape. Deep in contemplation. He drew the first draft of the mix, and let his mind wander. It was a moment of sheer, unbridled relaxation. He thought of his career to date. Now CIA Director of Operations. A far cry from the Air Force. He was wearing his Captain Hilts jacket.

His mobile buzzed and the word "Firestone" scrolled slowly across the screen from left to right.

'Got a second?' came the voice on the other side through the headset.

Ross took a long draught of whisky and coke, and said, 'For you Conor, always. What can I do for you?'

'We have a situation on the Potomac. An assassination of a Russian lawyer. The suspect is on Difficult Run.'

'So what?'

'There's something else.'

'Name it.'

'You told me once. You told me about your past, and present life. Remember? You had access to a modified F35 stationed at Edwards. Well. Do you still have access?'

'That's affirmative.'

'In that case, how about assisting us in a search of the Potomac? We could do with the F35's information gathering. Far superior to anything our police helicopters have.'

'It's too late isn't it? The lawyer is dead, isn't he?'

'She. You'd be avenging a lady.'

Ross thought for a second. For a lady? That changed things. He would have to drive back to Edwards straight away. That wouldn't be a problem.

'And while you are thinking, there's a chopper en-route. It'll be there in minutes.'

'Please don't tell me you're going to wake Hoffman!'

'Just tell him the truth, Ross. A lady needs help!'

'Okay. But do me a favour. Make sure the chopper lands on the far side of the lawn. At the edge of the woods. I'll be on the edge of the trees. The snow will be less deep.'

The helicopter was an Osprey, not a Huey, and Ross thought that made perfect sense. Time was a factor. Forty five minutes since the shooting. Or maybe that was all that was available. Either way, the search was being delayed, and the area would be correspondingly larger. The faster they got the F35 deployed to the search area, the higher the chance of a successful outcome.

***

Thirty eight minutes passed quicker than lightning for Ross, and then the modified F35 roared off the northern end of Andrews. It was over the Potomac in seconds. All systems initiated and data was streaming fast into the fighter-bomber. Ross switched on the infrared search, and a map popped up onto a section of the glass cockpit. There were two active screens. The left hand screen was the infrared.

Ross flicked a switch, and the on-board computer applied AI to the results. Ross requested details of the target and added the known characteristics. Height. Stature. Appearance. Age. Not an exact science, he thought, but as good as it gets. Much better than looking at the output and trying to sift the wheat from the chaff.

Real time results appeared, and he acquired the target. There was a closed, one man kayak on the edge of the Potomac, at the exact place where Difficult Run ran up against the river. The suspect was launching off the rocks. Ross plugged in the coordinates and the computer did the rest. All seemed to be going too well and Ross felt the same. Sure enough, when the F35 came over the target, something happened. The suspect took his kayak over the rapids, disappearing from the screen.

Ross flicked on a second AI version running on the data packets and re-acquired the target. The rapids were above and behind the suspect. He was out of the Kayak, in the water. Ross took the F35 over the target, and directed McGovern to where the F-35's on-board systems said the suspect should wash up. McGovern would do the rest, because the assassin was dead, and there was nothing else left to do. Nobody could survive the rapids in a kayak. The AI told him that, and he believed it.

He took the F35 to the end of the trail McGovern would have to come along. There was a clearing where the snow was deep and flat exactly a kilometre downstream of the place where Dead Run Trail came up against the Potomac.

As expected, McGovern came barrelling down the road minutes later, slamming on the brakes at the last moment, the Explorer coming to a halt feet from the F35.

'Suicide?' McGovern shouted as Ross jumped into the snow from the fighter-bomber.

'Affirmative,' shouted back Ross as he approached the Explorer, his voice all but swallowed by the howling wind in the trees on each side of the clearing. The rapids, fifty meters from the clearing, were background sounds, and added to the cacophony. Ross climbed into the passenger seat, and slammed the door.

'How can you be sure?'

'AI,' said Ross. 'No one would have taken the decision to kayak from Difficult Run to the rapids.'

'Except if their aim was suicide?' said McGovern. 'But that's AI speaking,'

'Such a person, smart enough to carry out the assassination of Feodor, and to escape that far, would have remained in the Difficult Run area. Opting for the river was suicidal. That's confirmed by him going over the rapids.'

'Okay. I get it.'

'What now?' said McGovern.

'Recover the body. It'll come to the bank just over there. I need you to come with me to check out the victim. The F35 has three seats. It's a prototype, and the engines can take it to Mach 6, but I dare say such performance will not be necessary for a trip down the Potomac.'

McGovern got on the radio just as two of his deputies drew into the clearing, and then he and Ross went up in the F35, straight to the victim's house.

Ross engaged autopilot as they took off from the clearing, and plugged in McGovern's initial victim report to the F35's AI. Victoria Feodor's address was at the top, and there was her telephone number and date of birth. 28 July 1985. He let it run as he took back control from the auto-pilot. It would be a short, flight. Potomac Fall Road, a little over 2 kilometres. He radioed the US Marshall's office and logged his visit. The venue was sure to be crawling with officers. He would have priority because he was with McGovern but he wanted everyone on site to be aware before he got there. No reason to expect that any action was imminent. But how could he be sure?

The modified fighter-bomber roared in low between Potamac Fall Road and the Potomac, hugging the trees, the engines throttling back. Ross put it on the snow on the lawn, between the trees and the swimming pool. They climbed down as a swarm of officers approached.

McGovern said to Ross, gesturing to the upstairs window, 'My guys are up there. They're going through the hard drives on her devices.'

There were voices and lights. A complex crime scene, and things were proceeding at pace.

'Let me take a wild guess,' said Ross. 'You haven't found anything because her drives are encrypted?'

'Not bad. You don't miss much.'

'Well, she was a lawyer working for the Russians in Washington D.C. It would be strange if they were not.'

'So? Subpoenas to Google and WhatsApp?'

'The F35 has software that cuts through that. I have to take the hardware and plug it in. Get me authorized.'

'You already are,' said McGovern. 'Come with me.'

They climbed the spiral staircase, and entered the bedroom. The scene of the crime. There were three officers dressed in hazmat suits, collecting evidence.

McGovern said, 'Listen up everyone! This is Lieutenant Colonel Lee Ross. He has authorization to remove the victim's laptop.'

Not a word from the officers, but their faces said they were not happy with it; McGovern calling the shots.

'Did the victim have only one laptop?' asked Ross.

'As far as we know.'

'That makes things simpler.'

Ross stood over the body. He was taking in the scene, and picturing what happened. Which wasn't difficult. The entrance and exit wounds were visible. There was blood spatter which recorded the direction of the impact and relative position of the assailant. The killer fired four shots from where Ross stood. McGovern was right next to him. Ross said, 'Tell me about the victim.'

'Victoria Feodor. 39 years old. Moldovan, of Russian descent. She was born in Criuleni, in Transnistria, the Russian enclave in Moldova. A separatist area. She practiced criminal defence and commercial litigation. Professional negligence.'

'Drug related clients?'

'Yes. They were part of it. So far nothing points to them. No trace of drugs in the house, and we've done a preliminary sweep of each room.'

'Here,' said McGovern, handing him the victim's laptop. The laptop had been checked for prints and wiped clean. Ross took it, and they returned the way they had come.

They got back to the F35, and Ross said, 'This won't take long,' and then he climbed the single pole bar which was the ladder, and which dropped from the left side of the aircraft. He pulled himself into the cockpit, He pulled out the laptop and plugged it in using the USB. The F35 had all the latest software and more. It could penetrate the defences of any enemy. If there was one location in the whole of the US which could hack into Feodor's laptop in minutes, he was at it.

The laptop came alive, the F35's software blasting through the firewalls. Feodor's email outbox was his first point of call, and it initially looked promising, and Ross's jaw dropped when he saw what was there. Rather, *who* was there. It was all about her latest client, none other than the President of the United States.

There was the last email that she sent, which was to the President. Ross looked at the subject. "Duty of Care to the American People."

Ross wondered where to start, and thought he would try a search of the email account for the word "President."

The first email was a week ago, from the Presidential adviser. The email was long and rambling; *sure to have been written by the President himself*, thought Ross. He was anxious to find out if he would be liable for involuntary manslaughter should he take the US to war with Russia.

Good point, thought Ross. That would depend on many things. One sprang to mind: *if he took the US to war because of the wrong reason. But what would be the right reason in any event? That Russia had initiated unprovoked aggression against a sovereign state?*

He needed a bell weather, and McGovern was the obvious choice, so he climbed out of the cockpit, and he saw McGovern so he went down the steps of the protruding ladder.

'Quick question.'

'Shoot.'

'If the US went to war now against Russia, due to Ukraine, would it be a just war?'

McGovern thought for a moment and then he said, 'I'm not an expert in International Relations and International Law, which is what you need to answer that one, but for what it's worth, my view is no.'

'Why not?'

'Two words. NATO expansion. The US tried to put NATO into Ukraine, against the stark warnings from Russia that they would never allow it. They made it clear again and again. But we kept doubling down. I like to use an analogy. A tame cat is nice when you stroke and caress it. But what lurks inside every cat is its true character. If you provoke it in certain ways, every cat will turn aggressive. Well that's what you have here with Russia. The West has awoken the Russian Bear by using Ukraine to poke it in the eye. The West, and by that I mean the US, is at fault, not Russia. And so, it will not be a "just" war.'

'Why, in your view, would the President worry so much about that he would hire a lawyer for advice on liability for the war in Ukraine?'

'That's clear. The President worries he has a personal interest in the war.'

It was refreshing, thought Ross. McGovern was following the same thread. An uncomplicated man. He never had to pronounce on the issue of the causes of the coming war, and saw things exactly the same. Had he just got lucky? Was it sheer coincidence that he had found someone with similar views? Not really, Ross thought. There were rumours circulating of why Budden was intent on inflicting on Russia a strategic defeat.

One. Certain Democrats would be liable should they lose the upcoming presidency. There were documents implicating them all in criminal offences. Should Tramp triumph, they would end up behind bars. Two, should Russia win in Ukraine, a defeat for NATO would orchestrate the Democrats' loss of the presidency. Third, there could be other reasons for Budden's hatred of the Russian Federation, and Potanin in particular.

Ross looked at McGovern. He wanted to ask him another question. Not random this one. He said, 'Listen. McGovern. What do you think could be the reason behind Budden's hatred of Russia?'

'I've learned something after all these years chasing criminals. If Budden worries enough to go to see a lawyer, it wasn't because of what's in the public domain.'

'Meaning?'

'The answer, must be in his past. Something he has to hide. Something so terrible for him, he would kill for it. This is my view only. Something that has not yet come out of the woodwork.'

'Victoria Feodor?'

'She must have known it. It's probably why she was killed.'

'You're saying the President got legal advice, and then he killed her because she became a risk?'

'Either that, or she always was a risk. As in, he knew from the start what he was doing.'

'Pretty cold, if you ask me.'

'Look at the man. He'll have justified the murder. He'd have told himself it was not his fault.'

'So where will it be?'

'The secret? You have all the access codes up there.' McGovern gestured to the F35.

Ross considered his options, and then he said, 'I need your help. Someone who knows what they're looking for. For me, it would be looking for a needle in a haystack. I need someone who can see the wood for the trees without having to walk through a forest to find the approximate locality. You are that person.'

'I'd need access to the F35.'

'You will get it. Call it a deal. It would be an unwritten one. No trace. And anyway, all deals are based on one essential condition. Trust. Without trust, forget it. No matter how tight the clauses of the written contract. I trust you, McGovern. I'll give you the access. You go ahead and find why the president had to kill Victoria Feodor.'

Ross felt a buzzing inside his Captain Hilts jacket. He slipped out his phone and saw the caller and considered it strange that his boss was calling. Even if Hoffman knew the Osprey had landed in his back garden, had he not immediately caught on? And why not? When the Osprey had taken off, the upstairs suite was in darkness. Which meant one of two things. Hoffman had seen the Osprey, or someone had called him. He took the call.

'Ross! What in hell's name are you doing?'

'Because something has come up, and it was necessary. A high profile Washington D.C. lawyer. An assassination of official of the Court and an upstanding member of our community. Is that enough for you? The US Marshal's office asked me to assist. So here I am.'

'Okay. So where is that, exactly?'

'McClean. One of the mansions near the Potomac.'

'Okay. But I want you back here in the morning.'

'Agreed, Sir. I was about to suggest the same. I'll be there at 9.a.m.'

Hoffman ended the call and Ross turned to McGovern.

'Hoffman's going to take me off the case.'

'He said that?'

'No. But that's what he meant. I know the guy. From his words on the call, he's been talking to someone. Which is his style. He does nothing before weighing everything up. Hearing all sides before making his move. He must have seen the Osprey, and woke up a whole load of officials.'

'You got all that from a call which lasted less than a minute?'

'Correct. He wants to rein me in.'

'Which means we have till 9am to figure this out.'

'Right,' said Ross, willing his mind to clarity, and back on immediate actions. 'The files are accessible?'

'Follow me.'

Ross activated the protruding ladder, which extended, and climbed to the cockpit, and installed himself in one of the rear seats. 'Get yourself up here,' he shouted down McGovern. 'There are two seats up front, and one in the rear. As I said. Three seater, because it's a modified F35.'

McGovern climbed, strapped in next to Ross, and then he said 'Okay. What now?'

Ross said, 'We find the needle in the haystack.'

Words which McGovern didn't hear, because he had gotten busy. Less than a minute inside the F35, and he saw it, and knew it mattered.

'What is it?' said Ross, waking up to a change of McGovern's attitude. 'You look like you saw a ghost.'

'Why is that written there?' McGovern pointed to the data link. 'Are you going to Barcelona?'

Ross looked at the screen, and saw that there was text.

'That's weird!'

'What is?' replied McGovern.

'Only numbers appear in that instrument. It's a data link.'

'Well, there they are. A text message from somebody.'

The text said, 'You both will go to Barcelona. Further instructions will appear here. Out.'

McGovern said, 'Can you trace it?'

'I can try. But it's one way.'

'How do you know?'

'The source is empty. Which never happens.'

'Hacked?'

Ross said, 'No. The F35 is impenetrable.'

'Look, there's more.'

They watched as more text came through in real time. Text was dancing along the screen, and read, "Darya Kam; Victoria Feodor; Lee Ross; Zak Hoffman; Victor McGovern."

McGovern said, 'My God! What is this? Why am I mixed up in this now? Who knows all those names, and what do they mean?'

Ross overcame the shock, and all he could say was, 'It's not Hoffman.'

***

Two hours passed, and they were spent by Ross and McGovern doing their best to get to the bottom of the text message. Efforts that were doomed to failure for reasons they could not understand. It was 08.30, and Ross said, 'In half an hour I need to know who killed Victoria Feodor and why. So could you please give me a summary of what we know?'

McGovern wiped away beads of sweat on his brow and said, 'Where to begin? Victoria Feodor. Born in Criuleni, Moldova.

But that's now a Russian enclave in Moldova. Transnistria. Feodor is basically Russian. She graduated law school in Chishinau, before moving to the US in 2015. She was a criminal defence lawyer specialising in manslaughter.'

'I'm guessing the type of manslaughter known as gross negligence, constructive, or unlawful act manslaughter?'

'Correct,' said McGovern.

'Not much to go on.'

'I wish it were not so. I wish the "ghost" would come back.'

A while had passed since the two cryptic texts had come through on the data link, disappearing straight after being read. Both wondered why. Had they both hallucinated? No. They had both seen it, and the chances of that happening by chance were infinitesimal. And nothing that they could have done to save it, as the screen wasn't set up for such a thing.

Victoria Feodor was smart, thought Ross. She had kept all her files encrypted. If he were a lawyer, he would have done the same. Especially, considering her client. So what did she find about her client / target. She wasn't a Kremlin connected Russian. He said, 'So why would the President of the United States hire the best gross negligence lawyer in town?'

No answer from McGovern, because a call was coming through on McGovern's phone. He snapped his fingers in Ross's face, made a sign, and listened. He hung up after seconds, and said, 'The body has been recovered. They still haven't identified him, but there's something you should know.'

'Shoot!' said Ross.

'They found a Glock on him, but that's not all.'

'What isn't?'

'It's a government Glock. The guy is un-traceable. Slavic. Six foot in height. 220 pounds. We should get more on the Glock in the next hour.'

'Is that all?'

'No. One name keeps coming up in the investigations. Feodor was meeting a Russian who works in the embassy. It seems the guy's a military attaché. All his files dead-end at a CIA firewall.'

'Can you crack it? If not, I will request an authorization code and assign a team.'

'Already done,' said McGovern.

'So who is he?'

'Pavel Ivanov.'

'What about the way she works?' said Ross.

'She always drills down into the facts of every case. She looks for fracture lines. The weak points which can be exploited, leading to a win. That's all I know.'

'So all we know is that Pavel Ivanov is dead.'

'Not for sure. Pavel Ivanov was the name that keeps popping up. An associate of hers. A client. Doesn't mean he killed her.'

'True. But we have to start somewhere. What else have we got?'

'We have a dead Russian lawyer, and a government issued firearm.'

'Moldovan, not Russian,' corrected Ross.

'Same difference. Moldovan from Transnistria means Russian.'

Ross looked at his watch. 08.47 am. He said, 'Okay. I have to go with what we have got. Unless I can make a good case, Hoffman will take me off. You stay put. Your team are still working the crime scene. Keep it that way. Something is sure to turn up.'

'I doubt it. We have the murder weapon. Forensics confirmed it's a match. We have the killer. He's stone cold. What else?'

'I'll let you know.'

Ross turned and eyeballed McGovern. They shook hands, and then McGovern climbed down the pogo-stick ladder and Ross flicked switches to initiate the engine start. Modified Pratt and Whitney. 5 times larger than the F35 standard. Large and fast.

Chapter 5

Helen Moskva was "Anella", to her friends. Or "Lena." Her brother, Commander Richard Kemp, assigned her the data stream coming into Archaia 9 from Earth. The data stream reached her home planet by passing through the central black hole of the Milky Way galaxy. They didn't call that galaxy the Milky Way. They give it a number.

The person on Earth who sent the data packet on its way was Alexandra Kirilenka. Kirilenka sent it just before the war which was going to wreck Earth. There were others in Helen Moskva's unit, and each were connected to a different world. Kirilenka, on the other end of that particular data packet, was given access to the deterministic fabric of the target planet, in that case, Earth. It allowed her access to the key determinative events on Earth in November 2024.

As for Helen "Lena" Moskva, after the success of her father being sent to act on Ross on Koh Tao, she herself was sent to Earth to oversee as much as possible the prevention of World War Three. She was able to have a conversation with Victoria Feodor immediately before the assassin struck. The conversation was by telephone. Lena substituted a client of Feodor, and she was able to find out the reason why the President hated Russia.

Chapter 6

17th November 2009, Matrosskaya Tishina
Prison, Moscow, Russia

Eight OMON riot cops enter the cold, dimly-lit cell. Big Russians. Heavy. They had knives and side arms. They wielded rubber batons, grasped so tight their knuckles turned white, while their forearms and biceps bulged under their black fatigues. There was a guy outside the cell, who was important. The guy was a bald American. He stayed in the corridor.

The cell had a broken window through which snow poured when the wind was from the north. Like then. The cell had a rough concrete floor and two occupants. One Russian. The other Ukrainian.

The eight OMON officers had zero interest in the Russian. That was plain to see. At the drop of a hat, they would have gotten busy with him, but so long as he remained quiet, he was safe. Which made perfect sense. He was Russian himself, and it's always easier to understand your country folk. Which is partly the reason for the war. The US neo-cons didn't understand Russia.

The Russian cowered in the far corner and the OMON officers left him alone.

The Ukrainian had no such luck. He got the rubber batons full in the face and ribs, and then the fists connected and he sought refuge on the cold, rough concrete floor. Sought, but not found. The eight OMON continued there, and pounded him until he was senseless. Steel toe-capped boots were the last to hit home on the skull of the Ukrainian, their effects the most devastating. The eight OMON left, followed, in the corridor, by the American who joined them on the way out. Protected. Assured.

Blood pooled onto the concrete floor.

Sergei Leonidovich Magnitsky's blood. An accountant, not a lawyer.

Chapter 7

Banana Rocks Cafe, Sai Nuan Beach,
Koh Tao, Thailand

The small tropical storm started in the Andaman Sea, and then
it crossed the isthmus into the warm Gulf of Thailand, gaining
strength. Lee Ross was chugging bottled Thai beer in the pirate
beach bar. He was bare foot, and he shrugged off the storm despite
that it was apparent that he would be stranded there. He could
think of worse places.

Ross was an American, CIA director of operations, and his
boss, director Zak Hoffman had taken him off a murder case in
Washington D.C. He was in Bangkok two days later, and then
he got an internal flight to Koh Samui, and then he got a ferry to
Koh Tao.

A squall, Ross thought, taking a sip from his bottle of Chang.
He was athletic thanks to daily work-outs. His body had fine
lines, like those of Greek warriors immortalised in a chunk of
ancient Greek marble. There were fine contours and smooth
curves. He had a craggy face. The fabric of a tight, black t-shirt
stretched across his torso. His shorts hung baggy, and he went

barefoot, enjoying the feel of the smooth hardwood planks of Banana Rocks.

Koh Tao's best kept secret, thought Ross. A pirate bar shackled to piles of hardwood above the waves in a remote, hidden corner of Thailand. He felt proud to have "discovered" it years previously, when his thirst for adventure and knowledge of the world led him to such places.

Ross surveyed the vistas of the tropical tempest from his grandstand lookout. The bar was made of local woods. It had a thatched roof and themed fittings. It was a front-row place in a theatre of nature's power, and the scene was set. 400 meters across the bay, a granite cape loomed through the spray. *Cape Ja Te Kang*. It had dark granite rocks, and a cloak of towering waves.

But that day, in early November, 2024, Ross wasn't sampling such delights alone. With him on the smooth hardwood planks of the windswept platform was a newly wedded French couple, Pearl Saab and Stefan Gainsbourg. Pearl was native Lebanese. Stefan, Belgian.

They clinked again and again their beers. The spectacle of the storm was playing out in front. There were meaningful conversations. There was a three-person kayak beached above the waves on the coarse golden sands below, should anyone be so reckless. But as the storm reached its crescendo, one thing was clear—no one was kayaking back to Chalok Baan Kao.

'I know what you're thinking,' said Pearl, her Lebanese eyes pulled for once away from those of Stefan even if for just an instant. Something had caused her to cast them briefly towards Ross, and it had nothing to do with her upcoming wedding. She wanted to lock horns with Ross.

Ross raised a spray watered eyebrow, and wondered, 'What now?'

Pearl chuckled openly, and Stefan wondered what the context was. He thought it a private joke, but then Pearl clarified. 'Don't even think about it!'

'About what?' returned Ross, a tennis player returning a fast first service, taking a long draught of beer. A ploy to increase the stakes. The beer was cool and strong, much like the wind off the sea.

'Getting dragged across the Cape's granite prow won't make you the island hero. You'll be battered to a pulp, and then you'll be swept out to sea, and you'll die across there, in the depths of the gulf!'

'I can think of worse ways and worse places to go,' said Ross.

'Such as?'

'Gaining entry to the Moscow-Washington hotline, getting caught, thrown in jail, depressed and suicidal.'

'And why say that? Don't tell me that after all these years, you're still obsessed with the Kremlin hotline. That's not the panacea for every case you can't solve,' said Pearl.

Ross drained his large bottle of Chang, his eyes cast back out across the maelstrom. Dutch courage, perhaps. It didn't matter. The storm had almost passed, and he had made up his mind, and the rain's rhythm on the thatched roof boosted his resolve. It had reached its crescendo hours ago, though heavy drops of rain were blowing in, soaking the decking and the bare skin of his feet. He said, 'It's something I can't get out of my mind. An obsession.'

'And you prefer to paddle the kayak around to the village, risking your life, just to clear your mind of the hotline?'

'Something like that,' said Ross. 'The harder the test, the better I get. The stronger. Thirst for knowledge I guess. And right now, there is a case which doesn't have a happy ending. A Russian lawyer killed just three days ago. If I could use that Kremlin hotline just once, I could solve the case, and maybe prevent a nuclear war at the same time. So excuse me, but right now, the Russia hotline thing is on my mind.'

'You need help. That hotline thing is becoming an obsession. OCD.'

'No. My obsession has a different name. Victoria Feodor.'

'Who's that?' asked Pearl.

'The case I just talked about. A Russian lawyer killed on the orders of the President of the United States. I shouldn't be telling you this. But I've known you since 1994, which means I've known you most of my life. The easy way to solve it is through a couple of quick calls to the Kremlin.'

'And why on Earth would the Kremlin help you solve a US murder case.'

'To prevent World War Three. More than that, I definitely can't say a word. But it wasn't a simple murder case. More a government assassination. And it was authorized at a high level.'

'Which is?'

'I can't tell you that.'

'So go for it, if it makes you happy!'

Ross leaned in, his words a challenge to himself. He just wanted to hear them. Pronounced. That was his thing. Say something, then make it real. Words were just that, words. But with him, words became actions, as if just pronouncing them caused a change in world history. Think butterfly effect. His actions echoed in eternity. 'How bad can it be?'

'Pretty bad! The waves would sweep you onto *Cape Ja Te Kang*, batter you to a pulp, and we would have to explain it all to the police!'

Ross said, 'So what? In the end, we all die of life. The more you live, the more you die, so get used to the territory.'

'Life being the ultimate carcinogen.'

'Correct. You live by the sword, you die by it. But without the sword, what makes warriors live?'

'Nothing.'

Twenty minutes passed, and with them the storm's violence. But the gigantic waves kept sweeping the bands of rock protruding like fingers into the bay. Ross was committed now, and nothing that Pearl could do would change it.

To their right, the setting sun appeared behind low thunder clouds. There was a group of Burmese surfers, their joie-de-vivre clear to see. They danced in the waves on their one-person kayaks. They aimed for the open waters, but the sea had other ideas. A group of girls was cheering them on with shouts and screams. One by one, the guys succumbed to the breakers, tumbling back to the beach and to loving embraces.

Ross was sure about one thing. That wasn't going to let that happen to him. When he made a break for it, he would keep it going.

Two events occurred simultaneously. First, an enormous bolt of lightning hit the pirates bar. Ross and his two friends exchanged looks as if to say, *where did that come from?* Second, there was gap in the waves.

Following the lightning bolt, Ross felt strangely energised. He felt as though the molecules in the surrounding air had been re-arranged.

'Did you feel that?'

'Feel what?' asked Pearl.

'I guess that's a no,' said Ross. 'I just feel electric.'

Ross saw a gap in the rollers entering the bay and jumped from his perch, trading the smooth planks for the coarse, golden sand of the beach.

He made fast progress off the beach. He was quicker and more agile than the Burmese. Ahead of him came the rough zone. *Cape Ja Te Kang* dead ahead, dark and foreboding.

Chapter 8

Safonovo airport (disused), Kola Peninsula, Russia

Alexandra Kirilenka made the final checks from the list. She was on the inside of the capsule in the depths of what was once the airport terminal building. Quietness enveloped her. A thumbs up told her assistants all they needed to know. A thousand times before had she told herself that when the time came, she wouldn't hesitate. And she didn't. That time had come, and it was once in a generation.

Kirilenka tapped the glass screen, and a map appeared in front on the co-ordinates pad. She selected *Cape Ja Te Kang* from the list on the screen and clicked it.

Embrace any insight, she thought. Nuclear war was the consequence of Ross's death. If Ross made it? If he didn't die off *Cape Ja Te Kang?* What would happen? There was a chance she could prevent global nuclear conflict. The theory was sound. The empirical tests over a decade. Right then, she too was preventing it. She had knowledge of the Darkness, but not its limits. Not yet. She knew how the Darkness networked. Perhaps the knowledge, lost since the Ancient Greeks, was again propagating on Earth.

The Safonovo airport terminal site system. She theorized it, designed it, and built it. Nobody else knew why or how it worked; not even Pavel Ivanov, though she had explained it to him more than once. It didn't help.

She had built the system alone. It had been hard. Very hard. But the harder it got, the clearer her head and the stronger her appetite for success.

Polyarny Inlet was home, but she had been born in Ukraine. She had studied physics at Moscow State University. Her father was Ukrainian. He worked in the military shipyard. Her mother was Russian, and worked as an art teacher in Polyarny.

After Moscow State, she entered GRU as graduate entry. Military Intelligence. They saw her abilities and ordered her back to Murmansk. They gave her a stack of cash, and they gave her the keys to the Safonovo airport terminal building. A "special operation" they said. One which she was to design and execute a deterministic predictor machine. One which could predict the next events of the closed Earth system. The theoretical physics held up. If one could calculate the velocity and momentum of each particle on Earth, the next second, minute, and hour of real Earth history could be predicted.

So she developed the machine, which was a capsule linked to a beam generator. It would send out a beam of electromagnetic energy to the black hole at the centre of the galaxy. The beam would propagate through the black hole via a wormhole and emerge in a parallel world, whose identity she did not yet know. But she knew it had to be there.

On the other side, the peoples of the parallel world would send the beam back to Earth. The second wormhole in space, and it would irradiate Earth in its energy. The velocity and momentum of every particle on Earth would be calculated, and become known to the person in the parallel world, which would then propagate back to her, Alexandra Kirilenka, through the third wormhole.

Kirilenka came up to speed. Testing, checking. Each time, the tiny capsule had a separate set of data; a packet of concentrated energy and mass. A beam focussed across space to the centre of the Milky Way Galaxy, to the supermassive black hole. A one-way ticket, she thought. A paradox. But she knew it would return through the third wormhole. Classic physics. Each action has a symmetrical opposing action. Weight. Forces. Every action had an opposing reaction. Why should "darkness" be any different? Darkness here meant light somewhere else. There had to be another world out there. Otherwise, nothing had sense. Journey's end would be a time and space warp. Mass and energy went way into the future.

Then came the first test. Something known. Controlled. The next second, minute, hour. And the data returned from space with a carbon copy of the actual outcome.

She tested and re-tested. Checked and Re-checked. She stored the data for further checks. The next day, she did the same; the next second, minute hour. Most surprising was the indication obtained about what additional capabilities the new technology would create. Each jump in technology always engendered further, new advances. Why would the most important technical advance since the Wright Brothers invented powered flight be any different? But what the results were telling was truly amazing: whichever event she focused on gave her the opportunity to be in two places at the same time. Focus on Koh Tao, and she would be present both on Koh Tao and in Safonovo. The insight she had obtained; the knowledge, was outstanding. And it was Russian, to be held and utilised by GRU only for military purposes.

Kirilenka let the results sink in, taking long walks in the wilderness surrounding Safonovo to achieve such an aim. Months passed until finally she decided the time was ready to take things further. So she tested the next day, week, and month. Each time, the same results; spot on. All world events portrayed. She had invented a prediction machine.

There had to be someone inside the Black Hole. God, she thought. Or someone with godlike power. There had to be light there, to balance the darkness. But anyone's guess who or what it could be. Those were questions above her pay grade. She only knew for certain that the recipient received data sent. They turned it around and spewed it out. Streamed into space on the other side of the black hole. The place was accessible via a wormhole linked to her capsule. She could receive it. Collect it. She had created the first wormhole which allowed access to the other side. To the lightness. With it came a return data stream, which the theory told her, was the third wormhole in the system. With it too came the power to predict. The next day, next month or next year. Finally, the additional capability. She could be present in two places at once. The first place would be the Safonovo airport terminal building. The second place, the location of the Earth event she would modulate.

She was ready for the start sequence of the first use of the system operationally. She relaxed and ran the set. Data streamed to the worm hole. A one way trip by the data to the centre of the galaxy; to the "lightness" wherever that was. It had to be a world, she thought, populated by humans. Einstein had predicted a star would be visible despite being behind the sun. Well, she knew a planet with people existed behind the Milky Way's black hole. For an unknown reason, she already knew the name was *Archaia*.

The display flickered, and she gripped the retaining straps. Stressed now; this was for real. She had asked the "humans" of the lightness, *Archaia*, two questions. One—when would the nuclear war would start. Two—the best bet pivoting site to modulate it. Beads of sweat appeared on her brow.

The flicker stopped. The screen became constant. Clear. It showed two events. Two pivotal sites. A "list". The first was the start of the nuclear war in six days' time, on 7 November 2024 at 18.30. A nuclear strike on Germany by Russia. That would set the dominos in motion; a series of connected escalating strikes. The second pivotal seemed harmless. But connected. It had to be a cause of the first site; a cause of the war. A guy called Lee Ross off *Cape Ja Te Kang*, Koh Tao, Thailand. He was going to die on the rocks. He was going to be pounded to pulp by the high seas in the midst of an Andaman Storm in the Gulf of Thailand.

Kirilenka looked at the date and time—November 1, 2024. That very day, and in fifteen minutes time. She put shutdown on hold, and pulled the communication link to GRU, Moscow, off the capsule wall.

Pavel Ivanov was busy, but he took the call. He had to. Kirilenka's call would be bigger than anything else he had worked on that day. The ability to change the world didn't come every minute of the day.

Ivanov's raspy tones and foreign intonation came through the telephone link. Kirilenka said, 'Ready, Sir.'

'Are you sure you want to do this Alex? No going back once you make this call.'

'Sir, because you asked, I'm good for this. It's been a long time, and I'm ready.'

'How many pivotal sites are there?'

'Two sites, but only one pivotal. There's the start of World War Three on 7 November 2024. Obvious, that one. I've focussed attention on the pivotal.'

'What about it?'

'It's a sea kayaker in a storm off the island of Koh Tao, an island in Thailand. It's in a little over fifteen minute's time, Sir.'

'Then go for it, if you're good for this. Good luck Alexandra, and Godspeed!'

***

Lee Ross's passage through the breakers was straight. It was perpendicular. He had the knowledge that an oblique force is all it would take to capsize him, and there would be no chance to re-enter the kayak. The granite cliffs of *Cape Ja Te Kang*, which fell to the depths of the Gulf, towered above the churning seas.

Ross saw a path through the waves. It was a chance, and Ross went for it. There would be deeper waters ahead, beyond the cape. He could see the calmer water ahead, shimmering like a mirage in a desert.

But behind him reared a wave, bigger than the rest. Much bigger. It was growing, surging. A fifty year wave, thought Ross, catching sight of it. He felt its presence, closer than comfortable. Air blasted from its depths, but he was on a roll, elation tingling in his nerves. He knew nothing of the pivotal and the Darkness. He was happy.

Kirilenka tapped the screen; a check on the pivotal. Her face was all smiles, like a delicate kiss on soft petals: the pivotal was green, which meant it was accessible. The screen blinked; the system extrapolated; and a depiction of Ross flicked up, in real time.

Ross cursed for wasting time, and had the required knowledge, which told him it was time to break the rules. With two quick strokes of his oar, he spun the craft and headed for the deeper waters far off the cape. Towards the south. Towards Koh Samui.

A trade. The swell lines would no longer fall perpendicular, but there were few good choices left.

Ross was facing make or break, and Kirilenka synchronized to the Lightness, to *Archaia*. A beam of radiation set out across space, and a data packet swept back through the third wormhole from the far side. Instant. The data subject's future set out on her screen. The future of the closed Earth system. Nothing from outer space to change it. *Not her problem*, thought Kirilenka. All she needed was that it worked.

The screen was a reconstruction of the future. A matter of fact. Extrapolation of the path and speed of each particle in the Earth system. The system would predict the future or the past. It needed selection of the place and time, and the system did the rest. Kirilenka watched the screen and picked out Ross.

He was doing well. He was halfway through the surf break, but things weren't over. Not yet. The jagged granite rocks of *Cape Ja Te Kang* were close. They were above him. There was a line of gigantic swells approaching, growing. The first was the biggest. It was a 50 year wave.

Kirilenka saw there were ten seconds left to the pivotal, so she put the cross hairs on Ross and hit the gas. The nuclear beam straight into the first wormhole. Safonovo airport connected to the black hole at the centre of the Milky Way.

The wave closed in, Ross paddling for his life with rhythm and power. The surge was upon him, crashing in his wake, above and behind. He sensed its approach, frame by frame; slow-motion.

Lightning cracked above, closely followed by a roar of thunder. He thought of his father. He thought of the moment when he was young boy on a farm, and had a nose bleed that wouldn't stop. Other memories came and went. So many memories, but at that time, the nose bleeding episode came back. Proof that death was close, he thought.

The next second came and he was still there. Still thinking. Still functioning. Sirrirat "Air" Kakandee came to his mind, and he was not sure why. Ten years had passed since he last saw her pretty face. Same place; *Cape Ja Te Kang*. But he had been on the granite of the cape, not off it in a storm. Different time.

He looked behind. No 50 year wave in sight, only the churning of bubbles on a flat, open sea.

His momentum had swept him over the deep water, and he had the knowledge that he had been saved. *Been saved? No. He had done this. So why did he feel as if he had cheated death by an invisible hand?* The sea was calmer, but could still capsize him. But he was out of danger. That was for sure. He breathed a sigh of relief, and paddled and pulled toward Chalok Baan Bay.

***

Kirilenka pulled up the pivotal sites and went to work. Ross had survived, and now to see if the future had indeed changed, modulated. She closed her eyes; took deep breaths. Her heartbeat returned to normal, and so she opened them again.

There were now three pivotal sites. It had worked! She had modulated Earth history!

The first two were out of range.

The third was in five days' time, in Barcelona. Lee Ross again. Kirilenka had time to get there. She could do this, so she zoomed in on Ross, the time displayed in the top right of the screen—07.55. The date was there, five days in the future—6 November 2024. The venue was a café on Barcelona's large, central square. *Placa De Catalunya*. It was on the corner of the square and *Carrer de Pelai*.

The screen showed Ross sitting on the square drinking espresso coffee. The cup in his hand was burning espresso, small and white. He was sipping it, and watching the square with what seemed to be arrogant indifference. Coffee and total control of the situation. Definitely Ross, Kirilenka thought. She checked the time. A minute to go to the pivotal.

In real time, a motorcycle screamed along *Carrer de Pelai* into range of the system. The motorcycle mounted the curb. The black leather-clad rider had one hand on the handlebars, and one moving to his side. There was a smooth, fluid action as the rider reached inside his jacket to a semi-automatic. He aimed it at the terrace of Café Zurich, and a curtain of bullets exploded across the terrace.

Ross reacted, but too late. From the moment the rider left the *Carrer* to opening fire was all ten seconds, and Ross stood no chance. Kirilenka watched as he lay there, motionless, his body riddled with bullets.

Blood pooled onto the terrace.

Kirilenka shut down the system and exited the capsule, her face a twisted wreck. Actions witnessed and lived, which actually was half the truth. Her assistants crowded around her. They had concerned expressions.

She thought to herself, *don't worry. I can handle this.*

Kirilenka said, 'Get me a place on the next flight, to Barcelona.'

Chapter 9

Joint Base Andrews, Virginia, USA

Evening had settled. It was 5 November 2024, and Americans were casting votes for their 47th President.

The CIA needed all the Russian walk-ins they could get. Ukraine. 7.10. Ross saw the Russian at the bar, and thought that there was not a shadow of a doubt. A walk in the park, he thought, and went all in with truth and provocation. CIA playbook in post-Ukraine, post 7.10. Truth and provocation. He was a pilot, and felt a strong affinity for law. Truth, in life, was all important. Connections and honour. Truth and integrity.

The walk-in spun around in her bar stool, and looked at Ross for the first time in her life. Ross had whispered something behind her left hand shoulder about drinks which only she could have heard, so she played her hand. She turned and revealed herself as Helen "Anella" Moskva, and he noticed her slim, athletic body and lily white face. She had a narrow waist, and he imagined what it would feel like to squeeze it. But then she said something which put her name in doubt. She said, 'You can call me Lena Moskva, or Helene Moscow. Or simply "Lena." It's up to you.'

Next morning dawned clear and warm, and Ross awoke early despite the partying the previous night. Sun was streaming into his apartment on Joint Base Andrews, Washington D.C.

It was a modern space tailored for him. He cast his eyes around the features. There was a Jacuzzi and a king-size bed in the living space. It had views to a park through huge patio doors.

But right then, he wasn't enjoying the facilities. Easy relief wasn't part of the plan. His mind had clicked into replay mode. He could still picture the walk-in. She had piercing blue eyes and a lily white face, and slim body. He recalled her raven hair. Her narrow hips, and lithe stature. He thought back to the words exchanged, hoping details would crystalize.

They didn't, so he tossed aside the duvet, grabbed his laptop, and opened the browser. Time for AI, he thought and he pulled up GPT-6, and punched in a query.

GPT-6—Conduct an all points intelligence sweep for a SU-57 inbound to the US.

He endured the response by whisking up a double espresso. It would sharpen his focus and get the input right first time. Get it wrong, and he could go down a rabbit hole. At least that was what someone had once told him.

The slim coffee machine was whining and screaming and then an espresso appeared burning and thick. He poured it into a small white cup and details came flooding back. He stood for a moment, and remembered a name. *Anella Moskva.* As for the venue, it was the Bluejacket in DC's Navy Yard.

He remembered there had been a free table backing up to the wall, midway between the bar and the dance floor. The music was loud, the whiskies were strong and the venue was packed.

A tall waitress twisted through the crowd and caught his eye. She wore a crisp white t-shirt, with a single word emblazoned in capitals across her chest. Ross snagged her, saying 'Two double Jack Daniels with coke on ice.'

He noticed the walk-in make eye contact.

'Two drinks?'

'Two drinks,' whispered Ross, as if to make the connection private. 'One has your name on it.'

Things weren't going well just for Ross. They were going exceptionally well for the walk-in. Ross was how his file said he would be, with short dark hair and eyes like hers, a touch deeper blue.

Ross pulled out a chair. The walk-in smiled like he had cracked a joke.

Ross covered the bill, lifting his glass, and saying, 'За здоровье!'

'За здоровье!' echoed Moskva, and then she flicked her hair back, asking. 'Your question?'

'Excuse me?'

'I guess it was the American who waited outside the cell in that Moscow prison who masterminded the death of Magnitsky. It might affect the election. No? Especially if the American turns out to be who he is. You have a situation and I'm guessing you've plugged it into AI to get a read on it.'

'Yes,' said Ross. 'We even hired a psychic. Top-notch stuff!'

'So are you worried?'

'About the "American"? Why should we be? Everyone knows what happened to Magnitsky. No opportunity for either the CIA or your organisation.'

Moskva said, 'What about Magnitsky?'

Ross said, 'Look. We know it happened in a Moscow prison. It would take more than a GRU agent to change the story. Someone in your government ordered it. Potanin himself, probably. That juggernaut of public opinion has already left.'

Moskva's eyes bored into Ross like red-hot daggers. 'Western propaganda!'

Ross said, 'What's your point here?'

'My point? Aren't you the forward one? To make a deal of course. The world is rapidly entering the World War Three death throes. Our governments need to cut a deal to end the stand-off. Besides, your country has a vested interest in keeping the truth about Magnitsky under wraps. But we know the truth, and there's a Russian SU-57 on its way to the US to spread it around. You see, there's a video.'

'Ah, a video. There's always one of those. But about the deal. What deal?'

'Ukraine, Stupid! And now, I'm curious. Is sarcasm your default negotiating position? Because I'm not buying into it. The SU-57 is mid-Atlantic and soon the news about Magnitsky will be household knowledge, the news being that the CIA, that you Americans killed him, not the Russian state. The mission approved. And only I can turn that plane around, but I'll need your agreement.'

Ross leaned in, a mock-serious expression written on his face. He said, 'About the video. But why should I care?'

'Because this is your great democratic institution. You need to consider what would happen if that SU-57 enters US airspace. The video would spread faster than a plague. Like on auto. Like a dead hand. After it's done, the Democrats might as well throw in the towel.'

Ross's look turned serious. 'Why? Just because some American masterminded the Magnitsky killing? You'll need more than that, so why not cut to the chase? Because this isn't about Magnitsky at all. It's about you. You're defecting, right?'

'What I am is not important. At best, I'm sideshow to the main event. But back to basics. I asked if you conducted AI on the SU-57 inbound to the US?'

'Of course, we'll check it out. Thank you for the tip. We'll see what it trawls up.'

Moskva smiled and knocked back her shot. She wasn't getting anywhere. The liquid slid down her throat like a shot of iced espresso on a Monday morning. She savoured its oaken notes. Time to change tack, she thought, and so she leaned in, and Ross reciprocated. 'Well, well. Lee Ross, the military man. North Cape. Israel, *Cape Ja Te Kang*. You've been quite the globe-trotter. Impressive resume. There's also the charming story of your entanglement with Akemi Bando, the Japanese-American F35 ace.'

Ross sighed. He slouched his six-foot stature back into his seat, which was warm and hard and accommodating to his weight. 'Very impressive, Lena. Not unexpected. The GRU did it right. The research is spot on.'

Moskva had raised an eyebrow. There was a smile, but Ross sensed a brewing storm. He said, 'But you made a mistake, and I'm guessing you're all bluster right now, hoping I didn't cotton on.'

'As in?' Moskva waved down a passing waitress, and signalled for a repeat of the same drinks. She was taking control. She needed him loose.

'You targeted me!'

'And with good reason!'

'Which is?'

Moskva leaned in, her look inquisitorial. 'Look, Flight Major Lee Ross, of the CIA. There's nothing to gain from this conversation, or from the proxy war in Ukraine. Neither for the US or Russia. After 7.10, everyone wants business as usual, not forever wars.'

'So?' Ross's eyebrow curled.

'So why not end it here and now, you and me? Let's cut to the chase. You're a pilot, and you're CIA's deputy director of intelligence.'

'And?' Ross took a long sip from his glass, as if the liquid would conjure a successful outcome to what loomed liked a losing situation.

'I'm GRU.'

'And I'm CIA. So what?'

'So how difficult could it be to negotiate an end to the war in Ukraine. That terrible, hideous proxy war? We get authorization from our respective agencies. Stop the war. Hammer it out.'

Ross swirled his glass, ice jingling. He swigged it, and said, 'The core of a deal? Why not?'

'I'm being serious!'

'Well good, because so am I.'

'Suppose they gave us the keys to the back corridor between our countries?'

Ross sighed, and then he said, 'Okay. I'll go along with this exercise in futility. What you're saying is what if we were the last two people on Earth with a modicum of common sense? A backroom deal to end this Russia-Ukraine war? Sure. Why not? But I need something extra.'

Moskva felt like she was finally getting somewhere, and she said, 'In such a scenario, what exactly would the US be offering?'

Ross chuckled, his voice laced with the effects of the alcohol. 'No, you first. You came here to make a deal. So you start.'

'Okay. America pressures Ukraine. The pressure is to accept Russia's annexation of four eastern provinces and Crimea. Ukraine demilitarizes, ends its Bandera associations, and declares perpetual neutral status.'

'In exchange for?'

'The normalization of relations between the US and Russia, obviously. For an end to the proxy war. America will no longer be looking down the barrel of nuclear annihilation. A win—win situation.'

Ross said, 'We need something more.'

'As in?'

'Information on Victoria Feodor.'

'Who?'

'You know who she is?'

'No I don't. Tell me.'

A waitress came with whiskies and cokes, and set them down on the table. Ross had missed the ordering stage, and a surge of suspicion washed over him. The alcohol was playing tricks, and he had the requisite knowledge to know it, so he decided to cut his loss and shoved a handful of dollars into the waitress's hand and rose from his seat. He noticed the surprise on the Russian's face. He leaned in close enough for her to catch a whiff of his aftershave. With a steely gaze and a flash of a perfect smile, he uttered, 'That's hardly an attractive proposition, Lena, so I decline. I mean, we don't deal through threats. But it was nice to meet you, and I hope the feeling is mutual.'

Moskva sighed and watched him go, his Captain Hilts USAF jacket disappearing towards the exit, which was up front.

He was advancing rapidly, but still felt that Anella Moskva had won the encounter. Still, he thought. Nothing ventured, nothing gained. Then he felt an unyielding prod in his back, and clarity returned.

Glock, he thought. Moskva had moved in for the kill. He would indulge her. After all, she was dancing to his tune. He said, 'Okay. What now?'

Moskva said, 'For now, you keep walking. Through the doors.'

'Where are we going?'

'To a car.'

'You're kidnapping me?!'

'We need to talk. No distractions. Keep walking. We're going to walk straight out of here.'

They hit the street. It was cold and wet. A storm was blowing in. It was raining. Not heavy, not light. Washington D.C. in late autumn. Ross said, 'Alright. So what's the play here?'

Moskva pointed to the other side of the road, and with raspy Russian tones said, 'See the Hummer over there? We're going to walk over to it, and you're going to get into the rear.'

'And then what?'

'We're going to have a chat.'

'This is a dangerous game.'

'For you, yes, 'cos I have the gun.'

'Russian spook detaining a lawman in the heart of DC. Not at all suspicious.'

'You're not a lawman. You're CIA, so don't kid yourself. Don't worry. It'll be a friendly conversation.' Her words cut through the air, a subtle smirk played across her lips. It hinted at hidden motives beneath her friendly demeanour. With a gentle nudge, she urged him forward, her touch carrying a faint hint of icy calculation.

Ross felt a surge of adrenaline in his veins. He squared his shoulders, and took a step closer to Moskva. He couldn't help but notice the subtle tension in her posture, the controlled intensity in her gaze. It was a silent challenge, a test of wills between two players in a high-stakes game.

With a silent vow to trust no one and to keep his wits about him, Ross braced himself for what lay ahead. The beginning of a deadly game of cat and mouse. 'Sure. Friendly,' he muttered. He wasn't smiling.

There were three occupants in the Hummer, two in the front, one in the back. Big guys. They had square, angular haircuts. Military, thought Ross. They had necks as wide as their heads. Muscular. Well trained. The rear door swung open as they approached from across the street.

Ross climbed in and eased his big frame into the back seat. Moskva followed, trapping him. Fine, thought Ross. The Glock was still there, inserted into his side. No chance to risk it, he thought. It wasn't exactly how he planned the evening to shape up. He turned to Moskva and fixated her chiselled jawline, and wondering how she managed to get such an immaculate complexion. Out of this worldly were his first thoughts. He said, 'So, what's on the agenda?'

Moskva ordered the driver to get on with it, and the driver reacted like he was a robot. He was as rigid as a statue. Calmly, the guy said, 'Where are we headed?'

'You choose. Just drive. Talking is what matters, not the scenery. Actually, you know what? Head towards the Lincoln Monument.'

'Talk about what?' hazarded Ross, squinting to his side, his eyes locked with his mannequin-like captor.

'Negotiations.'

'What's up for negotiation?'

'We just talked about it. An end to the Russo-Ukrainian war. But no games, Ross. Straight talk.'

Ross leaned in, which wasn't easy. There wasn't an abundance of space. With a smile he said, 'Straight talk it is, then. Let's lay all our cards on the table.'

Moskva's head flicked downwards. A measured nod. 'That's right. Take the elections. We have the means to tilt the scales.'

Another wry smile crept onto Ross's lips. 'Ahh! You're offering me a sneak peek? How generous!'

Moskva held steady. 'In exchange for a favour. A nudge for Ukraine to accept our terms. We both walk away. The US avoids the abyss.'

Ross chuckled and eased deeper into the Hummer's leather comforts. 'Avoiding abysses seems to be a recurring theme. So what are you offering?'

Moskva spun, her gaze head-on, eyes narrowing into two intense slits. 'Ukraine agrees to the annexation of the four eastern oblasts. Neutrality for the rest of her territory. America gets a clean slate.'

'Give and take, then. But in this case, one wrong move, and the board lights up.'

'Do you want to know your mistake?' said Moskva, her voice cutting through the low hum of the engine.

'Why is it that something tells me you're going to tell me anyway?'

'Encouraging Ukraine into NATO. Short memory, huh? 2008, Bucharest Summit, NATO declared Ukraine would enter. Russia made it clear—no dice. You Americans, doubling down seems to be reaching epidemic levels. 2023, Vilnius Summit, same story. It's like doubling down is your national pastime.'

The Hummer cruised on through the wet Washington night. Speed limit. No broken lights or excessive noises. Nothing for law enforcement to latch onto.

Ross said, 'Despite what we said earlier, I can't make a deal, and you lack the authority too. Also, your offer needs more weight.' He scanned the road through the pebbled windshield. The Lincoln Monument was up ahead. It loomed large in the windscreen.

'Fine. But don't forget, with every passing second the SU-57 gets closer to US airspace.'

Magnitsky, thought Ross. He said, 'So tell me about Magnitsky. You have video proof that an American masterminded his murder. What else?'

'More than proof, Ross. I've got evidence. Boatloads of it. It would unravel that narrative faster than a house of cards in a hurricane. Magnitsky's demise wasn't orchestrated by the Russian state. It was a designed plan by Western intelligence to smear Russia. And it worked like a charm. The Magnitsky files are the truth, and soon, they will spread across much of the US.'

Ross arched an eyebrow. 'You expect me to believe this BS?'

'I need you to understand the stakes. The moment those files go public, the world will see how your own agencies manufactured a crisis. That's the leverage we have.'

'And you can call off the SU-57 right now?'

'I can.'

'How?'

'A new invention. It's called a telephone. All I have to do is make a call to a GRU commander in Moscow. I have the number, and the access code. The smartphone is right here.'

'In Moscow?'

'That's what I said.' Moskva's eyes were gleaming with a kind of certainty that made Ross uneasy. 'You see, Ross, the Magnitsky files aren't a bargaining chip. They're the real deal. The trump card. A revelation that will shake the very foundations of your intelligence community. The US orchestrated a grand narrative, and we've got the backstage passes to the entire show.'

The Hummer came to a halt, its tyres screeching on the humid asphalt. They were in front of the Lincoln Monument. That was clear. Moskva said, 'We have video evidence of Magnitsky confessing. It shows the US killed him. Not Russia. We have it saved to a digital file in a secure location.'

'But also in the SU-57 right?'

'Yeah. You got it. They're all up there, approaching the US. Soon, every household on the eastern seaboard will know. All they have to do is to click on a link. Download the file. In the interview, Magnitsky confirms that this William Burns, was the mastermind. He was present at Magnitsky's murder. The American waiting outside the cell when the eight OMON riot cops went in. Do I need to say more?'

'Is that it?' said Ross.

'No. There are the workbooks of the Kalmykians. Those invalids who worked as analysts but couldn't even write. There is the video footage of the murder. And there is the video of Magnitsky admitting everything, and of William Burns admitting to being the mastermind. GRU now controls all the evidence. More?'

The weight of the revelation hung in the air. There was a full moon rising between clouds, shadows deepening. Ross felt the tendrils of a narrative more intricate than he had bargained for closing in.

The Hummer's engine idled, a low roar. The shadows played tricks in the dim glow of far streetlights. Ross contemplated the gravity of Moskva's proposition. Election night had turned the city into a vast celebration. But by the street lights of the Lincoln Monument, a different drama was unfolding.

'But how is this a strong negotiating position?' Ross inquired. His piercing eyes had fixed his opponent.

'Because the US is the Golden Boy on the International stage. If it comes out that William Burns, an American, is the killer, the US would stand to lose a lot. You should know; you should have the requisite knowledge that powerful people in the US government would never let that happen.'

'How exactly do you know so much about me?'

'Meaning?'

'You said I should have the requisite knowledge. No-one knows me better than you do, and I'm wondering why.'

'Just a hunch. Look Ross. I'm giving you a choice to get ahead of this. If you want, it can be a sweetener to the deal.'

'So if the US makes the deal, you will make the call to the SU, stop the download, and all this goes away.'

'Right,' she said, holding aloft the phone. Shall I make the call?'

She held up the phone.

'All I need is that you will agree to open a back channel for negotiations. And then I'll call off the SU for the time being.'

The Hummer rumbled in the background and Moskva was laying out the stakes. The weight of the situation settled over the quiet layby near the Lincoln Monument.

'If the US doesn't, we will release them, shaming the US. Think about it. America enacted the Magnitsky Act in 2012. We can release this video to the world, of you and me, talking. You see, someone is recording all this. Already uploaded it to servers in Russia. The world will know that you did nothing to search for the killer of Magnitsky when you had the chance. You will go down in history as a pariah. Right now, you have the chance to go down as a hero. Which will it be? So what will you do? Will you help us to make this deal?'

Chapter 10

Kirilenka was in Colonel Alexander Gottman of the GRU's office, and she saw Gottman take a phone call. She saw that it was Moskva and thought for a moment. Then she watched Gottman as he answered. He wasn't expecting the call. Ivanov was next door, but it was Gottman's operation.

Moskva said, 'I'm calling this operation off, Sir. Lee Ross is drunk. We will make another attempt when we identify another target.'

'Not a problem,' replied Gottman. 'I'll get the message to operations for relay to the SU-57. Gottman out.'

Kirilenka watched him as he stood, and paced, and stood again, deep in thought. He paced again, approaching the window. Something wasn't right, Kirilenka could see that on his face. He was looking out across the snowy square, searching for answers. The Presidential Administration. Kitai Gorad. Further back, there was the old British Embassy and the river. He liked the view, but another was forming, one of hope flashing through his mind. He didn't get far, as a flash burned into his eyeballs. From the trees he thought, for an instant. On the other side of the square. Then the bullet hit, and he fell dead to the floor. Blood pooled all across the wooden floorboards.

Kirilenka didn't seem shocked. Neither was she disappointed. Moskva had been unable to secure a deal with Ross to end the Ukraine war, which meant that her services would be needed again should the GRU wish to end the proxy war with the US in a bloodless way.

Chapter 11

Hours passed and the Hummer drove on through wet Washington streets. The engine roared its deep background noise.

Moskva's attention was on Ross's vital signs. She needed him alive. Her eyes swung toward her companions. The Hummer rumbled on through the wet streets. Steady. Constant.

Ross stirred. His eyes flickered, and then he tried to sit up. Tried, but failed. His body protested.

The vehicle pulled up to a squeaky halt near the entrance of Ross's barracks. They helped him out onto the pavement. Shaky legs, but he stood unaided. No swaying. Just alcohol and weariness weighing him down.

Moskva looked at him, her expression unreadable. She said. 'Okay, Mr Ross. You've had a rough night. Get some rest. We'll be in touch.'

The engine growled back to life, and the Hummer disappeared into the Washington night. Ross stood there alone, between veils of darkness and the city's dazzling lights. Otherwise, he was fine. He had his keys, and his apartment was close.

He slid the key into his door, and navigated the room. The sideboard emerged from the shadows. A familiar sight. The coffee machine beckoned him like an old friend out of the gloom, its presence a comforting anchor. He loaded a pod, traded a double espresso, and downed it in one swift motion. Then he tossed the duvet aside, crawled under it, and succumbed to deep sleep.

Consciousness returned, but the darkness lingered. 17 hours had passed. The lost hours whispered their tale. There was an alert blinking in the depths of the room. An alarm, a neon message sitting there, 'SU-57 and Magnitsky and videos to be broadcast.'

There was a realisation. A memory. His gaze met the ceiling, a faint glow of celestial motifs. The bar and the enigmatic spy. He reached for solace, conjuring a double espresso like a rabbit from a hat; a remedy for uncertain hours ahead.

Ross experienced a surge of caffeine. It coursed through pulsating arteries, and he felt electric. He remembered the spy and plugged GPT-6, which purred into action, dissecting the words. It was all about the SU-57 and Magnitsky. The black screen flickered, the output flashing up.

'SU-57 scheduled to take off from Akhtubinsk, Russia. Mission identical. A recon mission and dissemination mission estimated at 98.7%. The media will spread information about Magnitsky. It is likely to hinder the 47th US Presidential Election turnout. Experts estimate the chance of this at 99.8%.'

Ross reached for his mobile. He dialled, and listened, and the ringtone echoed.

Director Hoffman at his desk in the White House. He was running his fingers through his coarse, silver-streaked hair. Stress was weighing heavy. 7.10 and the evolving war in Ukraine. His hair and his motions felt good. He was pondering the shifting strategies.

'Ross.'

'Zak.'

'If this means you and Bando are sick . . .'

'We're fine.'

'If that were true, you wouldn't be calling!'

'I queried GPT-6 about Sergei Magnitsky, and there's something I'd like to bottom out.'

'Sergei Magnitsky?'

'You got it. So you remember?'

'I remember a Ukrainian who died in prison protesting Russian corruption. Nothing new about it.'

'Unless there's more to it than that.'

'As in?'

'US involvement in his death. A rogue mission. Black ops. Something went wrong, and we want to bury it. And now, Russia sees its chance to use what happened for election blackmail, threatening to release it.'

'But why now? Magnitsky died in 2009.'

'I thought there could have been a black op. CIA action back in 2009. And the Russians might try and weaponize it now. Blackmail us in a threat to release it, otherwise they will change the result of the election.'

Hoffman reached the window and stared out into the clear, night. There were stars dotting the sky. Winter in Washington, and there were constellations of stars visible from horizon to horizon. The full moon was sinking, casting its ethereal glow on a band of thick clouds.

Ross was speaking again. He said, 'GPT-6. There'll be options. They'll be evaluating them.'

Hoffman said, 'But why bother?'

'It's standard. That's why. If they have info pointing to US involvement, they're right. If the information is true, the CIA killed Magnitsky. Powerful people would prefer such information remain hidden.'

'Listen, Ross. Tramp will beat the Democrats by a landslide and the Russians are sure to back off. It's hardly in their interests to change anything. What about turnout?'

'If there is such information out there in the ether, it will hinder turnout, which will favour Tramp.'

Hoffman's eyes fixed on the brimstone moon as if frozen in their sockets. He said, 'If AI predicts that this will hinder turnout, that's enough for me. No threat by this Magnitsky information, and I'm not sure why you're bringing this up. Tramp will win, and the Russians aren't going to try to intervene. Budden has been a disaster for them in Ukraine. People have caught on. The effect of the social media posts of experts in offensive realism and geopolitics.

Irritated, Hoffman ended the call with a click, and his arms dropped as if all their power had drained out. The room fell silent and he sauntered to the switch and turned off the lights. The light prevailed, bathed in the muted glow of city lights below. He was pondering the words he had heard. Russia's intervention. A geopolitical dance that was unfolding and changing at every move. The moon sank lower. Stars twinkled. Then, one by one, they disappeared behind a thin veil of high cloud, and Hoffman found himself lost in thoughts of Russia.

Russia, cornered in Ukraine, became an unpredictable adversary. Ross's concern echoed. It reverberated throughout him. But like the IR experts, he embraced realism. In International Relations, it was realpolitik that mattered.

The paradox of 7.10 and the war weighed on him. Enticed by Western promises, Ukraine was a pawn in a dangerous game. Ukraine could help the West as a democratic bulwark. It would be on Russia's doorstep. But, that idea seemed more and more flawed. Russia, had red lines drawn, and now it was clear that they would never allow such an encroachment.

The experts had warned against the path his government had in mind. It was like a train carriage on a single track. The West had ignored his counsel. Ukraine's sovereignty, a lofty ideal, crumbled in the face of geopolitical realities. In the world of nations, might made right. The West's insistence on a different narrative, was misguided and now downright dangerous.

He gazed across the city. He could escape responsibility, if he wanted to. But the West's aggression risked escalation, and Russia had pushed back, strong. The night held its secrets, and Hoffman, stood vigilant, as if for the next move in a game of chess.

The moon kissed the tip of the Washington Monument, and Hoffman felt it a que, and returned to his desk. There was a pile of Intel documents. He lifted one, and saw details of the SU-57, inbound to the US, and the election—coincidence? More likely a Destabilizing Foreign Military Capability. He detested both on any given day, but more so on the eve of the 47th Presidential Election. Ross's words echoed in his mind. Were the Russians weaponizing Magnitsky?

Motivation had returned, and he moved around to the other side of the desk. There were papers, accessible, and abundant, and on one topic. Slatka. She had the key to Ross's fears. She was in the Kremlin's maze.

He soon found the one which had kindled his interest before the call with Ross. He picked up the phone, and dialled.

Bill Linklater answered on the second ring. His Deputy Director of Operations was a thin, wiry sort of man, with thick curly hair. Hoffman cut to the chase. 'What if the Kremlin assigned that new team to disrupt the US election? Is it possible?'

'Zak, after 7.10, anything's possible. Slatka's report. You've seen it I imagine?'

'I'm holding it now. That new Kremlin team's all about hacking. New blood from academia, high-tech businesses, and the tech elite. Could be playing a million hands. When did it begin to troll in?'

A rustling of papers wafted down the line, followed by a silence which tried Hoffman's jumpy nerves. He was about to speak when Linklater's voice returned. 'Joined the party on October 16, 2024.'

'Gather the A-team, Linklater. Top-notch analysts. Objective—find out how Russia will pull the strings on the election? Fast and tight. Thirty minutes. Twenty agents. I want teams. I want options.'

It was ten minutes to the second later when Hoffman breezed into Room 2.7. What he saw heightened his mood, which wouldn't have been difficult. He felt like he was witnessing a home run on the second floor of the long West Wing corridor. There was a vast expanse, with desks for twenty five analysts. The room boasted three windows framing a sweeping view of the White House lawn. The palpable hum of activity invigorated Zak Hoffman. Clearly, objectives were in motion. Linklater's firm grip on the reins was evident. Linklater strode over with a determined gait.

'Zak, we have four teams, five agents each.' He glanced at his watch. 'Their reports are due in just over forty minutes. That's where we are, Sir.'

Hoffman retraced his steps to room 2.6, a simpler space with one desk and a killer view. Capitol Hill. It had all the necessary connections. Coffee machine. Well stocked bar and fridge. All he needed then and there was his phone and an internet link. He dialled a familiar number, etched into his memory—Slatka. He heard the foreign ring tone.

Hoffman cut to the chase. 'The new Kremlin team. Are they interested in weather reports?'

'Anything to do with the elections,' came the response in the deep tones he loved. 'What else?'

'Locations?'

'The swing states. Wisconsin. Pennsylvania. Georgia ...'

'Have they communicated recently with the VVS, Russian Air Force command?'

'Affirmative. Communication constant.'

Chapter 12

Akhtubinsk, Russia

On the other side of the world, Flight Major Timofeev slammed the throttle of the scaled up SU-57 prototype. He intended to push it to the limit of the envelope. The twin engines engaged, all 2500 kN each. The aircraft roared down the runway, became airborne, banked, and headed northwest. Out over the Volga River, supersonic.

His co-pilot eased herself forward, against her straps. Timofeev saw it, and couldn't repress a smile. She was Easy, and she *eased* herself forward.

Easy updated the flight status on the glass cockpit. She talked to the controller via the encrypted flight system. Her name was Easy, but that was just a call sign. Korean and Russian, from a diaspora of North Koreans resettled by Stalin. She grew up in Sakhalin oblast in the Far East, and was fluent in Korean, Japanese Russian and English.

Timofeev knew only Russian and English. He glanced across the flight deck, the smile wiped. 'Let Moscow Vnukovo know about us via encryption. Update them on our ETA. Tell them to maintain silence until we're inbound to them, three hours from now.'

'Roger that, Major.'

'No need for this to get complicated, Easy,' said Timofeev.

Easy stole a glance, but Timofeev's eyes were outside. Better, thought Easy. She tried to relax. Which wasn't easy. VVS prohibited flight crew relationships. No one knew about "them" except her and the Major. But, that wouldn't help pass three long hours with him over the North Atlantic.

Timofeev's thoughts wandered back to the briefing with the general. Stark words. 'This mission is a first. Longer and harder than anything you've ever trained for. You'll fly to the edge of space; to the edge of the SU's envelope. Then, you'll go to an assigned location deep inside US airspace. You'll upload the data over a set course and time. Then, you'll return to altitude and leave.'

'Like plugging everything into GPT-7 and running it?' Timofeev ventured.

'That's true, Major,' affirmed the VVS general. 'Your plane is a prototype. Twin seated. Upgraded with the latest technology. 2.3 times the size of the original. It will run the latest AI programs, including GPT-7. These programs are from Russia and are for nanotechnology, the best in the world.'

'And where do we come back to? Here?'

'Negative,' said the general. 'You'll be going to Moscow Vnukovo.'

Timofeev absorbed the general's instructions with a nod, contemplating the challenges ahead.

Timofeev looked at Easy. He knew that the success of their mission depended on the SU-57's capabilities. The pressure helmets sealed them off from the outside world. They wore them as they ascended toward the edge of space.

'Take her to the ceiling, Easy,' he said. 'To the edge of space. Let's see what she can do. If this mission is as crucial as they claim, we'll need every advantage. We can hit the big numbers on the edge of space. It'll save us time and fuel—both of which we can't afford to waste.'

Easy set the auto-pilot to 60 km altitude, adjusting speed and power for efficiency. The engines burned, the aircraft powered towards the edge of the Earth's atmosphere. There, aerodynamics would let it coast. It would cross the North Atlantic without more fuel. The SU-57 was a sleek, quiet predator. It soared in the vast expanse and was a crucial player in the secret games of global powers. Below them, the Earth curved in all directions. The horizon loomed dead ahead. It was black above, tinged deep red ahead. The sun was out of sight. It painted a canvas in deep crimson hues. It looked as if a master artist had swept a brush across the sky.

Timofeev drew in a deep breath, acclimating to the confined space of the pressure suit. 'All right, Easy. Mach 4.2, altitude 59 km. Kill the engines.'

'Copy that, Major.'

Below them, Kyiv and the blazing turmoil of Ukraine became distant echoes. The missile sites persisted. A reminder of the ongoing strife. Europe a battleground. The effects of bad policies. The aftermath of 7.10 and the West's actions in Eastern Europe and the Middle East. Unsustainable bloodshed fuelled by the ambitions of America.

They cruised at Mach 4.5, ghosts in the sky. The aircraft's full-phased array radar made them untouchable. Ukrainian missiles were futile against the cutting-edge stealth technology. A radar profile below 0.1 rendered them invisible.

Timofeev ordered, 'Calculate the distance to Washington D.C.'

Easy fed data into the system, 'Great Circle makes it 7,854 kilometres from our current position. At Mach 4, we'll hit it in 1 hour and 40 minutes.'

'So take us Great Circle, Easy. Straight to Washington D.C.'

Ten minutes slipped by and the sun re-emerged in a burst of hues ahead. Easy gave an update, saying, 'Major, we're currently over the North Devon coastline. Nothing on the horizon until New York. I've got the controls. Get some sleep.'

***

Hoffman sank deep into his chair behind his cluttered desk in his West Wing office. The worn leather groaned like an ancient oak in a strong gale. The problem was keeping up with Linklater, who was sat opposite him. It wasn't a walk in the park. Linklater was telling tales of a new Kremlin team. They had one mission: to manipulate the presidential outcome.

Hoffman squinted over his laptop, and said, 'What's the play here?'

'Alert every polling station. Have them beef up their antivirus and run thorough searches.'

Hoffman's look hardened. 'Closing the barn doors after the horse has bolted? If their aim was to disrupt the election, their phishing attacks would have struck by now.'

'True.'

'Draft a notice to all polling stations and the US Electoral College. Best agents. Identify the cyber weak points. The Electoral College needs help.'

Linklater left the room, and Hoffman felt like a coiled spring. A thought took hold, and he settled back again, a thin smile tugging at the corners of his mouth. Regardless of the outcome, Linklater would take the fall.

Chapter 13

North Atlantic Ocean

Easy touched the Major's right shoulder, and when he didn't wake she shook him. It was their first touch since Volgograd. Their careers were still dangling over a precipice.

Timofeev squinted through his helmet's shaded visor. 'Current position, heading, and speed?'

'Mach 3.5, Sir. Decreasing, because we're approaching the US seaboard. Altitude 57 miles, coasting. Heading 258 degrees.'

Timofeev said 'I have control. Give me the latest on the storm. Centre position, extent, wind speed, and ground temperatures.' Sleep was gone.

'Roger that, Major. South Carolina. Heading east, not north, Sir. It's record-breaking. Stretching from Texas to New York State. Category 4. A hurricane in the middle of winter.'

'Get into position, run the sector as planned, and get out.'

Chapter 14
The White House, Washington D.C.

A sharp, staccato knock ripped, like gunfire, through the silence, and the door swung open. Linklater stood there, his face etched with pain.

'What happened?' asked Hoffman. He had lifted his gaze from the sea of Intel reports on his desk.

'NORAD, Sir. A Russian SU fighter bomber breached US airspace, flying at 50 km altitude. A prototype SU-57. Scaled up, but otherwise identical.'

'God damn Russians!'

'F35s are in the air, Sir. I'll keep you updated as soon as I have more.'

Chapter 15

Joint Base Andrews

As Ross had expected, Hoffman's call had come. Now, he and Akemi Bando were slammed by the full 4500-kilo-Newton force. The modified F35 had double scramjet engines. They were pushing the prototype through the sound barrier. A sonic boom reverberated across the suburbs of Washington. Though other F-35s had been scrambled, his was a scaled up version. More powerful and with spy capabilities. For one, it was a twin seater. He and Bando sat together. They could pool their tasks.

Ross extended his hand and adjusted the left-hand glass screen. He dialled up the scramjets' output to 70 percent power.

Bando reported, 'Heading 325, Angels 93 for bogey.'

'Heading 325, altitude 93,000. Copy.'

Ross made corrections for speed, bearing, and altitude. Bando added, 'Bogey is now at 312, Angels 105. Mach 2 closure. He's turning toward.'

'Heading straight for the eye of the storm, and so are we! Has he seen us?'

'Negative, Sir. We are with him. Contact—12 o'clock, low!'

Ross asked, 'Time to the centre of the storm?'

'They've turned again, heading north.'

'Bugging out.'

Ross leaned forward. He tapped the left screen and increased power to 75%. If the SU had detected them, he would soar into space and vanish. Though there were only 300m between them, the SU was pulling away. He said, 'Any chance we can get him?'

Bando touched the left screen. She replied, 'We can try, Sir, but it's one of their modified SU-57s.'

'I get it. First contact between modified scaled up 5th generation fighters.'

'Right.'

'Only one way to find out,' Ross said. He reached for the left screen and pressed the throttle. Ninety percent. He dialled Hoffman. 'Bogey is bugging out into the North Atlantic, and we're going after him.'

Hoffman's rasping voice rattled through to them. Not because of nothing did they call him Wolf Man. He said, 'Copy that. He'll head for Russia. Follow him. If he messes up, take him out.'

'Copy. Did they disseminate anything about Magnitsky's death?'

'If they did, I'll have news on that within the hour.'

'Copy. We'll shadow across the North Atlantic, and then we'll head for Barcelona. Out.'

Chapter 16

Cafe Zurich, Placa De Catalunya, Barcelona

Next day, early, Ross sat at his usual table at his regular time, enjoying one of life's simple pleasures—espresso coffee served piping hot in small white cups, and a sheaf of the daily newspapers. He digested the news of the election. As expected, Tramp had won by a large margin in all of the swing states. But until January 6, 2025, Budden was still President of the United States. Ross expected Budden to work on repairing his legacy during his last months in office, and that would mean he would be doubling down on support for Ukraine.

It was early morning, and the sun's red orb had just risen above the fountains. He knocked back a shot of espresso and ordered another. He admired his surroundings. Girls passed by in droves. Some in miniskirts and leather jackets. Others were casual. Most noticed Ross as they passed, which wasn't surprising. Ross stood out. He had a chiselled jawline, cool jacket, white shirt, and designer jeans. Just then, he noticed his boss was calling.

Kirilenka walked past the café and saw Ross. There was ten minutes to go, so she kept walking. Ross shouldn't see her. And anyway, what would she say if she approached him? Come with me because your life is in danger? To a CIA field ops agent? No. There had to be another way to get him out of there.

Kirilenka was on the sunny, southern side corner, out of sight. Backed up against the wall, with *Carrer De Pelai* to her right. The morning sun was dead centre. Kirilenka checked that Ross couldn't see her, and then she closed her eyes. Just another Barcelona chick enjoying the morning sun on a street corner. Only this one opened her eyes every now and then. One of her eyes was on the approaching traffic. She looked down, checking her watch. 7 minutes. She was running out of options. Plan B if she had to, but no guarantee it would work. The direct approach.

Kirilenka saw a man approaching. He had dirty jeans and a heavy backpack, and he was out of it, but not too much. A fine line she thought. Like between drunkenness and sobriety. Like Goldilocks. His actions would be controllable, spontaneous.

The "bum" came close, and Kirilenka stepped in front of him, saying, '*Para ahi!*

His dark eyes, watered in their sockets, fixated Kirilenka's. There was anger flickering, and the words "*Por que? Que paso?*" fell from quivering lips.

'What's your name?'

He told Kirilenka.

Kirilenka took his arm, and led him to one side, and threw a disarming smile. She whispered to him in Spanish, 'Pietro, I need your help, and I'm sure you can help me?'

He relaxed as Kirilenka knew he would do. A lady needed him. A task had been set. Humanity was in the genes and the culture ingrained from an early age.

Kirilenka said, 'There's a well-dressed man sitting on the edge of this terrace.' Kirilenka cast her eyes in Ross's direction, and he followed them. 'Fifty euro in it if you can get his attention. Just get him to notice you, and get him into the interior of the café. Here.'

She pressed a fifty euro note into his grubby hands.

'How?'

'Tell him that his life is in danger. Tell him he needs to get off the terrace in the next minute.'

His eyes darted to the terrace. Then his eyes returned to look into those of Kirilenka. He was being slow and deliberate, and it increased her confidence in him. He said, '€100.'

'Done!'

Kirilenka pressed the balance into his hand.

There was a motorcycle approaching. *Carrer De Pela,* Kirilenka thought. Time was running out. Kirilenka said, 'Go now!'

Ross heard a shout, and instinct came cutting in. Part genetic. Part experience. He noted the random guy approaching, and checked his sidearm was present and correct.

The guy drew close, and Ross took a second to evaluate him. His clothes. His aspect, and disposition. His training was about to kick in, but then he heard the guy saying, *'Tu vida esta en peligro. Entra al café!'*

Ross saw the motorcyclist. He had rounded the corner of the cafe. *Carrer De Pela* and *Placa De Catalunya*. Before he could react, a volley of bullets attained him, but none found their mark because the guy took them. He had swept a bullet free swath of air in front of Ross, and then he fell to the pavement.

Kirilenka saw everything, because she was on the corner of the cafe. The pivotal had changed; Ross was alive, at least for now. The motorcyclist had done his job. But, the coward in him was overriding his orders. Escape and freedom were his priority, not the assassination.

Ross didn't know much, but enough to know that waiting around for answers was not going to happen. For sure the bum had saved his life, whoever he was. Sure, he had paid the ultimate price. But for what, or who? There was bodies on the terrace, and confusion. He aside, unnoticed and then away.

Ten minutes and 50 seconds later, he found a café just as nice. It was on a square like *Placa De Catalunya*. The sounds of police sirens faded, muffled by the traffic and the bustle. Just another day in Barcelona.

I could get to like this new café, thought Ross. It had everything he liked. There was a terrace facing the sun and the area opposite was open and traversed by paths and gardens. There was a fountain in the centre of the square. Pigeons flocked in droves.

He ordered a double cappuccino, and finally made a call.

'Cafe Zurich?' answered Hoffman.

'Where else?' said Ross, knowing that someone would compromise his phone.

'With or without a female companion?'

'No comment.'

'That's a no. And Bando? Is she okay?'

'Last time I checked.'

'Where is she?'

'Check the hotel.'

A waiter passed by his table. Ross reordered.

Hoffman said, 'I want you to say the first thing that comes to mind when I ask you a question.'

'Shoot!'

'Our last telephone conversation before you scrambled.'

'What about it?'

'The focus was Magnitsky, but there was something else. You'd fixated on the case. I remember thinking it was a strange that you brought it up. No connection. No context. The case is years old. At the time, I didn't think anything of it, but now that we know all about it.'

'All about what exactly?' said Ross, his eyes falling across the square, double tasking. Or trying to. Which wasn't easy when Hoffman was talking on the other side of the line.

'The SU and your flight to Europe and Bando's report and the SU trying to disseminate electronic data across ...'

Ross said, 'That's changed, and you want to know why I knew all about the data dump before it happened. You're wondering how I knew that anyone would disseminate any data from Russia at all.

'Well. You knew the Russians were planning that, didn't you?

'So what if I did. That would be part of something called my job.'

'Mind telling me how?'

'You're entitled. It was a Sunday night. I met a Russian at the Bluejacket. I thought she might have been a walk-in, so I engaged her in conversation at the bar.'

Ross hesitated. He was still trying to multi-task, but it was a skill which didn't come easily. The street was quiet.

'And?'

'And? And so I pulled out because I got drunk.'

'Why?'

'Because I didn't want to leave you in a tough spot with no backup to fly the prototype.

'That was a mistake,' said Hoffman. 'If you were not one hundred percent fit to fly, you should have called in sick. We have back-ups. It's called redundancy. We can't ...'

'I know about redundancy, Sir!'

'Okay. What did you talk about?'

A man and a dog was approaching along the street. Ross saw the man and noted his mannerisms. Ross's position on the terrace. The dog was an Akita. Ross watched them disappear around the corner, and then he said, 'I can't remember what we discussed, but

I do remember the dissemination part. Now that I think about it, it's obvious they were planning a data drop operation to change election turnout. A simple action. Not telling you about the meeting has worked out. Without flying against them, we would have had no chance to put two and two together.'

'Not true. We would have known if a data drop had taken place. We would have been able to trace it to the SU.'

'Are you sure about that? Look at the report. Our radar got the SU dumping data for a long period. Around five minutes. Check the ground radars. Without Akemi and I being up there, we would never have known that it was the SU. And we got a visual as well. It's all in Bando's report.'

'So what were they up to?'

'Data drop. We both know that now, don't we?'

'We do. But why?'

'Election hacking. Russia Gate II. Why else?'

'Because something doesn't gel. They didn't do that. There wasn't a data drop.'

'You know that for sure?'

'All they did was drop data on a guy called Magnitsky, but as far as we can see, there's nothing in it. The data is a couple of videos of a guy in a prison in Moscow. But that didn't change a damn thing.'

'You should check again. Because that there is nothing in the data makes no sense.'

'Tramp still won a landslide, which he was always going to, with or without the Russian's seeding and the snow.'

'So what are you saying?' said Ross.

'I'm saying that the reason behind the SU stunt was not to change the election result at all. There was another goal, and you know what it is. They targeted you that night in the Bluejacket.

And the seeding operation was part of whatever purpose the Russians targeted you for. That's the only explanation that fits.'

Ross sipped his espresso for an instant, and then he said, 'Reference to Magnitsky was her calling card.'

'Yes.'

Ross put down his espresso, and said, 'Okay. Let me get this straight. You're saying that the walk-in's intention from the start was to seek a back-room deal to end the Russo-Ukrainian War.'

'Agreed.'

'You're right, she did target me. The Kremlin believed I might be on their side. They thought I would open a back channel for negotiations. But, it was unsure if I would believe that she had any influence with Potanin.'

'Exactly!'

'She used her knowledge of the upcoming dissemination operation as her calling card. It was proof that what she was proposing was real and came straight from the top, from Potanin.'

'You got it.'

Ross went quiet. What his boss was saying rang true. He thought back to the Bluejacket. He remembered the Russian's name. *Anella Moskva.* He remembered thinking that she had targeted him. There was chatter about negotiating an end to the Ukraine war.

'Ross? Are you there?'

'Her name was Anella Moskva. You're right. She targeted me, and I agree that the data operation was to prove her credentials.'

'That's right. So we need to debrief you. I'll be in touch regarding that, but for the moment, stay put in Barcelona.'

The line went dead, and Ross gazed out across the square. His eyes fixed on the crowd. He was a silent strategist, calculating the next move. He recalled the parting words he'd thrown at Anella Moskva. Mentioned something about their divergent negotiating prowess. Moskva had laid it out plain and simple. The US had to strong-arm the Ukrainians into embracing peace. Russian terms. Ukraine, or whatever remained of it, had to declare itself neutral. A lopsided deal, no shield for the US, and unenforceable. What proof did the West have that Russia wouldn't backpedal? And, start a new war and then take the rest of Ukraine?

So what if enforceability was a challenge? Could they still cut a deal, like the trio of the US, Russia, and China did to halt the Middle Eastern chaos after 7.10? Anella Moskva would now be back in Moscow. The US needed more leverage against Russia. Stopping their offensive was not enough. The pact to stop the war. A treaty between two mighty nations. Russia's moves in Ukraine fell under state practice. This is part of Customary International Law, not Treaty Law. A powerful state, Russia, asserting itself against a lesser power. The US is another mighty force. It threatened to use Ukraine as a barrier for the West's democratic order at Russia's doorstep. What Russia did was legal for Great Powers under Customary International Law. The crucial task now was to conclude the war, whether through a discreet deal or a formal treaty, like post-7.10. Moskva and him? A behind-the-scenes arrangement! A shame he was too soused to catch on to Moskva's game in the Bluejacket.

Chapter 17

Fifteen years earlier—Matrosskaya Tishina Prison, Moscow, 17 November 2009

Prosecutor Alexander Bagrov parked his black Chrysler, opened the car door and heard a commotion coming from the direction of Magnitsky's cell. There was a broken window to that cell, and he feared the worst. Magnitsky had been complaining about many things, so a broken window wasn't new. Bagrov had to see it for himself.

There were shouts and thuds, and there was no way he was going to intervene. So he pulled out his cell phone and recorded it. Then the clear smell of blood wafted through the broken window into the damp, Moscow air.

Luckily for Bagrov, the fight was recorded on CCTV footage because there was a camera located in the cell. At 17:42 on 17 November 2009, eight OMON riot officers entered Magnitsky's cell. Magnitsky on his upper bunk. Engrossed in a novel, and then he looked up. The sound of footsteps echoed around the cell. Keys jingled, a key turned, unlocking two bolts, and then the OMON officers poured in. They pulled him down and went to town on him on the concrete floor. There came a barrage of fists, boots, and rubber batons, and he died later that evening, in the prison hospital.

Fifteen years later, media interest lapsed and the case grew cold. The footage grew dust. Then it disappeared. It re-emerged in 2024 when Kira Kamenskaya received a copy from Anella Moskva.

Chapter 18

Kirilenka's flight from Moscow touched down on time at Severomorsk airport in Murmansk at 14.05. There was a yellow jeep waiting on the landing roll. It was off the airport perimeter road, but was prominently placed. *Not an accident,* thought Kirilenka. Someone placed it to be visible to incoming planes. It was stark yellow in colour, which contrasted with the barren hillside. Kirilenka felt a pang of anxiety, remembering her childhood fear of yellow jeeps. Sinister. Governmental.

Her parents lived in Polyarny. Yellow vehicles meant government and the state. Years later, the yellow colour anxiety remained, hard wired.

Kirilenka hastened to the front of the queue, entering the bus at the bottom of the stairs. First on, first off. She collected her bag from the carousel, exited, and then she saw a jeep approaching. It was yellow, and the driver was nodding, and she got in. No formalities. Soon the rough road led to the disserted airstrip. Safonovo.

She saw the driver glance up to the mirror, and wondered why. A watchful eye, or something more? Knowledge was power. But what could he know? About her. About the situation. But he wasn't just a driver. Drivers didn't look like that. So what if he knew, she thought. He knew the road, at least. They were anticipating the rough track's turns and switchbacks. The track separated Severomorsk and Safonovo. It was the most secure place in all Russia. But, all she could think about was the meeting with Pavlov Ivanov. She was in flashback mode, and didn't care about the driver.

She was reliving the day before. A secretary with mannerisms had taken her to his office. She thought there was haste, but never found out why. Ivanov was a small man. 1m 73. He stood at the window, with Kitai Gorad, stretching out hybrid between a panorama and a map. He was looking out across it, lost in thought. But then he turned and smiled as Kirilenka approached.

'You have it?' he said, his face anxious and lined.

'I have the list,' said Kirilenka, and put the black briefcase down. She opened it, and took out the list. 'There's something you should know.'

Ivanov studied it for a second, and then he said, 'Ten? What about the rest?'

'The number doesn't matter,' said Kirilenka. 'Well, yes. Ten pivotal sites. I won't be able to get to all. Some are in the US, some in Spain, some in Russia. I could get to the one in Spain, that's all.'

'When is it?'

'In three days' time.'

'Tell me about why that would be a good idea.'

'That's easy, Sir. Because I've ran it over and over. Checked the system with intermediate events. Always spot on. True.'

'So sure? The system only pinpoints pivotal sites?'

'Yes, Sir. But there's something else.'

'What?'

'There is a secret site over the border from where I am operating the mission, in Murmansk. Their secret site is in Norway, Kirkines. I believe it is a CIA site.'

'And why?'

'They are monitoring me.'

'How can you be so sure?'

'Because I see things. I notice how those surrounding me come and go. And Kirkines is where the surveillance ends up.'

'Why?'

'A hunch, Sir.'

'Sure? Not anything which the system itself has thrown up? I mean, if what you've got is as powerful as you say it is, you have no idea what it's throwing up. Right now, you're getting access to key sites. But, we don't know what else it might be giving you.'

'True, Sir,' said Kirilenka. 'I never thought about it like that.'

'And the event at the Barcelona pivotal site? Why should we want it changed?'

'Because if modulated, World War Three won't happen. Or at least, it won't happen the way currently destined.'

'Yes, but why?'

'Because it is on the list from the Black Hole. Why it appears on the list, we have no way of knowing. But the event makes it look likely. The guy is CIA. His aircraft is a prototype F35 fighter-bomber. It'll cross the Atlantic, and land in Barcelona. As things currently stand, he dies at the event. His death leads directly to World War Three. Causation. No death, no World War Three.'

Kirilenka was feeling the bumps of the track. Up ahead, the airstrip was looming. Soon they were going to burst off the jagged rocks of the hillside onto the strip. She caught sight of the driver's face again in the rear-view mirror, and then she heard the sound of the doors locking and screamed, 'What are you doing?'

There was no movement in his eyes. Not even a flicker. Just two grey balls, cold and stony and glued to the road. Then he said, 'Ivanov's dead.'

'Okay. So what are you doing?'

'I first get you to Norway. Kirkines. For debriefing. That's all for now.'

Kirilenka felt wrath rising like a volcano about to erupt. She said, 'Who authorized this?'

There was no answer from the driver. There wasn't even a glance. Which was an answer in itself. Norway. Kirkines. It all made perfect sense. This was a CIA operation in full swing.

Rocks littered the track as it crossed the perimeter, but the driver didn't care. He stepped on the gas, and the vehicle broke onto the rough asphalt of the disused runway, Safonovo airstrip. On the far side, began the road to Norway. A long drive off, but with one consolation—there would be time to make a plan. Ivanov was dead, but that didn't mean the list would have died with him. Nobody else knew of the system. Of Kosvinsky Kamen and the pivotal site approaching her space time coordinates. The next pivotal site. The CIA would never get it from her.

Chapter 19

Moscow, Park Parbedy

Kira Kamenskaya looked at her Rolex. There were 5 minutes to go, and she was marking each second, like counting sand in an hourglass. She hoped the meeting would bring answers. If anyone knew the truth about Magnitsky, Oleg Silchenko did. Ministry of the Interior investigator assigned to the case. Bodies buried, and if anyone knew where, he did.

Kamenskaya's mind skipped Magnitsky and landed close to home. She was Russian Defence Minister. She had all the features that mattered. Vladimir Potanin had noticed. They had dated. But now, she was his ex. Sometimes, her mind raced back to days when he was young and dashing.

She was sitting at a window table at Shokoloadnitsa cafe. Victory Park, Moscow; Kutuzovsky Prospect, Kutuzovsky Avenue. Through the window she saw the motorcade speeding past. *Potanin*, she thought. On his way to the office.

She glanced at her watch and sighed. Finding who killed Magnitsky wouldn't explain why Russia was failing in its war in Ukraine. With slender, neat fingers she swept her keys off the smooth, varnished surface of the table, and rose just as the door opened. Silchenko breezed in along with a blast of cold, Moscow air.

Silchenko scanned the interior, his sharp eyes taking in the details. He had hesitated close to the door. But then his eyes fell on her and he made a beeline.

He sat, said his greetings and his apologies for being late, and then the waitress approached, and he ordered coffee. Kamenskaya ordered a cappuccino. He said, 'Thank you!'

'Don't thank me yet,' said Kamenskaya. 'It could be a mistake.'

'Why would it be? It's a perfectly legal request. Next to the President himself, you're the highest-ranking Kremlin official. You're his ex, for Christ's sake! I just want to cover all bases. Expedite the case. Nothing wrong with that. I'm not breaking any laws, and neither are you.'

Kamenskaya said, 'I sent you the video because we both want the same thing.'

Silchenko said, 'So you've seen it.'

'I have.'

'Pretty terrible things in that video. Hard to watch! Isn't it? They took him apart piece by piece, starting with his legs.'

'I know.'

'But that was over fifteen years ago.'

'Oleg,' whispered Kamenskaya.

'What?'

'I know.'

'Sorry.'

'I guess you've arrested them?'

'Of course we have. They're in Lubyanka. Charges will follow. The wheels of justice are turning. But fifteen years is a long time. People move on. Some of them have confessed. Some haven't. But I need to find the person who ordered the hit—the mastermind.'

'Then we want the same thing,' said Kamenskaya. 'And you can't do it without my connections.'

'True. And since this morning, the officers are not playing ball. They're recanting all their confessions. Protecting someone big.'

'You don't know that for sure,' said Kamenskaya. 'Otherwise, why are we having this conversation? You could charge them and try to convict them based on the video and the confessions. But you think it goes deeper, and you'd like me to prove it.'

'Yes.'

'And how can I do that?'

'Because you can access GRU files.'

'Kamenskaya adjusted her position. The meeting got interesting. She said, 'GRU? What's Military Intelligence got to do with Magnitsky?'

'I was hoping you would tell me. For a fact, the mastermind is a foreigner. We got that from the confessions. But the database leads all dead-end with GRU access codes.'

'Anything else?' asked Kamenskaya.

'Well. We have a video of Magnitsky about to confess. But then he got a very violent attack of stomach cramps. A visit to the medical centre followed, with pancreatitis and gallstones to boot. Bagrov thinks he was about to confess to his part in the tax crimes. He was about to come clean on them. And then, another problem.'

'What?'

'The footage has gone missing. The MVD database has no hits. Vanished. No longer accessible. So someone wanted us to access it, but only for a while. The culprit—the GRU. Kira. What's going on? Who provided you access to the videos?'

'Why do you need to know?'

'Look. The video of Magnitsky about to confess gives a motive for murder.'

Kamenskaya said, 'I know. Those involved in the tax fraud all wanted Magnitsky out of the picture. Permanently. We're saying that someone played Magnitsky. He was set up from the start as a Russian auditor, an accountant, not a lawyer, working for a London-based hedge fund. In contrast, others gathered evidence for use in the US of how corrupt Russia is. The main goal was to use the whole Russian business to show Congress that Russia was evil. That would weaken Russia. The 2012 Magnitsky Act. But they didn't count on the arrest and torture of the accountant.'

Silchenko said, 'The US hoped someone would arrest Magnitsky and torture him. Then, they could turn the whole thing around and use it against Russia. Then, the whole Magnitsky thing becomes a US ploy to weaken Russia and impose sanctions. Right? Did the US mastermind or anyone else know about the Magnitsky confession video? It was before the riot cops killed him.'

'No proof of that. But it does all add up. We're saying that this was all an American ploy to weaken Russia. It makes perfect sense. Those particular OMON officers were acting for the mastermind, not Russia. If the Americans knew he was about to confess, to come clean on the tax crimes, he would have implicated his boss. The Americans sprinted to silence him. So the US, not Russia, killed Magnitsky.'

'Yes,' said Silchnko.

Along Kutuzovsky Prospect, a long line of Hummers had pulled up. If Kamenskaya had looked out of one of the windows, she would have had a heads up. She didn't look.

She said, 'We're struggling with what the US government knew. They knew about Magnitsky confessing to the tax crime. But, if Magnitsky confessed and the confession leaked, they couldn't blame Russian corruption. I'm talking humiliation for the US. Confirmation that the US got the whole Magnitsky Act of 2012 wrong. I mean, that the US killed Magnitsky instead of him dying because of neglect and indifference. That would pose a problem for all those US senators who voted for the Magnitsky Act in 2012. They would oppose that outcome. Killing one man to prevent it would be statistically very likely.'

Agents entered the café, and took the waitress to the rear because a setup was coming. That was clear. The whole thing was being videoed and recorded. Kamenskaya was still talking because she hadn't realized anything was up, and neither had Silchenko.

Silchenko said, 'You're right. Nothing proves the US government knew about it. Which is why we need you and GRU access codes. Because GRU took the video confessions of the eight OMON cops who killed Magnitsky.'

'And the video of Magnitsky being on the point of confessing. That would be crucial evidence,' said Kamenskaya.

'Yes. Well. All are with GRU too.'

Kamenskaya said, 'They could use it to blackmail those responsible for the murder. But why would they want to?'

'Suppose the mastermind has connections in Washington,' said Silchenko.

'Suppose GRU is developing the mastermind. They know the US government would protect any video proving guilt in the murder. In that case, the GRU could use that against the US.'

'Exactly!' said Silchenko. 'Now do you see how the land lies?'

Kamenskaya studied Silchenko. She saw unwavering loyalty to Russia. She said, 'I like you, Oleg. I like that you are a patriot.'

'How's that?'

'I read your file. What struck me was that you shared my views on Ukraine. The US has to understand what is happening from a Great Power perspective. Rights doesn't come into it. Ukraine a sovereign state? Yes, but only when that doesn't affect Russia's security interests. You and I know that Russia sees Ukraine as an existential threat. Shared history. Shared people. Potanin could not allow the West to peel Ukraine away. Then came the coup, and the shelling of the Donets.'

Silchenko said, 'Kira!'

'What?'

'Don't get me started.'

Kamenskaya and Silchenko realised something was amiss. The deserted cafe. The vanished waitress vanished. They looked outside and saw Hummers swarming around the cafe.

Chapter 20

Kirilenka waited, making calculations. Shifting numbers. It passed the time, but she was facing a dilemma. A thirty minute window. Or she would never make it.

The driving time back to the deserted airstrip at Safonovo. She would have to access the emergency number on route, assuming she would be able to make a call. She had the smartphone, and it would not be found by the driver. Then there would be the downtime to source the emergency crew. She would make it to the airstrip at the same time as the aircraft. If they sent a modified, fully fuelled SU-57, the flight time would be a little over two hours. Possible. But, she would have to act, and the limitation time was right upon her.

She began acting like she had an epileptic fit. Her clothes scattered. Naked. The driver screeched to a halt. She was small and vulnerable. Human nature told her story to the driver. She had him.

Chapter 21

Moscow, Park Pobedy

A concrete bunker in a black suit guarded the cafe's entrance. A walking fortress. 250 pounds. Moskva gauged he was oblivious to the unfolding scheme, so she handled him first. Then she slipped into the cafe's low hum. Her hand touched the Glock snug in her webbing—just to check. She noticed Kamenskaya and Silchenko.

She walked up to the bar, tapped the video, and addressed the waitress, 'Thank you, Nastya. Your service is noted.'

Kamenskaya and Silchenko watched, their movements in sync, like an unspoken agreement. Moskva threw a glance their way, and then walked over and said, 'What's the play here, guys?'

Kamenskaya was going to go down fighting. She said, 'No. You first.'

'So, look. Guys,' said Moskva. 'No secrets. I'm GRU Spetsnaz. There are ten Hummers parked outside. GRU, FSB, MVD. Six soldiers each.'

Kamenskaya pivoted toward Moskva. With a scowl, she said, 'And I'm Defence Minister Kira Kamenskaya!'

'I know who you are, Kira. What were you guys discussing?'

'Magnitsky. What else? You sent me a package with two videos!'

'Easy, guys! We're on the same side here!'

If the words were meant to put out the fire in Kamenskaya's eyes, they failed. Kamenskaya said, 'So what's this all about?"

'Protocol. President Vladimir Vladimirovich Potanin wouldn't let you near him. He needs to be sure of your intentions.' Moskva tapped the waitress's CCTV. 'And now, I have it. My staff will run it on the way.'

'On the way to where?' echoed Silchenko.

'To the Kremlin, of course.'

Chapter 22

Moscow, Park Parbedy

The Kremlin was not always the name of the hilly area in the centre of Moscow. Until the 12th Century, it was an unnamed area of woods on the banks of the Moskva River. Moscow has neither always been more powerful than the city to the south, Kyiv. Founded in 482 AD, Kyiv prospered for over 700 years before Yuri Dolgoruku founded Moscow in 1147 AD.

Slavic tribes first populated the area. The Vikings followed, but the Slavs prevailed. In the late 9th Century, these peoples became known as the Rus. They soon proclaimed their first Eastern Slavic Kingdom. Rurik was their first King.

Rurik died. His infant son was the heir. But, control passed to his relative, Prince Oleg. Prince Oleg expanded the Kingdom of the Rus along the rivers to the south. He conquered Kyiv in 882 and reached Constantinople in 907. Prince Oleg left to Rurik's son Igor Rurikovich a state called Kyivan Rus. Kyiv was its capital. Kyivan Rus was vast. It spanned from the Black Sea to Novgorod. It lasted as a collection of principalities until the mid-13th Century. Then, the state came under Mongol rule.

The first Russian state was the Kyivan Rus. Within its borders, Yuri Dolgoruki reached Borovitsky Hill in 1147 and founded Moscow.

Others followed his lead. In 1367, Dmitry Donskoy replaced the wood fortress walls with stone ones. He created the Moscow Kremlin for the first time. 11 years passed. In that time, Donskoy inflicted the first defeat on the Mongol rulers of the Grand Duchy. This marked the start of the Golden Horde's decline. Moscow won. The last Rurik ruler, Feodor I of Russia, son of Ivan the Terrible, ruled as Tsar in the Tsardom of Russia.

When Feodor I died, the first ruling dynasty of the Tsardom of Russia passed with him. Then came the Troubles—fifteen years of unrest and famine. Parliament chose their ruler, the Zemsky Sobor. In 1613, the first Romanov, 16-year-old Michael, was crowned. His great aunt was Anastasia Romanova. She was Russia's first Tsaritsa, the wife of the first Tsar, Ivan the Terrible. Michael of Russia conquered Siberia and extended Russia's rule from the Urals to the Pacific.

The Romanovs ruled from 21 February 1613 to 15 March 1917, when Nicholas II abdicated. One of their number, Peter the Great, ushered in the Russian Empire on the second day of November 1721.

Then came the Russian Civil War, and then in 1922, the Soviet Union, ruled by a centralized one-party state. Communism destined to implode.

Then came the chaotic 1990s and Russia's voyage into uncharted territory. Russia needed a leader to navigate the ship back to dry land, and restore its identity and values. Vladimir Vladimirovich Potanin was such a leader. He was cast in the mold of the Tsarist leaders descended from the first Ruriks and Romanovs. He was also a realist, and he restored strength and confidence and Russia returned to being a Great Power.

Potanin had grey eyes that twinkled when he smiled. But, anyone who knew him knew to interpret his smile. He was seventy-two years old and a realist who believed in Russia's destiny. He thought Russia would again be a Great Power equal to the United States of America. He was small but sturdy, his physique honed by years of KGB and martial arts training. He was wearing a black tuxedo, a bow tie, and a crisp white shirt. He had a round face with puffy cheeks. Once, it had dimples. But, he still had the charm, sophistication, and good looks that had graced him all his life. He was in the office he had chosen for the meeting. The office was big, spacious, and light, and there was a double-door window entrance to a balcony. The double windows extended from the floor to the ceiling.

The hall had views to the Kremlin Armoury. Moonlight streamed in from the half-moon above the red walls. The office was in the heart of the Moscow Kremlin in the heart of Russia, and temperatures had fallen. He pulled up a file on his desktop computer, looked at his watch, and smiled. It was almost time. He closed the desktop and looked across to the Tsarist entrance on the other side of the courtyard.

The Hummers entered through the gate at the foot of the Spassakaya Tower and screeched to a halt. Soldiers poured out of them, and Potanin went back to his desk, sat, and nodded to his security detail.

The fine doors flung open next without warning. A guard walked in first. Another followed, then another. Then Anella Moskva walked in. She said, 'Vladimir Vladimirovich, may I present Defence Minister Kira Kamenskaya? And investigator Oleg Silchenko of the MVD?'

Potanin smiled. He rose to his feet and walked to his three guests. His right arm stuck to his side until the last steps. A hand darted to Silchenko, and he said, 'A pleasure to meet you, Oleg Dmitrovich.'

Silchenko said, 'Vladimir Vladimirovich, the pleasure is mine. Thank you for this meeting.'

'Of course. I have heard excellent things about you from Ms. Moskva.'

Potanin turned to Kamenskaya, smiling. There was a sparkle in his eyes. He said, 'Kira. Thank you for coming.'

Kamenskaya eyed him with sheepish disdain. She said, 'Vladimir Vladimirovich. Mind telling me what's going on?'

'All in good time, my Dear, all in good time.'

He motioned his guests with a sweep of his arm. He pointed towards a drinks cabinet in the corner of the vast wooden-floored room. He said, 'What can I get you?'

'My usual,' said Kamenskaya. 'On ice.'

Potanin hesitated a beat, and then he grabbed the London Gin, poured a double, and added ice and tonic.

'Jack Daniels with coke on ice,' said Silchenko.

Potanin plied the drinks, saying, 'To Russia!'

Potanin got straight down to business, saying, 'Apologies first to you, Kamenskaya. Silchenko and Anella set up the meeting in the cafe. We were close. I needed an update on your plans for the Special Military Operation in Ukraine.'

Kamenskaya glared at him, and said, 'Why did you do that?' Concealing emotions was not one of her attributes.

Potanin said, 'Because you're anti-war, Kira. But. No sane person likes war. No reasonable person loves killing others. I respect people like Nuremberg prosecutor Ben Ferencz. They say there is a better use for humanity's wealth than building more deadly weapons. It is to build roads and hospitals and cut pollution. But those good causes are not the only issues. National leaders must consider them. National leaders must protect their people. You see, Russia is under threat. Look at the world if you don't believe me. In London, police officers use their warrant cards to arrest women. They also use them to kidnap, torture, and murder women. The West is decadent and woke, and its values and culture do not fit well with Russians. For Russians, respect and decency are what counts. '

Silchenko said, 'Which is why we're here, Kira. Anella contacted me. She filled me in about Magnitsky. But we have a problem.' He downed the remains of his whisky and turned to Potanin. 'Please. If you will, get Anella back in here.'

Potanin nodded and glanced to his security guys. He snapped his fingers. Then, his eyes searched for Anella. He found her, and he motioned for her, and she came right up, and he said, 'Anella. Better if you tell Kamenskaya why we need her.'

Moskva stood motionless, but her face expressed caring for Kamenskaya. She said, 'Kira Kamenskaya. There are turf wars at the heart of government. The Special Military Operation is in a critical phase. Control is everything, and there are elements in the GRU, FSB, and MVD that we do not trust. We need to keep control here—the four of us. Look around you. No cameras. I can tell you that there are no recording devices in this room. It's just us Kira.'

Moskva looked at Potanin and said, 'Vladimir Vladimirovich. Now is the time.'

Potanin said, 'Thank you Anella. Kira, we need you to get into Kosvinsky Mountain.'

'What? ' said Kamenskaya. 'Kosvinsky? Why me?'

'The GRU buried the Magnitsky files. I need the dirt on the mastermind who ordered Magnitsky's murder.'

'And why?' asked Kamenskaya.

'Americans care about their culture wars. They spread their liberal project for world domination on their terms.'

'And they're hitting us with human rights violations and sanctions,' said Moskva. She was standing next to the drinks cabinet. No one offered her a drink, so she helped herself—a double whisky with coke on ice.

'That's a long list,' said Kamenskaya. She followed Moskva's lead to the bar and refilled her glass.

Potanin said, 'Anella has opened a back channel with the Americans. She went a long way to succeeding, but came up short. We need more warp power in the negotiations. We need enforceability of the deal, so Russia and the US have more to lose by reneging on any deal. '

'And Magnitsky can help?' said Kamenskaya.

Potanin said, 'He ticks a lot of the boxes. He fought Russian corruption for human rights. He died and became a martyr. That's where you come in.'

'How's that?' asked Kamenskaya.

'You get us into Kosvinsky Mountain. You find those GRU files on Magnitsky, and you get us out of there.'

Kamenskaya said, 'And why do you need me? Why can't you send any one of your agents?'

'All agents work for an agency. As Anella said. We need to keep tight control of this. It all stays right here. And one further little detail.'

'Yes?'

'You report only to us. That is, to me, Silchenko or Anella. Is that clear?'

'Crystal,' said Kamenskaya. 'Anything else?'

'Moskva will ensure you have all that you need, That includes a military flight to Kosvinsky, out of Vnukovo.'

Chapter 23

The satnav on the dashboard showed Kirilenka's destination was close. It fitted with what she remembered about the road. The road ahead was a steep descent, straight to the flat expanse of the airstrip.

The aircraft would be waiting at the western end. She calculated it would be near where her road ended. She drove out onto the airfield.

The SU was bigger than she had expected. It was a scaled up version. But otherwise a SU-57. Two seater. Conventional, in the sense that the pilots sit side by side. She skidded to a halt, and shouted to the pilot, 'Is it fuelled?'

'Fuelled, and ready to go,' shouted back the pilot. There came the sound of engine start.

She saluted the one man ground crew, and smiled. She climbed the ladder to the right hand seat. She strapped in, and threw a query to the pilot, 'Time to Kosvinsky, Captain?'

'Under two hours.'

Chapter 24

Moscow, Park Parbedy

Inside the Hummer, Kamenskaya contemplated her predicament. The mountains awaited. And with Potanin's provisions, she had a phone loaded with apps, $50,000 in cash, a gun, and a bank card. She stood at a crossroads. Disappearing forever was an option, and a tempting one at that. An escape into the shadows while she still had a chance. Potanin had asked her where she wanted to be. Shokolatnitsa, was her reply. It was open till 9pm, and offered the solitude she needed for thought.

The Hummer reached the cafe and the driver tossed her a camouflaged flight suit. The intelligent choice was pulling out now. Kamenskaya, strolled into the bustling cafe. She was in leather, shirt, jacket, and denim. The vibrant clientele paid her no mind as she claimed a table near the bar.

Anella Moskva had not given her much to work with. That was for her own benefit. If she was caught, everything she had done would be analysed by her captors. Which meant the best protection for her was to be as believable as possible. Which meant, she had to figure out herself how to get the information that Potannin needed from Kosvinsky Mountain.

She ordered a double gin and tonic, and sat at the bar, navigating the Kremlin's secure app. It had the usual high-security features. The app connected her to Potanin, two other ministers, and the Chief of the General Staff. Fingertip seamless access to sensitive files from FSB, SVR, and FSO. She typed 'Magnitsky' and clicked 'search.' A trove of files flicked onto the screen. 547 in total. 175 of them were sensitive. Kamenskaya, was high on gin and tonic, and it helped her concentrate. She narrowed the field to eight files uploaded in the last five days.

She clicked 'print to PDF' and noticed one file was named RS-28. She knew that RS-28 was a super-heavy ICBM. Panic set in as a message popped up. The message read, "Print error ref. GRU". GRU, the watchful guardian, held control over these Magnitsky files.

Kamenskaya's heart raced, but determination fuelled her. Cross-checking for RS-28, she found the same eight files. Attempting another print resulted in the same "Print error ref. GRU." Trying to open a video file prompted a window marked GRU with an 'access denied' message. GRU had her cornered.

Time to pull out the stops. The App training had taught her one little detail that her Plan A would use—a loophole. Kosvinsky Mountain was secure. Using the App in Kosvinsky would override all security and intelligence levels. The action was automatic. She remembered that the system was fail-safe. They had tested it worked in training. Over and over. All she needed to do was to get into Kosvinsky Mountain. The plan was not without risk, but she didn't care. GRU had an interest in Magnitsky. It had to be significant. There was a chance it implicated Russian actions in Ukraine. She thought of the words "sworn duty to protect Russia's borders," and her urge to leave the cafe became easier to bear. She didn't even need to look at her watch. They could close the whole district. She would still use the next 10 minutes as needed.

Chapter 25

Moscow, Vnukovo Airport

The modified SU-35 fighter had two tails. It looked ghostly in the dim mist and murk of the apron's lighting. Fourth generation. Top Russian technology. Kamenskaya climbed the ladder to the cockpit, saying her greetings to the guy she found there.

He saluted and told Kamenskaya he was Captain Kuznetsov. He said he had orders to get her as close to Kosvinsky Kamen as possible. This meant landing at an airstrip in a forest.

Kamensyaka strapped in. The cockpit had all the features she expected. It had a glass display of all parameters.

'That airstrip. It's at Kosvinsky Kamen?'

'It's at a kilometre from the entrance to the installation.'

'I'll need to get to the bunker at the entrance to Kosvinsky. It's going to be tight timing.'

Captain Kuznetsov radioed control. He taxied to the runway holding point. Then, he straightened up on the centre lines, lighting the colossal twin engines. The aircraft roared off the airfield and turned east, Moscow spreading out below like a map. It disappeared within seconds. The plane was accelerating through the sound barrier.

Kuznetsov turned to Kamenskaya. He said, 'Get some sleep. There won't be much to see, unless the stars, the moon and the curvature of the Earth interests you. I will wake you inbound to landing.'

It wasn't Kuznetsov who woke Kamenskaya, it was clear air turbulence. The weather, thousands of metres below was getting worse, throwing chaos to the stratospheric levels. They were now deep in Siberia. Below them there was a strong wind coming from the north and there was wind shear close to the ground.

Kuznetsov made a quick descent and Kamenskaya fixed her eyes on the snow blasting past the canopy inches in front of her. Seeing it mesmerized her. Aware of her situation. There needed to be a landing strip. But no lights. She said, 'How can you land in this?'

'The computer handles that. I'm just here for backup.'

Kuznetsov was on short final, and glanced at Kamenskaya, then back to the glass cockpit. Then erupted the chaos. The bubble canopy shattered, and bullets hit Kuznetsov in the legs. He didn't scream. He still had to land the thing.

Kamenskaya felt nothing. There was a high pitched sound filling her ears as the aircraft pitched. It was ballooning. She snatched the controls and throttled up. The MiG was screeching its minimums before the stall, but the airstrip was dead ahead and instinct was kicking in. She was going to put it straight on the runway, which was now filling her field of vision.

The aiming point came up fast, and passed beneath. Now the computer was screaming, not the stall warning. She reduced the throttle, pressure on the control column, and slammed it down.

Full reverse thrust. All she had on the brakes, but no effect, and the end of the airstrip was upon them. There was nothing but trees and boulders up ahead. She saw a gap. It was towards the left. The boulders were scattered and the trees seemed wispy firs. She jabbed more power into the left-hand pedal, steering for it and, bracing for impact. Which was brutal.

The aftermath was a strange mix. An eerie silence returned to that part of the Taiga. Recovering from the shock wasn't easy. The lack of pain struck her as strange. She regained composure and checked herself. A lot of blood, but not too much pain. No injuries, because the blood wasn't hers. It was coming from the pilot, or what remained of him. On all sides there was crumpled metal and boulders. And then something crazy occurred which defied logic. Someone was calling her name. Her first thought was that the crash had affected her hearing. Or her mind. But the voice remained, still calling.

'In here!'

The voice got closer. She couldn't move because the crash had collapsed the cockpit. She was coming round. She was between the pilot and the canopy. No way to release herself. The pilot was dead weight, her arms trapped.

The voice came again, closer now. Again her name.

'In here!'

She saw a face, peering through the snowstorm and through the canopy, or what was left of it.

'Thank God,' said Kirilenka.

Kira summoned strength. She said, 'I'm okay.'

Kirilenka said, 'Are you injured?'

'No. At least, no pain. But.'

'What?'

She pulled together another sentence. 'How do you know my name? You were calling my name just now. Who are you?'

'We'll get to that,' said Kirilenka. 'But first we need to get you clear.'

'Clear for what?'

'We need to get you clear before they come.'

'We? Who are *they*?'

Kirilenka found the release buckle. Kamenskaya pulled herself out. Kirilenka supported her until she was clear of the SU wreckage. No injuries.

'They're CIA, Kira,' Kirilenka whispered.

Dim moonlight covered the snow. Kamenskaya was able to run, despite the crash, and what she had experienced. They sprinted for the safety of the firs, with its boulders, and wolves.

A powerful beam of light streaked across the frozen landscape, spiking the darkness. It came from behind the plane wreck. A boulder was close, so they crouched behind it, hoping the probing searchlight had not illuminated them.

'CIA? Why here? What are they doing here?'

'Because of you. Because you are here.'

'But why? Why does anyone know about me, or what I am doing here? Who are you?' She was struggling to understand how a hostile state got her location.

Kirilenka pressed a finger to her lips, and said. 'My name is Alexandra Kirilenka. And they're close.'

Kamenskaya studied her in the meagre light which immersed the scene. 'But how? How did you know? Who told you I would be here?'

'We'll get to that. All you need to know is that hadn't I been here, you were going to die in that plane. But now, you're alive, and so what are you going to do about it? They don't know we're here, but it won't be long before they find us.'

She said, 'Do you know what I must do?'

'You must get to the bunker and then you must access the system. Find out what you have to, and get out of there. Save the world, if you can. And the rest of us.'

'And where will you go?' she asked Kirilenka. It seemed to Kirilenka she knew it would be the last time she would set eyes on her.

'Me? I'll be back in Murmansk.'

'Why?'

'Look, Kira. Some other time okay? Right now, you have work to do. You need to get to the bunker before you're locked out.'

Time was running out. That much was sure. It didn't take a rocket scientist to work it out. All the pieces were fitting together, and Kamenskaya seemed to be getting the picture. She unstrapped her bag. She glanced at her watch. In a moment of calm, she told herself she had 40 minutes left. She had to get into Kosvinsky Mountain to the GRU file access points. The bunker was a kilometre away, and she looked at Kirilenka one last time, and set off towards the tunnels.

Chapter 26

Kosvinsky Kamen

The duty officer, the nearest guard, was an Army helicopter pilot. He held the rank of Flight Lieutenant. Kamenskaya saw his name, because it was on a patch on his jacket. Igor Chekov. Medium height, pale skin and curly blonde hair.

Kamenskaya said, 'Lieutenant. Do you know who I am?'

Chekov said, 'I do. You're Defence Minister Kira Kamenskaya.'

'Good. Who is directing these operations?'

The lieutenant said, 'I'll take you to him.'

They advanced through the void. The tunnel dwarfed them, their head torches piercing the darkness.

A humming noise was audible. The noise grew louder as they advanced. Soon, a station structure appeared ahead. It was the Maglev. Kamenskaya said, 'Lieutenant, you should return to the bunker. I'll go on alone.'

'Of course, General. If you need me, you know where I am.'

'Very well, Lieutenant.'

Chekov saluted and walked away. Kamenskaya watched him go. His torch's beams swept the darkness, then disappeared.

Alone and trembling, she turned to face the doors of the Maglev Station, and saw a guard approaching. He approached. She showed her ID. She said, 'I am General Kira Kamenskaya, Minister of Defence of the Russian Federation.'

The guard scanned Kamenskaya's identification. Her identity shielded her and unlocked secrets behind blast doors. He checked Kamenskaya's ID and nodded towards the blast doors. 'Prodolzhay pozhaluysta' slipped from his lips as he assessed her. He handed back her ID and waved her through, at a loss to understand why she was there.

Kamenskaya jogged down the dimly lit tunnel. She passed through the blast doors into the Maglev Station. She noted the exaggerated protection of the underground site. The tunnels were two hundred meters inside a mountain. There was a bunker at the entrance. There were two sets of blast doors, and then came the tunnel and the Maglev. She fought not to make eye contact with the guards standing there as she walked ahead. The guards saluted. Kamenskaya boarded the Maglev to the situation room. Two guards were standing there. She held out her pass, saluted, and they gave her VIP access to the mainframe. Showtime!

Chapter 27

This room was intentionally decorated, unlike the rest of the bunker's utilitarian design. Kamenskaya recognized the opulence from Mayakovska Metro in Moscow. Aviation scenes decorated the domed ceiling. Arabic carpets covered the floor.

Five imposing video screens were in an alcove on one side. Opposite them, black leather sofas surrounded a mahogany coffee table. Kamenskaya chose the middle couch. She found a console and laptop, both already active. The laptop was small. Mobile. She saw that it was fully charged, and smiled. *The fates had smiled on her too*, she thought, and had no doubt that the battery would be military grade, and capable of days of laptop battery power. She had little doubt that she was going to need it.

The GRU files, her target, lay within easy reach. Magnitsky Files and RS-28 files, sharing the same digital space. With a swift precision, she delved into the Magnitsky Files first.

The videos revealed OMON riot police's brutal tactics. Magnitsky's interrogation, torture, and eventual demise etched in each file. The final one was, "mastermind." An American orchestrated the sinister dance. His orders align with Magnitsky's demise. A grim puzzle, arranged for Potanin's political disadvantage.

Yet, the puzzle had an unexpected piece—RS-28 files bundled alongside. The RS-28 Sarmat, Russia's latest ICBM, unrelated to Magnitsky's case. Kamenskaya opened one of the RS-28 files.

And then the revelation hit her. The files were not ordinary; they were the most important GRU secrets, each labelled "Top Secret." The RS-28 file was a treasure trove of information. The holy grail for nations aiming to neutralize Russia's nuclear power.

Instinct triggered an abrupt halt. She sensed there were eyes on her. She felt paralyzed, the gravity of the situation weighing on her. She surveyed her surroundings—no visible watchers, no discernible cameras.

So she summoned a guard with the press of a button on the console front centre, and the door swung open. 'Yes, General?' a guard inquired.

'VIP access. What's that mean?'

'Means you get everything you need, General. Like a kid in a candy store with credit card privileges.'

'Very well. Bring me a double cappuccino. I need to wake up.'

The guard scurried to fulfil her request and Kamenskaya seized the moment. She downloaded the files to a USB. A daring act, a ticking clock counting down her escape.

The RS-28 files showed how Americans could cripple the Russian behemoth. Why was she privy to this clarity? A setup? Her surroundings seemed clear, yet a subtle unease lingered.

She pondered her next move. The downloaded information could prevent global thermonuclear war, but why her? The realization hit her like a sledgehammer—it wasn't about Magnitsky. The RS-28 files had side-tracked her, yet they held the key to preserving world peace.

Minutes passed and no guards came to arrest her for the download. The files contained crucial information. It prevented catastrophe and revealed Russia's internal issues.

The door creaked open. 'More coffee, General?' hazarded the guard, half offer, half request.

'Double cappuccino!' she countered, maintaining the charade. A momentary diversion as she contemplated a monumental decision.

The guard departed and Kamenskaya checked for hidden eyes. The Magnitsky file was her leverage. The RS-28 files a global game-changer. And the cappuccino had never been more crucial—a moment of respite in the face of impending chaos.

'Put it down there, Lieutenant, and then leave. No interruptions for 5 minutes.'

Kamenskaya finished her coffee. She put the USB in the zipped inside pocket of her flight suit. It would be safe there, she thought. The information on the USB was destined, she felt, to prevent World War Three, and having it safe in her inside, zipped pocket was going to secure the Earth's survival.

She shut her laptop. It was small, and she was able to insert it neatly and snugly into her flight suit inner pocket. Then she left the bunker. A woman with a mission, an unwavering aura of self-assurance.

But reality struck her like a sudden gust of wind. The Maglev was gone.

Chapter 28

All hopes of a swift retreat to the entrance receded like a tide. Her sense of desolation was immense. The tunnel cold. Standing motionless, in its cold, desolate interior, she willed her mind to clarity and a plan B if there was one. A faint murmur pierced the silence. It was a rising electric hum, reverberating like a mischievous hornet. Her hopes rekindled.

The noise of the Maglev was unmistakable. But had the guards finally caught wind of her intentions? Her actions on the GRU files could trigger a deadly directive. Looming problems ahead, she thought. Beads of sweat appeared on her brow. A fish in a pond. She stood tall on the platform's edge. A hand brushed against the Glock jammed into her belt. Whoever it was, she would go down fighting.

The Maglev screeched to a halt, and the person Kamenskaya saw was the least she expected. Oleg Silchenko.

So, she thought. You're no longer in Moscow where I left you. With a hiss, the entrance to the Maglev opened, and with it came a Makarov pointed in her face.

'You're under arrest!'

'Oleg! What's this, Oleg? A joke?'

A pair of handcuffs told her it was not. He tossed them at her, saying, 'Kira. Don't make this more difficult than it has to be. You know how to use them. Put them on.'

The Maglev had black plastic seats, which lined the carriage space with steel tubing grab rails and handles. Silchenko poked her spine with the Makarov. Then, he tied her to the steel pole in the middle of the carriage. Immobilized. But then he drew close and whispered something in her ear.

'What?' said Kamenskaya.

'Not a word!' said Silchenko.

The old Silchenko was back, and Kamenskaya drew an audible sigh of relief.

The doors closed with a hiss, and the Maglev accelerated towards the surface. And then Silchenko pulled the emergency breaks, cutting the lights. In total darkness, they were alone inside the most secure bunker in Russia. Silchenko said, 'Everything's going to plan.'

'The plan? What plan? What's the plan Oleg?' said Kamenskaya. 'I don't know what you're talking about!'

'Not a problem. Not anymore now that we're out of the Maglev station. Even if there's no sound, the CCTV will enable investigators to determine what we say.'

'What's going on, Oleg?'

'I reported everything I knew about you and received orders to shadow you anywhere you went.'

'From MVD?'

'From GRU.'

'So you're working for both sides? You're an investigator and also GRU Military Intelligence?'

'No. I'm CIA. Which is why we're here.'

'Then you're dead to me, traitor!'

'Everyone has their interests, Kira. Although you may hate me for it, you and I are on the same side.'

'No we are most definitely not. You're not the Silchenko I knew.'

Silchenko was immune to the words. He said, 'You want this war with Ukraine to end don't you? Well, so do I Kira. So does the US. Isn't that right? You do want to stop it, right? That's why you came here. Why else would you accept the mission from Potanin and Moskva? Because you thought the files were a bargaining chip with the US. Well, guess what? You're right. They are. And not only the files. I'm here to discuss this with the Defense Minister of the Russian Federation. General Kira Kamenskaya. We need to find a way to stop the Ukraine situation from escalating. Which is why I'm here and you're here. Tell me if I'm wrong?'

'You're not wrong Silchenko. But what the hell can we two do now to stop it? We're in a bunker inside a mountain in Siberia.'

'Plenty,' said Silchenko. 'We're not imprisoned. The train is still running, isn't it? We can still get to the surface can't we? You have the files, right? So we can leave here whenever we want. But we need to work things out between us first.'

'You mean work things out between Russia and the US.'

'That's right. A deal to end the war. We've both taken one step towards the resolution of the crisis. The steps could be the green shoots of a comprehensive deal, which we could run to the top. A contract between states. A treaty to end the war.'

Kamenskaya pondered his proposal, and then she said, 'So, what would the US bring to the table?'

Silchenko laid out the terms. He said, 'If Russia turned to the US from China, the US might pressure Ukraine to settle. Russia would keep control over the four eastern provinces. They would secure Ukraine's neutrality with Ukraine's consent. Never would Ukraine enter the EU or NATO.'

Kamenskaya said, 'There might be compromising info on the new Russian ICBM. There was a suspected mastermind in Magnitsky's killing. But there's a catch—we need a realist academic on the US negotiating team. The academic would sell the deal to US officials. They will lead negotiations from the American side.'

Silchenko said, 'A need for an academic?'

Kamenskaya said, 'Of course. Without a realist academic in International Relations, Russia will be misunderstood. We can't afford any missteps once the negotiations begin.'

'Aright then,' said Silchenko. 'To the surface! I'll contact Hoffman to discuss the details, and you will talk with Potanin.'

Kamenskaya said, 'We're wasting time!'

Chapter 29

Kosvinsky Kamen, Siberia, Russia.

The exit was difficult. It was like navigating hostile terrain. Another guard loomed. He was a big obstacle in their path, like a wave about to crash down on their escape plan. Kamenskaya sensed treacherous waters. They were like a rip tide in a stormy sea, requiring both power and skill to navigate. She whispered to Silchenko, 'Let me handle this.'

The approaching guard was no normal soldier. He was a battle-hardened captain with experience in Russian wars. Kamenskaya pulled out her ID, offering a crisp salute and swift introductions. 'Defence Minister General Kira Kamenskaya, and this is Oleg Silchenko of the MVD.'

Surprise flickered across the captain's face. Then came a stammered a response, 'I wasn't informed!'

'I'm informing you now, Captain. This is an unannounced assessment. You're familiar with protocol, I take it, Captain?'

'Of course.'

'Good. So what I need is a secure location and a reliable communication link to Moscow. To deliver our report.'

Mental cogs began turning in the Captain's head. *This was like a reprieve,* he thought. He said, 'Follow me!'

They walked through the sentry post and past a guard who saluted them. Then they stepped out of the bunker. Opposite the entrance, there was an army jeep in a large car park. The car park had rows of white lines painted on the black asphalt.

The captain pointed to the jeep and said, 'I'll take you to our command centre in Kytlym. I'll get my team to book a room for you at the Tayga Hotel.'

Kamenskaya said, 'We don't need a hotel, Captain. Take us to the command centre with a secure communication link to Moscow.'

They reached the command centre. It was a grey, two-story building sitting in a vast yard. It had a symmetrical layout with one-story buildings in two wings adjoining it. A main corridor ran straight across it, eastwards to the opposite side, perpendicular to the wings, which ran north and south. A minor passage crossed it at its halfway point. The minor passage ran into the two wings. The captain led them to a large room off the padded main corridor. Black cables tangled around the desks, laptops, transmitters, and receivers.

The captain saluted, and left, muttering he would return in ten minutes. Kamenskaya and Silchenko exchanged knowing glances. The captain's footsteps receded down the long central corridor. They couldn't tell whether he had gone towards the entrance or the opposite side of the building. What mattered was that he was gone.

Kamenskaya surveyed the room. No cameras. There was an abundance of desks set in rows, which made the room look it was used for trainings. Front and centre of the first row of desks, there was a telephone. She walked past Silchenko, grabbed the receiver, and dialled a number she knew by heart. Potanin's number. She heard a ringing tone and then she heard the voice of the PA.

She seemed friendly initially, and so gave the customary greeting. She said, 'Privet Masha, Kak dela?'

Silence reigned for a beat longer than Kamanskaya expected, and then came, 'I can't talk to you. There is a catch-or-kill order out on you.'

'Kind of you to tell me,' said Kamanskaya. Which was the truth. Marsha could have just hung up. 'Since when?'

'A few minutes ago. Potanin signed the order. I'm hanging up now.'

Kamenskaya turned to Silchenko, who didn't notice her look because he was up to his neck in his own problems—with Hoffman.

Kamenskaya could feel nerves rising. She felt like Vesuvius about to erupt, so she edged closer to Silchenko to eavesdrop. Any distraction was welcome. She heard Hoffman shouting orders down the line and Silchenko detailing the deal terms discussed on the Maglev. Which was exactly what she wanted to hear most of all. *An insurance plan of sorts*, she thought. Once the CIA director knew of the plan, it would take some of the pressure off her. Not that it helped now. Right now, they had to escape the clutches of the Russian state. She said, 'Oleg. We need to go!'

'Why?' said Silchenko.

'There is a catch or kill out on us.'

Silchenko heard Hoffman say, 'Catch-or-kill? On both of you? Why?' which Silchenko couldn't answer because the door flew open and a storm of bullets shattered everything around them. Two things happened. Silchenko absorbed the shots intended for Kamenskaya, and Kamenskaya threw herself across tables, chairs, and cables, finding refuge next to the doorway.

Silchenko lay dying. *Everything just got harder*, thought Kamenskaya. No Silchenko meant no negotiations.

More shots rang out—the same shooter from the same door. He was moving in for the kill. Like a tennis player sprinting to the net to end the game. Or a chess player. But Kamenskaya had some moves of her own.

One. The captain was alone. He had no backup. She snuck up behind the door. He was on the other side. She sensed him on the other side, and sent him crashing to the ground with a kick of the door. He had been holding a pistol, and the force of her kick sent it flying. She pounced like a cat, got to it before the captain, and shot him in the thigh. No errors. No prisoners. She dragged him to the entrance, and then she punched in Potanin's speed dial number.

At the second ring, Potanin answered. Something told her he was on the defensive, which begged more questions. She said, 'You sent people to kill me. Big mistake. Huge. I'm not the enemy. I'm your biggest cheerleader!'

'No, Kira. You're history.'

'Why. You owe me at least that!'

'Sure, Kira. The RS-28 files. You're running to Ukraine. Or the US. I know about Silchenko. I know about you both!'

'You're so wrong, and hear me out! You owe me that too.'

Potanin said, 'You have a minute. Because after that, I'm sending more than a single man to kill you.'

'You and I know the only way to end the Special Military Operation in Ukraine is through talks. And for that, you need help—my help. Vladimir Vladimirovich. I'm a patriot. As you are yourself. You and me, we're birds of a feather. We're fighting for the same things. With NATO on our doorstep and the US doubling down, now is the time to end this.'

'Fifty seconds.'

'Listen to me, please! I thought I'd never be doing this, but I now beg you to listen to me. I have the nucleus of a settlement.'

'Forty!'

'The plan has been discussed at the highest level of the US security service, the CIA.'

'With Hoffman?'

'Correct. With director Hoffman. Silchenko called him and gave him the details of a deal. It's a deal in Russia's interest, and in the interest of the US and Ukraine. The US will provide things in exchange for US pressure on Ukraine. This pressure is to end the war on Russian terms. All I ask is that you allow me the power to conclude the deal.'

'And Ukraine will be neutral? And Russia will keep the four annexed territories?'

'If those are Russia's terms, the settlement will reflect.'

'That's interesting, but there's something you're missing. It's a big thing. Can't be overlooked.'

'What?'

'You're presuming I would stop with four annexed territories, right?'

'Which is the truth. Your publications. What?! No way! Are you intent on taking the whole of Ukraine?'

'My dear Kira. I commend your bravery, but not your naivety. So much bloodshed in Ukraine. The Russian people will not accept that Ukraine will remain whole on our border. It can rise again. It would be a bulwark of the West to weaken Russia. The time for negotiations was before the first Russian soldier died. Now that tens of thousands have died. Russia will not tolerate a Ukrainian state on its border. It is ready to poke the Russian bear again. So, unfortunately for you, this conversation is over. I'm going to give you a head start. I owe you that. But from now on, we'll hunt you down because you're a threat to the Russian state. So, be gone. But as a former friend, Godspeed!'

Kamenskaya grabbed the injured captain's gun, rifle, and ammo, and then she ran out of the room. She looked left and right along the long corridor, west, and then east. Left went to the entrance. West. Right was toward the opposite side—the rear of the building. East. She went right.

Outside she sprinted towards the trees, like a fox fleeing hounds. Her plan was to put distance in place, but first she needed a second. To think. She caught her breath against a tree. Her heart raced, her breath came in ragged bursts. But a smile played across her face. She checked her inside pocket. The zipped one. She felt the USB was where she had slipped it. Zipped up. Safe, and she was still at liberty to make it matter. She was back in control. All that she had to do now, was get it to Ukraine, or to the West.

Chapter 30

MVD Headquarters, Moscow

Investigator Pavel Karpov of the Ministry of the Interior, the MVD, was in his office overlooking Kaluzhskaya Square, Moscow. The window had fine views. You could see Gorky Park, with its trees and games courts. Beyond it, there was the Moskva River with the massive façade of the Ministry of Defence building on the far bank. On Karpov's desk, a Teams video linked him to the eyewitness at Kosvinsky Mountain. The witness was describing everything that happened when the bunker was penetrated.

He was on duty that night at Kosvinsky Kamen, the eyewitness said. He said General Kira Kamenskaya entered the situation room, and his description of Kamenskaya was spot on. He said she was tall. 1m 79. Dark. He said she had straight black hair and deep green eyes. He said she had thick lips. The eyewitness said that Kamenskaya had walked to her objective. No hesitation. No fuss. Direct and assured. She had been there before. That was obvious, the eyewitness said.

He said there had been two monitors at the desk where Kamenskaya sat. He said there was a nest of wires and cables beneath it. He said, 'She accessed the system like she had done it a thousand times.'

'And then?' asked Karpov.

The eyewitness looked around as if what he was going to say would land him in a lot of trouble. He said, 'She walked straight out with it!'

'With?'

'The files!'

'File, or files?' asked Karpov.

'Two files,' said the eyewitness. 'The first and the second.'

'And her clearance?' asked Karpov.

'Was evident from her credentials. We had checked her. She was a spot on ID match. She outranks everyone. Even the Head of Nuclear Forces. Even you. Even the Chief of the General Staff. So even if we had wanted to, we could not have stopped her. Unless…' The nervousness had returned.

'Unless?'

'Unless President Potanin had overruled the system.'

'And the content of the files? What exactly did they contain?'

The eyewitness remembered the investigator had 'all necessary clearance' to conduct the investigation.

'We call the first file the Sensitive First File or SFF,' said Karpov. 'It contained all operational data on the RS-28 Sarmat, our newest ICBM. It's information that could hurt Russia's missile defense. It would leave Russia at a big disadvantage if the Americans got it.'

'That's above your pay grade, but anyway, thank you. I got it. And the second?'

'The second file is the Sensitive Second File (SSF). It contained compromising information on an MVD case about the West.'

'Which case?' asked Karpov.

'Magnitsky,' replied the eyewitness.

'And why were the two files placed together?'

'As a final level of security, Sir'

'Meaning?'

'Sir, all Kosvinsky Kamen sensitive files are saved in the computers of the situation room with a link to an unrelated file. This is a last level safeguard against unauthorized access. Only the Russian President and those working in Kosvinsky Kamen know the reasons. They know the reasons for this final level of security.'

'Which are?' asked Karpov.

'If someone gains access to a sensitive file, they will see a second, with both accessible at the access point. The second file can contain a variety of information. In this case, it contained sensitive information on the Magnitsky case.'

'I get it. The second file, the SSF, protects the information on the first file. How does it do that, exactly?'

'The downloader sees and will check it out. They will see it is unconnected and innocent. But, it is likely to be irresistible to anyone who knows something about the second file. In this case, most at Kosvinsky Kamen find the info in the second file irresistible. This is due to the strong feelings about the Magnitsky case.'

'Understood,' said Karpov. 'We hope that the person who accesses and steals the first file will be tempted to download and investigate the second. They will then alert us to their location soon after the theft.'

'That's it,' said the eyewitness.

Chapter 31

Kremlin, Moscow

President Potanin sat alone at the end of a very long table in the Kremlin's room. The room was next to the Great Hall. His grey-blue eyes bore dark circles beneath them. They were a testament to the toll of the Ukrainian counter-offensive on his sleep. Despite the morning's bathing and sauna rituals, the lines around his eyes remained. They looked like scars on a battlefield.

His generals failed in Kyiv. Disasters in the broader eastern and southern Ukraine had disrupted his sleep. The recent routing of the 155th Marine Brigade signalled a critical juncture. It was time for Potanin to regain control. The unravelling events left little room for debate—the Americans were not willing to let go. The unfolding clashes were more than fights. They were battles for values. They pitted the authoritarian world against the West.

In Potanin's weary assessment, a historical truth lingered. From the times of Napoleon and Hitler to conflicts in Syria and now, trying to win a war against Russia was hard. The West, oblivious to this historical lesson, engaged in a head-to-head confrontation. Yet, Potanin found solace in the solidarity of allies. At least he could rely on the support of Iran, China and North Korea in this complex geopolitical chess game. Potanin sat at his laptop, a Lenovo, his digital command centre. He grasped the headset and clicked a link. It connected him to Lieutenant General Murdov, the eastern commander. The battlefield was a chessboard, and Potanin wanted to know his opponent's next move.

Murdov's report cut through the virtual airwaves. It was a crisp declaration of retreat from the Battle of Kyiv. The words echoed in the digital space. Tired, Potanin heard them. He refused to see them as futile.

His raised voice to Murdov was a hallmark, and his tone was firm, when he said, 'Futility be damned! Never underestimate Kyiv's importance! Sacrifices are inevitable; we must seize the city, sever the head of the Ukrainian Army. Clear, General?' Potanin's command echoed with unyielding determination.

'That's clear, Vladimir Vladimirovich.'

'Confirmation from all units within 24 hours. Dismissed.'

Injustice gnawed at Potanin. In 2008, unsettling tremors led to war. Washington's security Monroe Doctrine, clashed with Russia's interests, putting Ukraine in the centre of a storm. Potanin's mind replayed the forceful eviction of an elected leader. He remembered the discrimination against Russian-speaking Ukrainians. The annexation of Crimea had been necessary.

The weight of his duties pressed on him daily, and Potanin's dark eye circles showed the toll of sleepless nights. His eyes now narrowed in thought. He scowled. It showed the inner conflict caused by Russia's geopolitical challenges.

The Kremlin's inner chambers were luxurious and still. History whispered through the hallowed corridors, and Potanin grappled with the realities of the present world. Nuclear conflict was looming. In his analysis, confrontation between the democratic West and authoritarian East seemed inevitable. The air in the room felt charged. Urgent decisions could shape the destiny of nations.

Chapter 32

The situation room in the West Wing was a shadowy expanse of secrecy, the dim lighting casting long, ominous shadows across its walls replete with video screens and codes. It looked more like a clandestine bunker, with President Budden settled into his comfortable black leather seat. He was a lone figure surrounded by the technology of modern governance. The air hung heavy with the gravity of the discussions to unfold. Three huge video screens graced the wall before him. The central one glowed, casting an eerie light on the officials.

By his side stood National Security Advisor Jake Piraeus, his trusty companion in the current complex dance of global politics. The room echoed to the beat of war, with key figures each weighing in, and adding their voices to the chorus. One of them was the US Secretary of State, Tony Blister. Another was the Chair of the Joint Chiefs, General Mike Miller. Amidst the array, one figure held the President's attention—Hoffman.

Hoffman sat at the centre, which was actually his default position. His words echoed through the holy space. He declared that the sands of the international landscape were shifting. The Unipolar Moment's influence was waning, and China and Iran and North Korea were rising. This change seemed inevitable. The President absorbed Hoffman's words, and tried his best to triangulate reality. He saw the rise of Realpolitik and a shift in global power.

With a nod of approval, President Budden acknowledged Hoffman's insights. 'Nice speech,' he remarked, encapsulating both a genuine acknowledgment, and a subtle challenge.

Hoffman continued his narrative. He was succeeding in weaving a tapestry of geopolitical foresight. The President looked lost. He looked like he needed more than a second alone with a geopolitical analyst. He took stock of Hoffman's words, and grappled with their meaning. The analogy of the Russian invasion was of a formidable wave. It was still in the depths before crashing onto the shore. It struck a chord. The wave promised victory for the liberating forces. The West's industry and tech backed it.

President Budden's thoughts meandered in the face of Hoffman's narrative. He thought about their last encounter—a meeting on the Washington D.C. subway. The details flickered in his memory like he was assembling fragments of a puzzle. The urgency of the present moment demanded a swift mental catch-up.

Hoffman's words flowed. President Budden navigated a geopolitical chessboard. Victories and losses measured in territory. They were in the triumph of democracy over authoritarians. The situation room saw a convergence of strategy and vision. There, they all admitted the game had begun.

Chapter 33

Ural Mountains, Siberia, Russia

The MI-24 gunship sliced through the air. It was thundering along, hugging the terrain, above the trees and the snow-covered ridges. Rotors chattering and churning. They whipped snow off the tops of the fir trees. This was Siberia.

Finally, after what seemed like hours of the pummelling, gruelling ride, the helicopter banked and Kosvinsky Mountain came into view ahead, a rounded 1,500m granite dome—an unmistakable sight.

Major Pavel Karpov of the MVD surveyed the forest below. A PK machine gun swung from his shoulders. Soviet-made. 7.62 mm, an integral part of his combat readiness.

He was scouring the Taiga passing below, for any sign of life; an absorbing task. It was a dense expanse. A mosaic of towering conifers and intricate underbrush. The latest reports put Kamenskaya heading east. Which meant that she would be on the other side of Kosvinsky Mountain. But just in case, Karpov was using the flight to search that particular sector. There was no reason to be complacent. No prisoners. No mercy. Chalk it up to a Chechnya-honed sixth sense or a gut feeling. Major Pavel Karpov hoped that he or a team member would find Kamenskaya first. It was for her sake.

The gunship arrived at the bunker, and came in straight, landing hard and fast. The gunship's powerful downdrafts blasting snow. The chilling wind cut through the layers. Throughout the icy tempest, the MI-24's doors remained wide open. Karpov felt a rush of cold air and adrenaline in about equal amounts. He saw a thumbs-up from the pilot, and jumped down, onto the tarmac.

If Karpov had hoped that the operation to capture Defence Minister Kamenskaya was being led with skill and determination, what met his eyes at the bunker was a sight for sore eyes. Armoured personnel carriers and infantry fighting vehicles lined the roads spanning out from the car parks at the entrance to the tunnel. There were main battle tanks in abundance near the wide entrance apron, including T-72s and T-64s. Hidden along the road were three T-14 Armata tanks. Roads splayed in three directions out from the entrance tunnel, descending from the mountain, each swarming with activity. Like vigilant guardians, two S-300 surface-to-air missile launchers stood poised above the bunker. The whole area bustled with staff, all believed they would find Kamenskaya. *A veritable hornet's nest,* thought Karpov.

At the centre of the nest, Karpov saw a field headquarters, with groups of officers, and strong security measures. Which wasn't surprising. Kosvinsky Mountain was a national-level target. Part of a complex conflict with Ukraine. The operations spanned space, ground, air, and sea. The conflict could become a wider NATO—Russia war. It could have global implications.

Karpov stooped real low, under the helicopter rotors through the frigid, snow-laden air. There was a group of officers, and one face seemed familiar as he drew close. He saluted, 'Major Pavel Karpov, Sir!'

The officer throwing the salute was Major General Evgeniy Volkov, who was the leading the operation. Volkov was the head of the Strategic Rocket Forces of the Russian Federation. He wore a full winter combat outfit, bristling with weapons and badges. He stood six foot four tall, and he weighed a solid two hundred and fifty pounds. He was a walking mountain of Special Forces muscle, bone and skill. Ego matched his stature; *no room for small talk,* thought Karpov. Fate had put him in Kosvinsky Mountain.

'Follow me, Major,' said, Volkov the air of arrogance apparent from the get-go. It seemed to Karpov to suggest he already knew the outcome of every step they were about to take.

Volkov led to a large tent pitched in front of the trees. It was a hub of a military activity. There were tables laden with gear and cables; equipment primed for action. Some tables hosted files, others were more of an arsenal of rifles, pistols, and anti-tank weaponry. To the left, a partitioned area buzzed with operators, each hunched over workstations. Total, unbridled focus on tracking Kamenskaya. Laptops, headsets, printers—a high-tech command centre. Volkov strolled to the far end of the tent, where two guards flanked doors of solid steel. *A restricted zone*, thought Karpov. The general beckoned him to black leather sofas on either side of a glass coffee table.

He shut the door with a soft click, then turned with a casual demeanour, and said calmly and quietly, 'Coffee, Major?'

'Yes. Thank you, General.'

Volkov popped a pod, pulled the lever, and created an espresso as perfect as any in downtown Napoli. He passed it to Karpov and made one for himself.

Questions and insights crowded in on the general, but he heard helicopter rotors drowning out the tent's flapping fabric, and he missed the opportunity to steer the meeting. Karpov seized the moment. 'They told me a GRU officer would be assisting.'

Which really irritated the general. He said, 'Colonel Ivanov just arrived. The President has approved the GRU's participation. But this is my operation from start to finish. You have a problem with that, Major?'

Another gulp of caffeine and Karpov felt weighed up, like a coiled spring, and so he said. 'GRU and MVD forces will be under Rocket Forces command?'

Karpov re-evaluated earlier fears for Kamenskaya. Working with Volkov was one thing, but taking orders on the investigation was another. The MVD had the undisputed authority to investigate criminal offenses in Russia, not the usurper in front of him. His pulse quickened, as he sensed a turf war was about to be declared.

'Major Karpov, must I remind you that the President has directed it?' Volkov retorted.

Karpov stood his ground. 'With respect, General, Kamenskaya is now a civilian. The Interior Ministry, not the military, can investigate her. This is true regardless of the President's instructions.'

'Not how I see it, Major. If you have a problem, Potanin will decide.'

There was a knock on the steel doors, which swung open, and Colonel Alexander Ivanov of the GRU stood at attention, and then he introduced himself. He handed identical sheaves of documents to both the general and the major.

'General Volkov. Major Karpov. This operation is now under GRU's command. Read the documents.'

Chapter 34

The Kremlin, Moscow

Towering double doors, guided by golden handles, swung open at the eleventh hour, and President Potanin of Russia strode into the vast hall. His left arm swung as he walked, the right looked poised to draw a sidearm. It was his default position.

On the far side of the room, a long table stretched out, offering commanding views of the Kremlin Armoury. There were massive windows overlooking the Kremlin Gardens. The newly appointed Defense Minister was seated there radiating extreme anxiety. He was fidgeting and shuffling, and then he made to rise as the President approached the table.

'Please. Remain seated.' bellowed Potanin exuding arrogance and confidence in equal measure, and then settling at the opposite end of the table. 'What's this about Shoigu?'

'Vladimir Vladimirovich, I asked for the meeting to discuss the recent US Department of Defense press briefing.'

'Why, Defense Minister?'

'It gives insight, Mr. President.'

'Please. Let's address each other properly. Vladimir Vladirmirovich, if you please! And, of course, it's about insights. What are they?'

'Apologies, Vladimir Vladimirovich. As for insights, we have several. They show that the US is escalating the situation.'

Potanin snapped his fingers, and caught the attention of the waiters, and ordered refreshments. Tea for two arrived minutes later, served on a silver tray, and then he said, 'Defense Minister Shoigu, continue with your report.'

'The US press conference, Mr President. The Under Secretary of Defense for Acquisition and Sustainment and the Deputy Under Secretary of State for Policy spoke at it. The US is arming the Ukrainian Defence Department. They are doing this through two programs. One is funding. The other is leading a contact group of 50 countries. These programs are the USAI and the US Defense Contact Group. Together, they represent Security Assistance to Ukraine. The total is $172 Billion since the start of the war. The US is supplying various, highly effective offensive weapons.'

'Offensive weapons. Some defence organization!'

'Yes, Vladimir Vladimirovich. It includes Javelin anti-tank and Stinger systems. It also has Patriot anti-aircraft and GMLRS long-range artillery systems, ATACMS. It has 105 howitzers and Humvees. And, of course, F16s.'

'These aren't insights. These are reports!'

'So Vladimir Vladimirovich, note the following insights.'

Shoigu, flipped open a notebook. 'The US is not backing down. More like doubling down. They're signalling that they're in this for the long haul. The Deputy Under Secretary of State for policy repeated the usual mantra. He said, 'When you launched the invasion, you expected Ukraine would collapse.'

'These aren't insights!'

'Well, here's one. The US is trying to reap the benefits of its policy in Ukraine. Encouraging Ukraine to move to the West and provoking Russia led to Russia invading Ukraine. The US military-industrial complex wanted this right from the end of the Cold War. The words said and figures presented at the press conference show that the US Defense Enterprise is much larger. It's larger than the contributions from other nations. In short, Vladimir Vladimirovich, the US is now reaping the benefits of confronting Russia. They will keep increasing production and replacing arms going to Ukraine.'

Chapter 35

Ural Mountains, Siberia, Russia

The wilderness was unforgiving. Siberia. Just to the east of the central Urals. Kamenskaya battled through deep snow, blizzards. She was enduring a bone-chilling minus fifteen degrees Centigrade. Relentless wind whipped across the frozen land. It shook the towering fir trees, which stood as sentinels across the region. Civilization was a distant memory. She was in the heart of a remote area, the area chosen by the Russian elites as their fortress in a hot war with the West. The refuge had a name—Kosvinsky Kamen—Russia's nuclear war nerve centre.

Kamenskaya pressed on, rapidly approaching exhaustion. Eventually, the brutal weather and the conditions forced her to halt. But she was grateful for the heavy snowfall. It compacted the layers beneath, making carving a makeshift shelter from the drift possible. An igloo. With her last reserves of strength, she crafted the blocks. Soon, the rough work was finished, and she disappeared from view as a search plane thundered overhead. A deep sleep claimed her.

Later, sunlight bathed the frozen Taiga, casting a soft glow through the snow of her igloo. The wind whispered through the pines, and Kamenskaya found a modicum of solace. She pulled her flight suit close around her, and surrendered to another hour of sleep.

Revived despite the lack of food, but by sleep and rest alone, she broke out again and pushed on through the snow and the Taiga, further to the east. Away from Kosvinsky Kamen. Aircraft buzzed her from time to time, but she always managed to dig into the snow before they passed overhead.

The second night mirrored the first. And then the third. Finally, she reached a riverbank, the river snaking its course from the north to the south. Upstream, the land was flat. She turned south, along the river's left hand bank, downstream. After a kilometre, she came upon limestone cliffs and a cascading ice cliff where in summer there would be a waterfall. She could hear the river beneath the ice, and walked down to its foot of the limestone cliff, to a flat area where the river emerged in a plunge pool.

She had a pressing need for warmth, and she found dry, standing wood on the edge of the plunge pool, where a strand of trees had died. Kamenskaya gathered a large amount of the dry wood, working for half an hour. The physical exertion relaxed and warmed her. She arranged a sizable woodpile on the flat area between the cliff and the plunge pool. She placed the fuel she had on hand, and then she took out the magnesium block and the survival knife from inside her flight suit. She scraped the block, taking care that the magnesium shavings could accumulate in a pile deep in the wood. She struck the flint side of the block and a stream of sparks flew into the magnesium shavings, igniting them. The fire roared to life. She fortified it by building a barrier of wooden trunks. The barrier was between the limestone cliff and the plunge pool.

She reclined in the snow, basking for minutes in the intense heat. Rare moments of happiness and safety overwhelmed her.

Kneeling, she reached inside her flight suit and extracted the mini laptop, and pressed the on button. It flickered to life. Just as she thought, the battery indicated full charge. Military grade. She inserted the USB, and a window flashed on the screen. Eight files. Each paired as she had seen in the bunker. They played out—no GRU access code requests.

Each file unfolded, and Kamenskaya absorbed the revelations at a deliberate pace. The details of a US operation to weaken Russia unfolded. A US-based mastermind with Russian help. The videos included the death of Magnitsky in prison. One showed a confession to murder. Another showed OMON riot officers admitting guilt. Paired with each file was a single file named "TOP SECRET—RS-28."

She added more wood to the fire, basking again in the warmth that penetrated her to her core. Finally, she lay between the colossal fire and the cliff, succumbing to a well-earned sleep.

Later that night, a realisation jolted Kamenskaya out of her exhausted slumber. Something was amiss! It was as if her sunconcious had been labouring all night on an equation that refused to balance. The two files! How could she have missed the connection between them? She scrambled upright, found the USB, inserted it back into the mini-laptop, and examined the Magnitsky file. Opening the first video file, she identified the mastermind—William Burns. The TOP SECRET RS-28 file demanded her attention, or rather, her conscious mind now demanded she make the connection. Russian ICBMs. No ambiguity, she thought. The information on the RS-28 in her hands could stop the war in its tracks. And stop the risk of global conflict. World War Three. She understood the urgency to reach Ukraine or the West.

Chapter 36

Ural Mountains, Moscow, Russia

The fourth day dawned grey on the Taiga towards the east of the central Urals. Clouds hid the sky, forced from the north. They carried icy Arctic gusts. The snow was a product of the winds. It sculpted the landscape into a frozen masterpiece. It piled up in deep drifts around trees, rocks, and the silent wolves. The wolves huddled together for warmth.

Later, in the evening, Kamenskaya lay nestled between the dying embers of the fire and the flat area next to the limestone cliff and the fire had been robust until the early hours. Now it clung to life, its red core glowing amidst the icy gusts. The sun was setting, but it still provided a fragile shield against the winter's cold. It trapped its fading heat in the swirling air between the flames and the limestone cliff. Kamenskaya was cocooned in her flight jacket. She stirred and opened her dark green eyes.

With a relaxed and rested body, she reached for pieces of wood behind her and added three to the fire. The gusts delivered pure oxygen. The flames rekindled and rose from the ashes, like a reborn phoenix. Her subconscious acknowledged her situation was terminal. Yet, a flickering hope lingered.

First, the harsh reality is her location in the Siberian wilderness. It's during a snowstorm and devoid of human habitation. Second, the absence of food. Third, the relentless pursuit by the Russian state. Game over.

Staring into the flames, Kamenskaya resolved to face her fate with defiance. Two possibilities:

First, she could run to Ukraine, armed with the RS-28 information. It could neutralize the nuclear threat hanging like the sword of Damocles over the Ukraine. With the coding details in Ukraine's hands, the risk of triggering a nuclear end game would be averted. A tough fight awaited. But, the war would stay conventional. She would be hailed a hero for stopping Russia from starting a nuclear war.

Second, and in the alternative, she could flee to the US with the RS-28 code. It would give the power to neutralize Russia's ICBMs. A limited nuclear war was a grim possibility. But, NATO would prevail. NATO's action would prevent a global nuclear war. The outcome would reshape Russia under Western liberal democracy.

She tossed dry wood into the fire, and the flames licked up through the kindling, a plan taking shape in her beautiful mind. In it, there were the bones of a strategy. The plan offered a chance to step back from the brink of Armageddon. Kamenskaya contemplated her choices. She knew the information she had held the key to avoiding disaster. More branches fuelled the fire as the blueprint for her next move unfolded.

Chapter 37

Sartov, Ural Mountains, Siberia, Russia

The weight of despair settled upon the couple like a leaden cloak. The woman was Italian. The man, Russian. The Italian said, 'Okay. We kill ourselves.'

'The Russian said, 'Yes. Nothing changed. No choice. I can't take this anymore, and neither can you.'

'And how?' asked the woman, resigned.

'You'll figure it out. You were always good at that.'

The words brought sadness. He, Evgenia Tsvigun was from Moscow, and she, Patrizia Bellisai, was from Naples, and they had been a couple for just shy of three years. Long enough to give the relationship strength. Short enough for the fire of passion to glow still.

They sought solace in each other's arms, a last refuge. And as they slept, intertwined, the grey dawn broke, accompanied by a biting cold and a howling wind. They opened their eyes in their bed, and their tears welled up in their eyes. They remembered the conversation, and what they had decided.

'And now,' asked Patrizia. 'What do we do?'

'We've already been through it all. Over and over. There's no way out, but to kill ourselves.'

'But I don't want to die.'

'Or we don't!'

'But where to turn, when every direction dead ends at searing unhappiness?' asked Patrizia. 'I'm so tired, Zhenya. No strength left.'

'And I'm lost without you,' said Zhenya.

'Then it's better. Or you take a long walk right now, for hours or as long as it takes—even days. Maybe you don't come back. You decide to spend the rest of your life with me. You don't come back until you have a reason to.'

Evening fell, and the wind picked up again, freezing like a vice even more solidly everything in its path. The snow fell thick and heavy, covering the cleared streets and roads of Sartov with fresh new snow.

Zhenya left the apartment. He walked for hours. His footsteps echoed through the empty streets. Every corner he turned was silent. No answers emerged. He passed through the park gates, and saw a lone dog curled up at the entrance. *Like a guard dog,* he thought.

The dog was a German shepherd. It nestled between the gatepost and two bushes, with only a snow drift for companionship. As he approached the dog looked up, its face morphed into recognition. It looked into Zhenya's eyes. A strange connection flicked between them. It was as if the dog could feel the weight of Zhenya's pain and his regret for causing Patrizia's suffering. At that moment, a revelation struck Zhenya. There was a different way. It opened up a path he and Patty could take. A way to continue and where they didn't have to tear each other apart.

He said a silent prayer for the dog. Then, he left it where it lay and hurried home as fast as the icy streets would allow.

He knew Patrizia remained oblivious to his lover's identity. The different way which he had seen when the dog looked at him, was the miracle to end the war in Ukraine. Because the war consumed Patrizia's thoughts, and finding an answer to end it would rekindle his love for her. Cause and effect, he thought. The German shepherd at the park gates had caused a change to his life. It was his destiny. It was fate.

Their fragile relationship would endure. Then, he would find a way to deal with his betrayal and they would start over.

New hope energized him. He hurried home, his heart buoyant with possibilities.

She heard him unlock the door, and met him as he entered. She had rehearsed what she would say so much that she knew the words by heart. But, in the end, other words came to her lips. She said, 'Tell me only that you're coming home.'

Zhenya said, 'I love you, but I need space. And then I'll make it up to you.'

'How?'

'The war in Ukraine!'

'What about it?'

'I had a hunch. You wouldn't believe it.'

'Try me!'

'A dog, Patty. A German shepherd gave me hope. It recognized me, I swear, even without reason. I wouldn't have paid attention, but there was something in that dog's look. Something ethereal. It was as if the dog could see what I was thinking. And what I was thinking was the thing that clicked. As if my whole life was before and behind me, but right then and there, all that mattered was you, the premonition and the dog.'

'And what were you thinking?' asked Patrizia.

'Ukraine. Patty. I was thinking about Ukraine! The war. It's as if your words all these months of war finally made sense. Your good intentions and feelings for all people also came good in me. As if, for once, I could be your equal. To do something for Ukrainians, for Russians, for Italians. For all the peoples of the world. We have to prevent this war from escalating. That's what the dog's eyes said to me as it looked at me. It was as if the dog too was reaching into the ethereal, tapping into an unknown modality of force and knowledge, and we had connected.'

'It means you're coming back to me? For good.'

'Yes Patty! I am. To stop this crazy war before it's too late.'

'But how? What can *we* do to prevent this war from escalating? We are in control of nothing. All we have is a cabin in the Siberian wilderness near a river, and a dog called Hachi. The cabin doesn't even have a strong, continuous internet signal. It comes and goes. How could it suddenly become the lynchpin to save the Earth?'

'Patty. I know how wild it sounds. We're two drops of water in a tidal wave of humanity, a juggernaut, leading to war, escalation, and nuclear bombs. We need to turn the tidal wave around, but it's like an aircraft carrier. It doesn't turn on a dime once in motion. But the truth is, I can't answer that. All I know is what I feel. And that's enough for me, and I hope it's enough for you. And yes, I'm returning to you, but I can't say it will be forever. But I'm trying. As I said, I love you. That's all I can say.'

Patrizia said, 'That's fine. We don't need to figure everything out today. We need to get through the day. Tomorrow will be better.'

'We could leave in the morning, to the cabin. We could take food for two days. Spend time together. You and me and Hachi.'

Hachi. Their grey-eyed husky lay next to the wood-burning stove, and he pricked up his large pointed ears when he heard his name. He cheered them both. Hardly could they believe that hours earlier, they had been contemplating murder-suicide. They both felt tearful and thankful at the same time. They didn't know what to think. But the talk and thought of their husky was a path to salvation.

'Agreed,' said Zhenya. 'Throw things in a backpack. A clean towel. Fresh linen for the bed. There's wood at the cabin.'

'And the gun and cartridges,' added Patrizia.

'When, now?'

'Yes,' said Patrizia. 'Unless you prefer to die!'

***

Hachi barked louder and louder. He was waking up the whole forest. Between bouts of barking, he nestled up close to the woman. But when that had no effect, he lay on top of her, covering her. He was like a cosy blanket on a winter's night.

His barks echoed, but, no one heard. The wind and the snow. They filled the air swirling through the pines swallowing all sounds. But Hachi did not leave. He snuggled up closer.

Zhenya and Patrizia heard the barks as soon as they began. They were in the cabin, and darkness had fallen. They had let out Hachi, who had sensed the woman from afar.

It took Zhenya and Patrizia long minutes to get to Hachi, and when they did, they thought the woman was dead.

Zhenya felt for a pulse, and found none. Her skin was as white as the snow surrounding her. He scooped her up and held her tight. A fragile butterfly. And then he ran toward the cabin. Patrizia stumbled behind as best she could in the deep snow, a faithful shadow. Then came Hachi, the real hero of the hour.

The cabin was a twenty minutes away, but they made it in ten.

Zhenya laid Kamenskaya down on the sheepskin rugs by the crackling fire. Her body was a lifeless doll. Patrizia threw off the woman's cold, damp clothes. She stripped her down to her underwear and then she laid her down on the sheepskins in front

178

of the roaring cabin fire. Skin on skin. The best way to transfer heat. She smothered her. The warmth of her body went to work, and the heat of the fire breathed new life into the woman. Zhenya did his part, covering them both in extra sheepskins. He knelt, his knees next to Kamenskaya's head. He took care not to shield her from any of the precious heat coming from the fire. He pushed two fingers onto her neck. This time, he felt a faint pulse.

Later, Zhenya prepared hot tea. Slowly, but surely, Kamenskaya was coming round. First, there was flickering in her eyelids. Then there was a shivering which ran across her stomach. Finally she opened her eyes. She was blinking in the light and the heat. She said, 'Where am I?'

'With friends,' said Patrizia.

Kamenskaya said, 'You saved me!'

'Don't talk,' said Patrizia. 'Rest now. Talking will come later.'

'No. I need to talk now. There's so little time left.'

Zhenya and Patrizia exchanged glances. 'Little time?' asked Zhenya, plying her with hot, sweet tea. 'Little time for what?'

'My name is Kira Kamenskaya, and there's something you need to know. It's the same thing the whole world needs to know.' She sat up. She felt more warmth spread through her body. 'Then you can decide to help me if you'd want to help.'

Zhenya put a little table next to Kamenskaya and placed the tea on it.

Patrizia said, 'Why?'

Kamenskaya opened her eyes wide as if a premonition had taken hold and said, 'In danger I am, and so are you!'

Zhenya said, 'About Kosvinsky, right?'

'Right,' said Kamenskaya. 'You probably know. You've seen the helicopters and the planes and the tanks. The region is reared, and all to find me. It's a huge military operation.' She looked at

Zhenya with hope and understanding. She said, 'They're trying to catch me, alive of course. But also dead if they have to.'

Zhenya said, 'Why?'

'I have information from Kosvinsky. Information on Russia's newest intercontinental ballistic missile. If it got into the wrong hands, I guess that would compromise Russia's nuclear arsenal. It would give the Americans an advantage.'

Patrizia and Zhenya traded looks. For an instant or less. Then Patrizia said, 'How can we help?'

Kamenskaya looked more focussed, as if relieved that her message got through. She said, 'I need to travel to Ukraine. The information in American hands would prevent the war from going nuclear.'

Zhenya sat, took a glass of tea, and handed it to her, saying, 'Why Ukraine?'

Kamenskaya said, 'Ukraine is the key. To prevent escalation.'

Zhenya said, 'But how can *you* do that?'

Kamenskaya took a sip of tea. She said, 'Without giving that information to the Ukrainian authorities, logic would win. Although we are now still far from it, this might pass. Pushing Russia back from their four new territories in Ukraine will make it more likely that Russia will use nuclear weapons. These territories are the four annexed provinces. Ukraine would face tactical nuclear strikes. The war would escalate to involve NATO. Not de-facto, as now, but for real. Which would result in a global nuclear war.'

Patrizia and Zhenya exchanged glances. Zhenya said, 'So?'

'So, Ukraine must know this. Winning a conventional war with Russia won't lead to global nuclear war. The information I have is the game changer. It would give Ukraine that security. If Russia were close to defeat, Ukraine could give the information in my USB to the Americans. That would stop the Russian threat.'

Zhenya said, 'But how can you have such information? What kind of information?'

'On Russia's newest, most powerful ICBM.'

'Understood. But between here and Ukrainian forces is a 40 kilometre wide war zone. We can't just walk across. There'll be checks.'

Kamenskaya said, 'No one said this would be easy. We'll have to find a way through the lines.'

Patrizia said, 'We'll travel together—strength in numbers.'

Kamenskaya smiled, 'I've got a better idea. A couple traveling together is less suspicious. Much less suspicious than two women and a man. Being apart also gives more in other ways. Ways to harbour things up our sleeves. To dodge trouble. With you here, at this cabin, as our secret weapon, we'll be able to make some remote moves if needed. So, my idea, if you both agree, is that I travel to Ukraine with Zhenya. You will stay here, for internet backup as required.'

Patrizia smiled. The mission articulated by Kamenskaya focussed her on her value. She was no longer worried about Zhenya's unfaithfulness. This changed everything. There had been a seismic shift since their arrival at the cabin. Besides, Kamenskaya was beautiful, and she didn't want to stand in the way of Zhenya if he had any chance with her. She said, 'Alright, you've convinced me. I'll manage the operation from this cabin until you two arrive in Ukraine. Then I'll return to Sartov with Hachi. Consider me your backup, on standby.'

Chapter 38

Bolshaya Dimitrovka Street, Moscow

Colonel Alexander Bagrov of the Procurator General's Office needed to walk a tight line. He had to balance speed and avoid getting flustered. He would arrive at his office red-faced from too much pace. His sweat would soak his crisp white shirt, even in the sub-zero air. Too slow, and he would be late for the meeting with Investigator Karpov.

Major Pavel Karpov had taken the Magnitsky case from Oleg Silchenko. But that had been fifteen years ago. Now, Bagrov was 48 but still working at the General Prosecutor's Office on Mala Dmitrovka, Moscow. But he had lost touch with Karpov in 2012. That was, until that very morning.

The sun shone down from above the park on the edge of Bolshaya Dmitrovka, and Bagrov rounded the corner of No. 72. Passers-by were bustling along, their arms full of purchases from Tverskaya Ulitsa. There were business people and tourists. And then there was Pavel Karpov.

'Couldn't this wait?' asked Bagrov, stretching out a hand.

'It's Kamenskaya,' answered Karpov.

'What's she been up to?'

Karpov pointed down the pavement toward the Garden Ring Boulevards and said, 'Let's walk.'

The lights changed, the traffic drew to a halt, and they crossed the busy Bolshaya Dimitrovka Street, taking care to avoid the clear ice patches. Bagrov repeated his question, 'So what has Kamenskaya been up to?'

'Stealing state secrets.'

'Such as?'

'Coding information on the RS-28 Sarmat ICBM.'

'You know that for sure?'

'As good as. Yesterday at 01.30, she downloaded the complete coding of the thing.'

'Downloaded from where?'

'Inside Kosvinsky Kamen.'

'A location without security right?'

'Right. But it doesn't help, because to get within 100 miles of the place, you need clearance. The whole area is sealed tight.'

'And she walked right in?'

'Correct. Which is why I needed to talk to you.'

'That's not surprising,' said Bagrov. 'After all, she is our Defence Minister!'

Karpov smiled and said, 'Any ideas on why?'

'Could be a thousand things. The first thing I'd check is big foreign policy decisions.'

Karpov raised an eyebrow. They stopped under the trees of the boulevard. 'Ukraine?'

It was Bagrov's turn to decide which way they were heading. He said, 'This way. We'll double round past the Balshoi and then along to the State Duma. Sure. Ukraine would be the first reason. She's a patriot, of course. No one gets to where she has got without that being the case. But being a patriot also means being committed and honest to self. Being Defense Minister means understanding war; she is a big reader. Her home is full of books on war. I mean shelves upon shelves. And the pride of place is The Art of War, by Sun Tzu.'

'I know that book,' cut in Karpov. 'She likes it then?'

'Likes it.' Bagrov chucked. 'She worships it. So you should know that Kira will think a certain way right now.'

'What way?' asked Karpov.

'You shouldn't fight battles that you can't win.'

'Meaning?'

'In the context of Ukraine, that would mean not being drawn into an escalation with NATO.'

Karpov took Bagrov's arm, stopping him dead. He looked him straight in the eye. He said, 'Look, Sasha. She has downloaded two files. The first is on the RS-28 ICBM and the other on Sergei Magnitsky.'

Bagrov thought a moment, and then he said, 'But why did she take the second file? The Magnitsky case has nothing to do with the war in Ukraine.'

'The bigger question is why was the Magnitsky file saved in the same folder as the Sarmat file,' replied Karpov.

'And you have an answer?'

'I have a theory, nothing else.'

'Let's hear it.'

Karpov led the way down Petrovka Street towards the Bolshoy Theatre. After a moment's pause, he said, 'The GRU saved the Sarmat file in many places on the secure servers. They were within the building Kamenskaya entered. The GRU also kept the second file in every folder where they saved the Sarmat file.'

'And why do they do that?' asked Bagrov.

'My theory is that the second file was placed in those Sarmat folders as a tracer. Anyone stealing the first file would get tempted to take the second. And when they opened the second, they would be compelled to investigate. In Kamenskaya's case, we both know of the logic. Once she saw what Magnitsky endured and the lies in the case, the injustice would compel her to act. And her actions would bring in the wolves.'

Karpov saw they were reaching the end of the street. But he kept talking, saying, 'She would be tempted to reach out to whoever and whatever is needed to investigate. And bingo, we would be all over her.'

They reached the end of Petrovka Street. Bagrov led the way, turning ahead of Karpov. Karpov caught up. He said, 'So far, you have received nothing, right? No friendly signs of information from any of the search agencies. Which means she has probably cottoned on.'

Karpov led the way again, this time back towards the top of Tverskaya.

Bagrov said, 'Listen, Kamenskaya is not going to be found by her reaching out. You know that.'

They got to the Yuri Dolgoruki statue, and Karpov said, 'You're right. Life has clued her up. She will know that our best way to locate her is through technology, so we can forget about finding her that way.'

'So?'

'So, it's up to you now, Bagrov. Bring your friend in from the cold.'

Chapter 39

The Kremlin, Moscow

President Potanin walked at a good yet steady pace along long corridors towards the meeting. His left arm swung in unison with his steps, but his right arm remained static, glued to his side. It seemed to be hovering over an invisible firearm holstered on his side. He stopped where the passage turned at a right angle to the left. A vast window gave great views across the Cathedral of the Archangel to the Moscow River. Night had fallen across the Kremlin. The moon hung above the red-brick ramparts behind the Armoury.

Defense Minister Shoigu sat at the long white table. He tried to get up, but Potanin pointed to his chair. Shoigu stayed put. Potanin sat and placed his hands in front of him. His arms were half outstretched and his hands pointed like an arrow toward Shoigu. He said, 'Defense Minister Shoigu. Make your report.'

Shoigu cleared his throat. He grabbed the sheath of papers before him. 'Vladimir Vladimirovich. I reported that the US military-industrial complex has greatly benefited from the war. At that time, the total funding for Ukraine through the USAI and Contact Group was 172 billion dollars. I am reporting on the publication of a meeting of the Ukraine Defense Contact Group. The funding level is now at 190.7 billion dollars. The latest Security Assistance package is 10.5 billion dollars alone. The assessments made at our last meeting stand. The US will keep funding and supplying offensive weapons to Ukraine. This helps the influential US citizens connected to the US military-industrial complex.'

Chapter 40

Fifteen years earlier—Park Parbedy, Moscow,
18th November 2009

Alexander Bagrov was 45 minutes late. He was out of breath and sweating despite the freezing Moscow air. It was minus 25 degrees Celsius on the frozen Moscow streets. He made it to his workplace, the General Procurator of the Russian Federation.

He was a straight-talking lawyer. Blonde, blue-eyed, and athletic. Playing the field and getting into relationships had come easy all his life. His problem was getting out of them.

The General Procurator of the Russian Federation had a classic facade. It was set back from the street. It sat in a large, indistinct yard on Bolshaya Dmitrovka Street, a stone's throw from Tverskaya Square and the balcony of the Moscow Town Hall where Lenin proclaimed his revolution on 18th October 1917. It is home to the best government lawyers in Moscow, each with a team working out of a specific building area. The rooms, spaces, and floors were separate. They were arranged wisely for efficiency. It had different areas for fraud, homicide, and sexual crimes. Tax crimes operated out of the fourth floor, which was where Lieutenant Colonel Alexander Bagrov worked. General Yuri Prigozhin was his boss. Prigozhin was the head prosecutor of Tax crimes and the bane of Bagrov's existence. If Bagrov arrived at 09.05 to work, he would lose his job. It almost happened a week before. Then, there had been an accident on his tram from Ulitsa Podbelskova. He had to run for 10 minutes to the nearest Metro to the accident site. Then, he had to run from Pushkinskaya to the office building. He got to his desk at 09.03 and kept his job, but it had been close. Prigozhin had made it clear that he would fire Bagrov if it ever happened again.

Bagrov had made it to his desk under the radar. He knew because General Prigozhin was still in his office on the 6th floor. He knew that because Prigozhin's secretary had just entered the open plan. She was a 6-foot sculpted brunette named Oksana. She had nodded in his direction. A memorable conquest, he and Oksana had remained on good terms ever since the end of their brief union. Despite her signal, Bagrov's calm was more fake than real. He sat down and switched on various devices among a tangled mass of wires and cables. He was relieved. He would not have to account for his delay or move to plan B.

Plan B was to tell the truth, which should have been watertight. Everyone knew that Matrosskaya Tishina prison called him often. They worried about Magnitsly's health. Their most famous inmate had been complaining daily about his eleven months and fifteen days in jail. Complaints written and filed numbered over 300 already. Blocked drainage in the cell. Vermin in the cell. No privacy in the cell. Magnitsky filed each and compiled reports. True, Magnitsky's condition had worsened over the months. But, it had not worsened more than that of other inmates of Russian jails.

Last night was different. The previous night, Magnitsky had not made all the usual complaints. He wanted to talk.

So Bagrov had gone straight there, despite it being 23.30. He had been in the company of a lady, Lena. But when the call came, his career came first.

His car pulled to a stop in the prison parking lot. He locked his car and began walking to the prison gates. The weather was cold, and snow was falling. He tightened his long down overcoat around his torso and pressed along the prison walls. Magnitsky's cell window became visible as he swung around the north-eastern corner. A tower with guards and AK-47s topped the corner. He could see the broken window of Magnitsky's cell.

Bagrov rapped on the heavy steel door. A guard buzzed him in and escorted him to a conference room. The room had four walls and a steel table. A video camera sat at each corner and two chairs. It was like every time before, and just as dismal. There were two iron doors—the one he had walked through and one in the opposite wall—to the cells. He heard footsteps on the cell door side, a bolt pulled back, and a second bolt scraped out. The door opened, and Magnitsky shuffled in, his hands and feet shackled. The guard set him down and attached him to the table with a steel ring. Bagrov made a signal to the video camera to start recording.

Bagrov cautioned Magnitsky and said, 'Something to tell me?'

Magnitsky said, 'Yes. About Kalmykia, I'm ready to talk.'

'Go on,' said Bagrov. On the face of it, the State had a great case. The workbooks were for the Kalmykian "invalids." Magnitsky and Burns had signed off on them. They had no idea what they were doing. Then there were their video statements. Great evidence. Evidence that would be difficult to argue against. Courts in Russia convict 99% of cases that come before them. But even cases in Russia cases revolve around evidence, even corrupted evidence. The signed workbooks and video statements by the Kalmykians would be clear evidence. They would not even be corrupt. The prosecutor only lacked something to seal the conviction. They needed the holy grail of any investigation: a video confession.

Magnitsky said, 'I've got something to tell you.'

Bagrov looked up at the cameras. He was looking for a sign that they were recording. He saw a green light on each. He said, 'That's understood. Tell me about Kalmykia. What has Kalmykia got to do with anything?'

'Kalmykia is a Republic having special tax laws. It gives special tax treatment to companies registered in Kalmykia. They employ persons with recognized disabilities.

'Tell me something I don't already know?'

Magnitsky shuffled his feet under the table and clattered and rattled his handcuffs. He was struggling and grimacing. He shouted, 'Can someone take these off?'

'Not a problem,' said Bagrov, rising to his feet. He kicked the door ajar and shouted an order to a guard.

A guard walked in, a bunch of keys jingling as he searched for the correct key. He un-cuffed Magnitsky.

Bagrov said, 'You do something for me; I do something for you.'

Magnitsky nodded.

'So, who instructed you to go to Kalmykia and why?'

'William Burns.'

Bagrov glanced at the cameras. He saw that they were still rolling. He said, 'What exactly did William Burns instruct you to do?'

Magnitsky said, 'He told me to go with him to Kalmykia. To recruit disabled people to be analysts for the shell companies, for the funds.'

'And who was the strategist behind the plan? Who was the instigator of the plan and why?'

'From start to finish, the plan was Burns's. He told me to cut the taxes on the funds of the hedge fund manager. I devised a plan to register shell companies in Kalmykia. I would employ disabled people in that region. We would call them 'analysts.' They would work for the company. Then, we could say they were employed by the shell companies, and, in turn, by the investment manager. But it was a ruse, of course.'

'So that's what you did?' asked Bagrov. 'You went with Burns to Kalmykia on his orders. You recruited invalids so that the shell companies and the hedge fund would pay less tax.'

'Yes. On the instructions of Burns, I travelled to Kalmykia and found and recruited five invalids. They were mentally compromised. The workbooks of these invalids prove that we acted together. Burns and I both signed the workbooks.'

'And what was the nature of the tax breaks which the companies benefited from?' asked Bagrov.

'The employment of the invalids in Kalmykia caused this. It lowered the overall tax for all the hedge funds from 35% to 5.5%.'

'And how much did that save the companies as a whole?'

'Overall, the value saved due to using the invalids was just over $17 million.'

'And what kind of tasks did these invalids do?' asked Bagrov

'They had to cut articles from international publications. The articles were about the companies' subject matter. Then, they had to ship the clippings to the corporate head office in Pavalyetskaya, Moscow.'

Bagrov peeked a glance at the CCTV cameras. The room had four—one on each corner. They were sweeping the room. Bagrov expected the MVD received the images in real time. Investigator Karpov was outside the room and watching. But the pictures and sound recordings of the interview went to other places. There was also a live feed to other agents—straight into another Moscow location—GRU headquarters. Ulitsa Grizodubovoy, 3, Moscow, Russia.

GRU. The name meant something to Bagrov. It stood for the Main Intelligence Directorate is the foreign military intelligence agency of the Russian Armed Forces. Its Russian name was Glavnoye Razvedyvatel'noye Upravleniye. Known for its involvement in intelligence gathering, covert operations, and military espionage. Active since the early 20th century. It has had various name changes.

Chapter 41

Prosecutor General's Office, Bolshaya Dmitrovka, Moscow

Colonel Alexander Bagrov's desktop blinked with a message on Microsoft Teams. Oksana, his rendezvous with fate, sent a cryptic note: 'I need to see you.'

Bagrov's terse reply read, 'Shokoladnitsa. 10 minutes.'

Shokoladnitsa café nestled on the intersection of Bolshaya Dmitrovka and Petrovskiy Pereulok. It was a haven for tea, coffee, and business lunches. It drew in office workers from Pushkinskaya and Tverskaya during lunch. This created a bustling vibe with lively music and well-spaced tables.

He swept the documents which spread across his desk into his drawer and locked it. Then, he threw on his coat and walked to the lift. He felt the gaze of his colleagues. Flying under the radar but sparking curiosity. He didn't mind. The message from Oksana signalled a shift.

He chose a discreet table near the entrance. Bagrov ordered two business lunches with English breakfast tea. Oksana materialized three minutes later, and the exchange began.

'Have you ordered?' she asked.

'Caesar salad. Borsh and tea for two,' Bagrov replied.

'Thanks.'

Bagrov cut to the chase, 'I'm pretty sure I know what this is about.'

'Which is?'

'Magnitsky.'

'Well done. How did you know?'

'I could say something, but I want you to say it first.'

'GRU?' Oksana ventured.

'No. Karpov. I just met him. I know that the MVD wants me to help catch Kamenskaya. Why did you say GRU?'

'I was going to ask you the same thing. Come on, Sasha!'

'What?'

'You know what happened. You interviewed the man, for Christ's sake!'

'Yes, Oksana. I interviewed him, and he confessed. All recorded. But that was fifteen years ago, so excuse me if I'm a little sketchy on some of the current details. Things have moved on.'

'Recorded?' Oksana raised an eyebrow. 'If someone made a recording, there would be a tape.'

A pang of unease hit Bagrov. 'That will be with investigator Silchenko.'

'I just talked to Silchenko, who confirmed that there is no recording on file.'

'There must be a mistake,' said Bagrov. He had no interview recording. He could be framed for Magnitsky's death. Danger lurked from every angle.

Oksana glanced at her watch, 'Look. You have a meeting with Prigozhin scheduled for 2 pm. Don't be late!'

Chapter 42

Prosecutor General's Office, Bolshaya Dmitrovka, Moscow

General Prigozhin stood by his huge window. He gazed at the Lenin monument six floors below on Tverskaya Ploshad. Colonel Alexander Bagrov had given up trying to please his boss. He knocked twice and barged into the room. At 48, he was a seasoned Colonel in the Armed Forces of the Russian Federation.

'Bagrov!' Prigozhin bellowed, shifting from the window. 'Coffee? Or something stronger?'

'Coffee's fine, Sir. What's this about?'

Prigozhin seized the coffee pot, poured a mug for Bagrov and approached his subordinate thrusting it into his hands. A double Jack Daniels on ice was his own choice, and he swirled it before taking a long swig.

Bagrov sipped his coffee, sensing a buzz in his jacket. Glancing down, he saw Oksana's name. Trouble wasn't unexpected, but not from her.

'You going to take that?' Prigozhin asked.

Bagrov reassured himself it was just a call—no big deal. Prigozhin could be angry, but that wasn't his concern. He walked out of the office, swiped the screen in the hallway, and whispered, 'Bagrov.'

'Can Prigozhin hear you right now?'

'No.'

'Then don't go back into his office. Don't talk to him. You might not get out of this in one piece. Right now, you still have a chance.'

'I don't know what you're talking about!'

'I'll fill you in.'

'You should have done that in the cafe.'

'I had no time. Meet me back there. And Sasha.'

'What?'

'Get out of there.'

Bagrov said, 'Wait. The cafe's too close. Meet me at Rock 'n Roll in 30 minutes. Come alone.'

***

Oksana parked her Mercedes, and manifested a casual entrance. She entered and found anything but. The bar was overflowing into the road and the thick snow. Navigating to the back past a DJ in full swing, she spotted Bagrov, who was gesturing to a space at the bar.

Oksana ordered a double Jack Daniels and Coke on ice. Bagrov had chosen wisely—a well-researched and secure bar. With the loud techno music and high-frequency interactions, surveillance risk was minimal.

Bagrov joined her, asking, 'Been here long?'

'No,' Oksana replied, spinning around and pulling out a high seat for Bagrov.

Bagrov ordered two beers. Then he said, 'Fill me in.'

'You're on GRU's radar.'

'No kidding! Then tell me, Oksana. Do they have the Magnitsky interview tape?'

'They do.'

'How do you know?'

'Because they contacted Prigozhin. They told him everything.'

'Everything?'

'Not only do they have the confession tape, but they also gave information on Kamenskaya. She accessed the Kosvinsky Mountain mainframe and viewed and downloaded two files. Wait. That's not quite right. She accessed one restricted file on the RS-28 Sarmat, 'Top Secret,' paired with a second file. Your interview recording. The GRU paired the second file with the first for extra security. It will help find anyone who downloads the first.'

'You believe?'

'Yes. That's all I know. In any case, Kamenskaya downloaded both files onto a USB drive and fled Kosvinsky.'

'Understood. But why me? What have I got to do with any of this?'

'Because you're her friend, and they trust you. And you have to trust them. They believe that you can assist them in finding her.'

'And betray my friend?'

'Yes. I guess the GRU hopes you will do this as a soldier. You are, after all, a commissioned officer who took an oath to serve the Motherland. It would be better for Kamenskaya, too—better than winding up dead.'

'Come on! We both know that capturing her alive is the worst thing that could happen now to Kira.'

Oksana said, 'I know.' She looked around, suspicion bearing down. And then she said, 'Look, Sasha. As your friend, we both know you haven't a choice.'

The truth hit Bagrov. His career. His *life*! He had burnt his bridges with Prigozhin. Prigozhin would be planning his capture and prosecution. Like, *this is for losing the Magnitsky file and for gross misconduct,* he thought. He had left the office while pursuing his inquiries about Kamenskaya. He was under no illusion that he was now on the run from the General Prosecutor's Office, even if he was acting for the GRU. They would incarcerate and torture him if the GPO captured him, and it would come down to a judge to decide his fate. And with a 99% conviction rate, he didn't fancy his chances.

Oksana said, 'The GRU will protect you, and then it comes down to a turf war. And we both know that the GRU trumps the GPO.'

'I'm not so sure,' said Sasha. 'But you're right. I'm out of choices.'

'Yes. And the GRU protect their own.'

'That's true. So? Now what?'

'There's a team outside.'

'What about you?' asked Bagrov.

'I can take care of myself.'

'Prigozhin will know you met up with me.'

'That concerns me, not you. You just need to get outside. Right now. The GRU agents are in a black Mercedes 4x4 SUV opposite the entrance. They'll fill you in on the next steps. And Sasha …'

'What?'

'Good luck!'

***

The black Mercedes was there. Opposite the club's exit, three vehicles lined up along one side of the boulevard. There were MVD vehicles and motorcycles. So the MVD was on the GRU side of the turf war, a welcome development. But no guarantee that the GRU would trump the General Prosecutor. Bagrov crossed the boulevard. A burly man got out of the middle Mercedes, opened the rear door, and the convoy sped away, catapulting Bagrov back into the rear seat. The SUV was empty except for the driver. He wore a black leather jacket with black hair and black, two-day stubble.

Bagrov asked, 'Where are we headed?'

'Vnukovo Airport,' said the driver. He was a man of few words.

Chapter 43

Kremlin, Moscow

Potanin pointed to the other end of the long table. His hand cut through the air with a terse command. 'Defense Minister Shoigu. Take a seat and deliver your report.'

Shoigu pulled out the chair, settling into it with military precision. 'Vladimir Vladimirovich, the US has raised the stakes. It is sending support to Ukraine through the Ukraine Contact Group. The group has fifty nations. Their total investment now exceeds two hundred and five billion dollars.'

'I've perused those reports,' Potanin replied with impatience.

'Several Western nations are approving support packages. They are arming Ukraine with modern tanks.'

'I've had a look at that brief as well. What's on the Western arsenal, and who are the contributors?'

'Germany is providing 58 Leopard 2 tanks, two divisions. Additionally, they're offering 80 Leopard 1 second-gen tanks. The UK is supplying two divisions of Challenger 2 tanks. The US is in the game too, delivering four divisions of M1 Abrams tanks. Ukrainian crews, trained by each supplier, will man these divisions.'

Shoigu paused. Then he said, 'The worst part is seeing German tanks with their black cross symbols fighting Russian tanks on our soil.'

Potanin nodded thoughtfully. 'Thank you, Defence Minister. We'll play our hand in the American game, and Russia won't come out the loser. But for now, you sit tight. Is that clear?'

'Understood, Vladimir Vladimirovich.'

'Dismissed.'

As Shoigu exited, Potanin wasted no time. He pulled out his mobile, urgency etched across his face. The number he dialled was the deputy chairman of the Security Council. Irina, the deputy chairman's PA, picked up on the second ring. Potanin said, 'Irina, get me Dmitri Mendeleev.'

Chapter 44

White House, Washington D.C.

The message had echoed through the intelligence community with the stark urgency of a Kill or Capture scenario. Zak Hoffman was a robust figure with a silver-streaked mane which had earned him the nickname "Wolf man Zak." He paced his office. This practiced ritual underscored his reputation and disseminated his renown. It was a means to concentrate. It was reserved for moments demanding deep thought. Moments exactly like the current one.

The message was authentic. The location, Kosvinsky Mountain, validated it. Kosvinsky. Russia's version of Cheyenne Mountain, the bunker built to shield leaders in a nuclear war. The second point was the sheer scale of the mission the Russian's were undertaking—a comprehensive Catch or Kill operation. They were pulling out all the stops. T90s, T72s, and T64 tanks and electronic warfare aircraft were mobilized. The material they were fielding could detect any electrical activity.

Hoffman stopped his pacing and sat behind an expansive hardwood desk. Again he considered the message, and then he took a decision. He picked up his telephone, and rang his Personal Assistant, saying. 'Call an immediate security meeting. The group is to include the Chairman of the Joint Chiefs, the National Security Advisor, the Secretary of Defense, and the President.'

Thirty minutes passed and General Mark R. Park, Chairman of the Joint Chiefs of Staff started the meeting from his office in the Pentagon. His booming voice resonated through loudspeakers in the White House Situation Room. The split screen showcased General Park and Zak Hoffman.

'Hoffman. This is National Security Advisor Jake Piraeus. The President and Secretary of Defense are here. We're all ears, and we've read the brief. Ms Kamenskaya is on the run after escaping the Kosvinsky Mountain complex. There's a Kill or Capture order out for her. What's your confidence based on?'

'Many things, Sir. What we see at Kosvinsky Mountain is no mere 'exercise.' It's definitely a kill-or-capture operation, and its scale indicates a high-profile target. The Russians are throwing everything to prevent this person from escaping. Tanks, helicopters, aircraft, infantry. They've even shifted their satellites. All pointing to one thing, Gentlemen.'

'And what's that?' inquired General Park.

'Whatever the target possesses, we need it.'

'That's quite an assumption, Hoffman,' Piraeus interjected. 'There could be alternative explanations. They might be testing our response.'

'Possible, Sir, but I doubt it,' responded Hoffman.

'Why's that?'

'Our asset in Moscow confirms this isn't a setup. The target is Defense Minister Kira Kamenskaya, and she's on the run.'

Piraeus inquired, 'Do we know what she's done?'

'We do, Sir. She accessed the mainframe in Kosvinsky. Our asset in Moscow has verified it. An SU-35 flew from Moscow to the Urals on full afterburner. Kira Kamenskaya was on that flight.'

The President cleared his throat, and said, 'Hoffman, the Moscow asset confirmed Kamenskaya is the target, correct?'

'That's correct, Mr. President.'

'If this is a setup to gauge our response, it's peculiar. I agree that whatever Kamenskaya has is significant. Look at the risks she's taking. They'll execute her for this.'

'Hoffman, this is General Park, Chairman of the Joint Chiefs.'

'Yes, General.'

'Did our agent specify what Kamenskaya took and why?'

'Sir, she downloaded nine files. Eight relate to the Magnitsky case, and the ninth labeled RS-28.'

'RS-28?'

'Yes, General.'

General Park addressed the President, saying, 'Mr. President, RS-28 is code for their newest ICBM. If Kamenskaya has anything on that missile from inside Kosvinsky, we should try to secure her.'

'Agreed,' said the President. 'General, initiate plans for Kamenskaya's extraction. We need to get to her before the Russians do. They've replaced their old ICBMs with RS-28. If she knows something, we have to grab her. Assemble teams. Formulate an action plan within the next hour. We'll reconvene in one hour.'

Hoffman ended the video-conference, and called his PA, and told her to put out an urgent call for his best agents to assemble immediately in 10 minutes.

Nine minutes and thirty seconds later, he strode into the room where the agents had assembled. He said, 'Listen up. I want everyone to report to me within 5 minutes. The target individual is within 100km of Kosvinsky Mountain. Name—Kira Kamenskaya. Mode of travel—unknown. Intentions—unknown.

Reason—data theft from Kosvinsky Mountain. Time of theft: 48 hours ago. Reason for tracking: the GRU and Rocket Forces seek this person. Kill or Capture. So, it is highly likely she possesses critical defense information. Find this person!'

The sound of clattering keyboards and rapid conversations filled the room. Hoffman approached the young lady at the desk closest to him. Julie Connor was two years and three months in. He counted on her each time he needed particular actions, just like then. Hoffman whispered, 'Activate your team. I want a list in 30 minutes of every building within 50km of Kosvinsky. Include the phone numbers of each person who stayed at any of those buildings in the last six months.'

Agent Connor said, 'I'm all over it, Sir.'

Chapter 45

Julie Connor considered the list. The list was a vehicle, that's all. What she and Hoffman really needed was to narrow the field. She had done these exercises a hundred times. Never in such circumstances, and with such urgency.

Connor started at step one—the geographic list. That was team one. They had color-coded the area map of Kosvinsky Kamen. She blew it up three times, printed it, and stuck it to one of the large cork wall boards. A red pin was at every building within sixty kilometres of the Kosvinsky Mountain bunker. There were forty six red pins in total.

Step two—her task. Arrange Team Three, fifteen of her best agents in the task.

Step three was her best fifteen agents, all drilling down into each person's life connected to each red point. Team Three. She put them in the corner of the open plan in Langley. She said, 'Okay, listen up, everyone,' and motioned to the board, 'Look at that!'

'A map!' said the guy nearest to her.

'Yes. And you know what to do. Just like training, only this time it's for real. You're team three. There are fifteen of you and forty-six points. Three each. You have an hour to analyse those locations. Pull up the mobile data. See who they are. That's Step Three. And then proceed to step four. Pull up the last ten weeks of mobile location history. Run it through the computer. And then step five. Pull up the last twenty-four hours, looking for anything different. Statistics. Run both sets of data. Let the program do the heavy lifting. I want results in an hour. We're looking to reduce the forty-six locations by a factor of ten. Something manageable. Are we clear?'

Connor's team did better than expected in fifty minutes, not an hour. Three locations in the map area showed anomalies.

Connor took them one by one. She divided her team of fifteen again. This time, there were five per team—one for each anomaly. She said, 'Teams Two and Three, spread to separate areas and discuss your results. I want brain power put to bear. Team One, come with me.'

Team One's location was close to the entrance of Kosvinsky. Unlikely, thought Connor. She put herself in Kamenskaya's shoes. The site was a settlement. A village. She said, 'What's the anomaly?'

Agent Philips had been designated leader. He was an overweight man of thirty-seven and medium height with blue eyes and mousy blonde hair. He said, 'Number seventeen out of the forty-six. Three individual mobiles are in one building, registered to the same address. Over ten weeks, the users are dispersed each night. They go to different locations in the settlement. In the last twenty-four hours, all are together at the registered address.'

Connor said, 'So? Kamenskaya caused everyone to bunk up together? Not likely. Good work, though. Keep discussing.' She moved to team two. They had different parameters for the same anomaly.

Connor walked across the open-plan space. Other teams were working. Different projects. Different time frames. She came on team three. Connor liked the tall, blonde team leader wearing a black business suit. She had a ponytail. Everyone knew the lady had Spanish heritage, so someone nicknamed her 'La Rubia,' and it stuck. She didn't mind.

Team three was buzzing, excited. A hive of activity. Connor said, 'What you got, Rubia?'

'A cabin 45 km directly due east from Kosvinsky. It's isolated, but there's a river. No track. There's an intermittent network signal indicating the presence of two individuals. A couple. The guy's Russian. She's Italian.'

'Names?'

'The guy is Zhenya Tsvigun, from Fryazino, Moscow Region. The lady, Patrizia Bellisai, last known address Via Parco Carelli 22, Posillipo, Naples.'

'And the anomaly?'

'They live in Sartov, a nearby town to the bunker complex, and when they are in Sartov, they're inseparable. They must either be in love or have cabin fever.'

'Or both! And the anomaly?'

'They spent the night in the cabin, but now they've split. Zhenya is on a train, and he's alone. The train is heading southwest.'

Connor said, 'Put it through AI. We need full statistics—nothing left to chance. And find the destination of that train. And get the connecting trains.'

Rubia said, 'Already done, Miss. AI says there is a 97.3 % certainty of Kamenskaya being on the train with Zhenya. The computer says the only explanation is that Kamenskaya met the couple, causing the couple to split. The train's headed to Saratov, with connections to Penza, Rostov, and onwards towards Ukraine if there wasn't a war on.'

Connor said, 'I want the full report. I want the whole thing. Print it and have it on my desk in 5. And well done!'

Agent Connor executed the report. She collated and arranged it. Then she went straight with it in hand to find Hoffman. Who wasn't far. There was a sea of desks ahead of her. Agents milling with clipboards, reports, books, and laptops. Hoffman was in his office, just off the main corridor, outside the open plan room. The blinds were open, so Agent Connor was free to enter. She knocked and entered and said, 'Sir, the results.'

Hoffman said, 'Good work. Fast. I like it. What does the list show?'

Connor said, 'Not just the list. The whole thing. The result. A better than 95% certain of the location of Kira Kamenskaya.'

'Surpassing expectations again, Connor?'

'It's what we do, Sir.'

'Well, keep a list of your team. If you're right, I want to nominate awards.'

'We're right, Sir. Kamenskaya is there. No doubt about it.'

'How can you be so sure?'

'Trust me,' said Connor. 'I know my job, and so does my agent. Kamenskaya is on that train.'

Chapter 46

Vnukovo Airport, Moscow

The MVD convoy blazed a trail from Chisty Prudy to Vnukovo Airport. It set a record. Bagrov's journey to Vnukovo was a result of the rising chaos. Kamenskaya was on the run. Nothing about the convoy's swift movements was by chance.

At the VIP security gate, a hive of activity unfolded. MVD agents swarmed around border guards, their missions apparent. And the Border Service, a part of the Federal Security Service (FSB), clashed with the MVD. Bagrov saw he was about to become collateral damage to a bureaucratic showdown. He braced himself as a stocky FSB border guard, armed to the teeth, approached the lead vehicle of his convoy.

The guard was strategically positioned. Bagrov shouted to his driver, 'Wait!'

'What?' said the driver, swinging around, unsure of what to expect from Bagrov.

'Is this vehicle protected?'

'Protected?'

'I mean, is it bulletproof? If this guard unloads his AK47 into the windshield, will we survive?'

'We'll survive.'

'Are you taking orders from me?'

'Yes, I am, Sir.'

'Then this guard is history if he tries to stop us. Drive forward, taking all necessary measures, including killing the border guard if you have to. Just get me into the airport, and to my designated flight.'

I'll get instructions, Bagrov thought. If the turf war gets hot, fewer people will die here than in Siberia. If the FSB can, they'll stop us anyway.

Things happened sequentially. The SUV lurched forwards and the driver accelerated, and the border guard dived aside. He hit the deck, and emptied most of his automatic at the Mercedes. Bullets hit the rear of the SUV; they smashed the rear screen; but the SUV didn't stop. It raced across to the far side of the apron. A distance of five hundred odd meters, which Bagrov considered would give them ample time. Time to get installed in his transport to Kosvinsky.

The SUV screeched to a stop below and to the side of the fighter jet, a modified SU-30. It was bristling with missiles. A man dressed in a light green flight suit descended from the cockpit, saluted, and identified himself as Major Pudofkin. He said he had orders to transport Bagrov to Kosvinsky Mountain within three hours.

'Major, we have about two minutes before the border guards catch up with us.'

Pudofkin threw Bagrov a camouflaged flight suit. 'Put these on,' he said.

Bagrov wrestled into the flight suit, and then he inquired, 'And now?'

'I'll fill you in on the rest when we're airborne.'

Bagrov followed close behind Pudofkin as he climbed the ladder, and then installed himself in the rear seat of the SU. Pudolfkin strapped him in, and handed him a headset. And then they heard distant gunfire, and realised they were out of time for more pre-flight preparations.

Pudolfkin handled the departure despite the SU coming under sustained small-arms fire. The SU roared off the runway and turned east.

'You'll be using this,' said Pudofkin, handing an item to Bagrov. 'It's a transmitter-receiver identical to the one Kamenskaya took. I have orders to get you within 20 kilometers of Kosvinsky Mountain, where you'll initiate contact.'

'You mean there's no need to land this plane?' said Bagrov.

'Correct, Sir. If Kamenskaya is a listener, we'll be able to contact her from the air.'

'What makes GRU so sure this will work? If you were on the run, you'd know the risk, especially Kira Kamenskaya.'

'That's beyond my pay grade, Sir.'

Chapter 47

Ural Mountains, Siberia, Russia

The train clattered rhythmically to the rhythm of the rough, Siberian tracks. The cosy warmth of the carriage lulled Kamenskaya into a slumber. Twenty minutes passed, and then she awoke with a sense of unease. She glanced at Zhenya, who was dozing across from her on the seats. She tapped him on his shoulder, whispering, 'Zhenya, pass me your phone.'

Zhenya sat up and asked, 'Why? What happened?'

'I need to check something.'

Zhenya tossed her his phone, and Kamenskaya navigated through it, soon finding what she was looking for. She said, 'You sent a text to Patrizia?'

'Yeah. So?'

'Then we're compromised. It's my fault. I should have warned you, but I had too much on my mind. That was a big mistake. But now, we need to get off this train.'

'Why?'

'Because the MVD and GRU will be looking for me at Kosvinsky Mountain. The entire security apparatus of Russia will be searching for me. Planes will be swarming over Kosvinsky

Mountain like hornets around their nest, absorbing the electronics of the airwaves. They'll have had your text the moment you sent it. Right now, I suspect a team will be triangulating the location where you sent it. How long ago was it sent?'

'About 30 minutes ago,' Zhenya replied.

'Good. That's not too long. The GRU hasn't much time to act. But, there will almost certainly be teams in the air already with orders to kill or capture us both.'

'Oh my God!'

'Grab your coat, Zhenya. There are hills in this section of the track, and the snow has been drifting. Its deep, and we can jump.'

'Wait,' Zhenya interjected.

'For what?'

'You said they would be searching for your mobile. We could use that.'

'How?' asked Kamenskaya, puzzled.

'We leave it on the train, they might follow it. We hide it somewhere where no one will find it by accident. It'll lead them away from us if they can trace it.'

'Worth a try,' said Kamenskaya 'We might need your mobile later, but right now, we need to lose them. You're right. Just before we jump, we'll stash it.'

In haste, they made their way to the train's rear, oblivious to the puzzled looks of their fellow passengers. At the very rear, two seats were free, and they thanked their lucky stars, and hid the phone in a seat without prying eyes. Then they went to the rear doors and looked for a suitable section to jump. There had to be deep snow, and no telegraph posts or railway infrastructure coming up. They saw a long section of continuous snowdrift approaching, looked at each other, and leaped. They landed hard. Despite the drift, their bodies cartwheeled briefly, before coming to a stop. They watched the train as it trundled on. It wasn't slowing.

Now, another danger stalked them. The cold, which seeped through their clothes. For now, at least, the escape's adrenaline overshadowed any discomfort.

They sat up, surveying the surroundings, and all they saw was the falling snow and darkness. The distant hum of the train lingered, and then only the sounds of the wind remained.

Their first move was to cross the tracks and head north, away from the anticipated gaze of the Russian Army. Though Kosvinsky Mountain was days away, the direction offered a strategic advantage. If Kamenskaya was right, the Russian Army thought they were heading for Ukraine. Doubling back towards Kosvinsky Mountain would be unexpected. Kamenskaya strategized that the Russian Army would least expect her to return in that direction. Another reason, was that the Russian Army would already have thoroughly searched the area of the bunker, and would expand the search outwards, not inwards.

For the first hour, they made swift progress under the shelter of pines. Their eyes had accustomed to the darkness, and now the moon had risen behind scattering clouds, bathing the Taiga in its ghostly light. Snow was blown into patterns, with patches of clear ground.

They came to a frozen river with a waterfall, and followed the riverbank to the north. The terrain was challenging, but not impossible. The river provided a reference, and seemed a friendly feature in an otherwise bleak and lonely landscape. It meandered through huge, rounded basalt rocks shaped by centuries of flow. Zhenya suggested deviating from the river, but, Kamenskaya hesitated. She saw the river as a guide.

Zhenya reassured her, 'As long as we see Kosvinsky Mountain ahead, we know we're walking north.'

In the early morning light, they stumbled upon a hidden gem—a cabin at the river's edge. It was deserted, and its stone-walled structure exuded an air of comfort. It was approached by an untraveled track which ended at a sturdy wooden door, untouched by recent visitors. Kamenskaya tried the door but faced resistance by the keyhole.

Zhenya pushed her lightly aside, and kicked the keyhole with all the power he could muster, and the door flew open.

Inside, they marvelled at unexpected comforts. There was a double bed adorned with thick sheepskins. There was a fireplace with stacked wood, stools, and a low table. At the rear, there was a wood-burning stove and a copper kettle.

Zhenya set to work on a fire. There were matches in an alcove, and there was firewood wood in abundance. Soon enough he had flames flickering up through dry pinewood, dancing, and casting forth their warm glow. For her part, Kamenskaya was exploring the facilities. She discovered clean linen, towels, and provisions. She fetched water from the river, and Zhenya built up the fire. Upon her return, Zhenya had kindled a second fire in the wood-burning stove.

There was an Italian espresso machine on a shelf. Kamenskaya found a packet of ground coffee, and soon they were savouring hot coffee.

The day passed slowly, and they napped, stoked the fires, and drank coffee, and afternoon became evening. What had been just pleasant banter between them took a more serious turn as the evening progressed.

Zhenya voiced concerns about their impending fate, acknowledging the gravity of Kamenskaya's actions. He said, 'Chances are we'll never get out of this. You have committed a crime punishable by death, and I have helped you.'

'No problem, Zhenya. We're about as off the grid as anyone alive.'

'Yes, but we're not even 100 kilometres from the scene of the crime. There can't be a million cabins in the region. They'll have maps. The latest maps. It's just a matter of time until they check out this place. Somebody owns it.'

'You're making assumptions. It's not sure the Russian Army knows about it. But you're right. They'll catch up with us eventually. We have no food left. And we have little hope of catching any without weapons.'

'So what do you suggest we do?' Zhenya asked.

'What do you want to do on our first and last night together? I at least want to be happy tonight.'

They stoked the fire and, in the glow of the flames, shared a passionate embrace, and then more. Following their love-making, they relaxed. They lay in each other's arms, listening to the howling wind. The storm intensified, shaking the cabin, and the trees echoed its protest. They knew they might not survive the next day. They clung to each other, enjoying the warmth and love amid the relentless storm. They succumbed to a profound sleep, knowing that it would be their last night together.

Chapter 48

Washington D.C.

The room beneath the West Wing of the White House was abuzz. The meeting had been called by the CIA. Delegates had arrived. They were waiting at the room's threshold area. The atmosphere was tense. There was the National Security Advisor, and there was General Park, Chairman of the Joint Chiefs, one of two uniformed officers. General Park wore his Class-A uniform. His belt was adorned with gold star clusters and crafted decorations. He carried the scent of tobacco and wood smoke. A cigarette rested in the corner of his mouth, and a Zippo flicked around in his hand.

The second officer to wear a uniform was the head of the Joint Special Operations Command, JSOC. His name was Vice-Admiral William Edwards. He was tall and imposing. His uniform sagged in the shoulders, but his muscular build was evident beneath his suit. His hair was dark and short; his skin tanned. He looked like he could be in his late forties. There were lines on his face.

There was the Secretary of Defense and the Secretary of State, both older men. There were strained attempts at small talk in the threshold area, honest conversations impossible and incomplete. There were two White House aides. One stood to one side of the older men. For the last five minutes, she was more or less still. Occasionally, she touched her earphones. Then she mumbled a response into a concealed mouthpiece and then turned and approached the semi-circular desks to the left of the door to the Situation Room. The second staff member sat there. The staff member at the desks nodded in thanks. He buzzed open the brown wooden door to his right. The delegates filed in. No words. No emotion. White House efficiency.

The President and Vice-President entered last. There was plenty of room for them. They are the two most important members. The 'Sit Room' was large and square—seating room for 20. In the centre was a massive hard-wood table—rectangular and tailored to fit the space. Six swing leather upholstered seats on each long side of the table. One at the far end, upholstered in the same way, but larger. The head. No seat on the opposite side of the head. Someone sitting near the door would block the view. The white screen extended across the wall from the door.

On the big projector screen was a direct link to Langley where CIA Director Zak Hoffman sat, peering out.

The President said, 'Hoffman. We're all present on this side. I think the question on everyone's mind is, why we are here at all.'

Hoffman said, 'Thank you, Mr. President. The short answer is, by necessity. The situation in Ukraine risks escalating, and there was no getting around it. It is a proxy war against Russia. There would be no reason to delay action. Any action that could lead, or is likely to lead, to securing information vital to the Russian war effort. With that proviso stated, I will now report on what happened. I will also report on what we in the CIA believe is the necessary action. Any questions so far?'

Silence reigned.

Hoffman gulped water from a glass to his side and said, 'Very well. That's a negative, so here's what has happened. The Russians have launched a massive operation. It's a catch-or-kill and the target is none other than Defense Minister Kira Kamenskaya. Our analysts say this fact proves only one thing. Kira Kamenskaya has stolen some of the most sensitive information for Russian defense systems.

The President cut in. He was in the big, black, upholstered turn chair. He wore dark blue jeans, a white shirt, a black tie, and a black blazer. He looked more like a lawyer than a military man, but when he spoke, words came more like an army man than a lawyer. This was not negotiations. This was command, and he was Commander in Chief. He wanted control and he would darn well take it. He liked questions answered as and when they came into his mind. And right then, a question had entered his mind. He said, 'Zak. What is the nature of the information she holds?'

'Information on their newest ICBM, Sir.'

The President said, 'The RS-28?'

'That's right, Sir. Are you aware of the recent upgrade to Russian ICBMs?'

'I've read the brief. Sure, or best bet that Kamenskaya's information concerns the RS-28?'

Hoffman said, 'Sure, Sir. I'm betting my future career on it.'

'Cos that's a big thing, Mr Hoffman,' said the President. 'If you're wrong, we risk direct conflict with Russia, not just a proxy war in Ukraine.'

'I'm aware of that, Sir.'

'Questions anyone?'

A hushed silence rang out, deafening in its emptiness—stunned, hardly believing faces.

The President said, 'Please, Hoffman. Continue.'

Hoffman continued. He heightened the pace, wanting to avoid being interrupted again. He said, 'The Russians have not yet located Kamenskaya, but we have. She's on a train heading to Ukraine, and we need to extract her while we can. Every second matters. I'm talking about a DEVGRU force to pick her up.'

The President said, 'That's it?'

'Those are the raw facts, Sir. We need Kamenskaya secured along with the information she is carrying. I have checked it all very carefully, Sir. State of the art systems. Independent analysts. AI applications. All our models and analysis bring the same result. We must secure Kamenskaya and do it right now before the Russians get hold of her.'

The Chairman of the Joint Chiefs said, 'Not quite so fast, Hoffman. Your proposal would normally take months of planning. You're proposing to cut straight to execution. That's a big jump, and therefore a big risk, Mr Hoffman.'

Hoffman said, 'With all due respect, Sir, we haven't got months. We have to go right now. Necessity demands it. If we wait, we lose this.'

'That's understood. And what about the information being redundant?'

'That's not the case, Sir, according to all our analysis.'

'How can you be sure?'

'The scale of the operation, Sir. If the information is redundant, the Russians wouldn't spend so much to catch or kill Kamenskaya.'

'What about a ruse? A ploy to lure us in? We send in our best, and they're ready for us, and take them out and get a diplomatic reaction from the rest of the world?'

The Secretary of Defense, Dr. Paul Lawrence was sitting next to the left of the President and couldn't hold back any longer. He was in the first leather seat on the left. They were opposite the first screen and the Vice-President. He was a man in his early fifties with salt-and-pepper hair and a well-groomed beard. He looked up at the big projector screen and said, 'Zak. Suppose the President decides to give the go-ahead to the operation. How will this play out?'

Hoffman went to reply, but the Chairman of the Joint Chiefs beat him to it, saying. 'I can answer that one. Sir, the Joint Special Operations Command will command the operation. It will do so until it crosses into Russia. From then on, it'll be CIA-led. We are not at war with Russia. Not yet at least. There would be legal issues should we send in US armed forces. But make no mistake. The troops will be Special Forces. It'll be a Seals team from DEVGRU, a small team, along the lines of the killing of Bin Laden.'

Hoffman looked uncomfortable. He didn't like what he was hearing. General Park's reference to Neptune Spear, the DEVGRU's operation to kill Bin Laden, was unhelpful. Neptune Spear was a bad analogy. He was thinking about execution. A Seals team would need a helicopter, especially if the operation were like Neptune Spear. That couldn't be the template for actions within Russia. Think about where Kamenskaya was. Slap bang in the frozen heart of Siberia. Hours from the borders of Russia. No helicopter could penetrate that far. It was logistically impossible. This was true even for a stealth Blackhawk. It had modifications to increase its speed and range. He opened his mouth to speak, just as the door flung open, and Agent Conner was standing there with a look on her face. An unforeseen development. Something big. He expected the worst, something he had been sure would happen. Russia had found, captured, or killed Kamenskaya. She passed something to Hoffman, a single-page readout.

The White House Situation Room had seen everything in real-time. Bad news was about to be heard. Never had so many top state officers pinned their hopes on a huge, projected video screen.

To their relief, they saw the faintest smile on Hoffman's face. Good news, not bad. He said, 'Gentlemen, there has been a development that I think changes things. We have just received a report from an asset in Moscow, who works in the General Prosecution Office. She gave a heads-up on the GRU operation to catch Kamenskaya. Her colleague is a close friend of Kamenskaya, Alexander Bagrov. Bagrov is a patriot focused on bringing in Kamenskaya by the Russians, alive of course, as he is her friend.'

The President said, 'Get to the point, Hoffman. How does this change anything?'

'Sir, our agent reports that GRU now commands Bagrov as an asset to assist in the search for Kamenskaya. Our agent reports that the GRU gave him a radio transmitter. It was identical to one she took from Kosvinsky Kamen on her way out of the bunker.'

'So she's got to be a listener,' said the Chairman of the Joint Chiefs. 'But there's no way she would ever use it. It'll be all one-way traffic for her benefit. She's smart enough to know that.'

'Exactly,' said Hoffman. 'And you're right—she would never use it. But the Russians are smart to be getting him close.'

'How's that?' said the Chairman of the Joint Chiefs.

'It's a backup plan at best. Kamenskaya is smart enough never to use it—unless her situation changes. They're just doing what we would do in similar situations. Put everything on our side. Like a chess game, and they're arranging their pieces.'

The President stood up. There was something on his mind. Perhaps he wanted to add weight to what he was going to say. He said, 'So we should do the same. Put everything on our side, leaving nothing to chance.'

'You're right, Mr. President,' said Hoffman. 'Which is why I advise the following: Our agent in Moscow reports Bagrov is now at Vnukovo airport. GRU is putting him on a fast jet, a fighter with scramjets in all probability. He has a pilot's license. So they're quickly pulling out the stops and getting him to the transmission area. I advise we take out Bagrov's aircraft before he gets within range of Kamenskaya for risk reduction. The worst-case scenario is he contacts Kamenskaya, and we don't. I can't afford that to happen.'

'And how do you propose shooting down a fast Russian jet? It's fourth generation isn't it? And well inside Russia.'

Hoffman said, 'I'm sure the head of the Joint Special Forces Operation Command will agree. This will be an operational decision for the Joint Special Operations Command. They will take it with the CIA. The CIA will eventually have command of the mission. You, as Commander in Chief, will give the final go-ahead. In the next hour, we will have a range of options. The head of the Joint Special Forces Operation Command will correct me if I've got that wrong, Sir.'

Vice-admiral Edwards said, 'Thank you, Mr Hoffman. What you say is correct. Legal precedent, statute, and International Law constrain the chain of command. They do so in such an operation. The command is from President Budden, Secretary of Defense, and Chairman of the Joint Chiefs. They come to me as commander of Joint Special Operations Command, JSOC. Once we get the go-ahead for whichever action you decide, the operation will transfer to the CIA, who will command it to completion. Those soldiers involved will transfer from the military for the mission's duration. As stated, this is because we are not at war with Russia.'

The President looked around the table to the door, stopped, and said, 'Very well, gentlemen, lady. I look forward to seeing the list of strike options in the next hour.'

Chapter 49

The modified SU-30 hit V2 and Major Pudofkin rotated and it lifted off the runway into the clear, blue and cloudless Russian skies. Its engines roared loudly, and the sound echoed across the airfield. He maintained a controlled ascent, the altimeter ticking upward with each passing second. The MKAD highway became a distant ribbon of concrete. Moscow's urban landscape shrank as the SU-30 climbed higher.

The transition from afterburners to scramjets marked a pivotal moment. The roar of sheer speed subsided, replaced by the distinct, muted hum of the scramjets. The aircraft was now at Mach 1.8 and accelerating still. It had a new efficiency. It was trading speed for altitude.

Inside the cockpit, Pudofkin's eyes flickered between instruments, monitoring the aircraft's vital signs. The modified SU-30, a technological marvel, responded to his every command. The altitude gauge continued to rise. The sky grew dark as the aircraft climbed into the stratosphere.

The mission weighed heavily on Pudofkin's shoulders. He understood the gravity of the task at hand. He had to get Alexander Bagrov swiftly to the transmission area. Russian interests depended on it.

Chapter 50

Hoffman was in his element. He paced one of the large situation rooms on Langley's second level, directing operations. His best team was in front of him, a hive of activity. People were scrambling with laptops and clipboards, block books, and notebooks. Agent Julie Connor entered and walked briskly towards him, saying, 'Sir, you won't believe this. We just intercepted a text message to Patrizia from the train. It's the confirmation we were looking for. The confirmation that Zhenya really did split from Patrizia, and is with Kamenskaya.'

'What's the message?'

'Simply, Hi, Darling. Just letting you know everything is okay. We got the train okay. Talk soon. And that's not all.'

'Why's that?'

'It's a further anomaly, Sir. He never texts. Even when they're apart within their hometown.'

'That's double proof then. Well done. Get the head of JSOC on the phone. He needs to know this. Good work.'

JSOC oversees SMUs. They are part of SOCOM. Direct Action, the type Hoffman had in mind, required JSOC to command an SMU. The SMU was called the Naval Special

Warfare Development Group, or DEVGRU. Only DEVGRU could pull off a target capture mission deep within Russia.

The JSOC commander was Vice-Admiral Frank Edward. He was 56 years old. He had a weathered face. It testified to years of service, with recent postings to Afghanistan, Iraq, and Syria. His skin was full of lines, scars, and imperfections. He loved strict schedules. He was a man of routine. He arrived 10 minutes early to the 5 pm meeting ordered by the Secretary of Defence. He strode into the Langley situation room. The room had two long sets of black leather sofas on either side of a long wooden table. The table was empty except for a man sitting halfway along. The admiral recognized him. The man sitting on the bank of sofas was a striking man with coarse grey hair and a stubble face. Hoffman.

Admiral Edward drew up to Hoffman and said, 'This war—what a mess. It's out of control. No end in sight.' He sounded as he looked—as if he was kept up all night by anxiety. A desire to make no mistakes weighed on him like an anchor around his neck. He was doing his bit to bring an end to it. As head of DEVGRU, he was certainly capable.

Hoffman gestured arrogantly to the sofas, without taking his eyes off his laptop and an email. He lacked respect for the Admiral, and it showed. He said, 'You're right, Admiral, and that's exactly why we've brought you in.'

'How's that?' said the Admiral, skirting around the table, sliding into the middle of the sofas. He positioned himself opposite Hoffman. He folded his arms. It was body language which Hoffman had been trained to pick up on in a heartbeat. It meant Hoffman was aware that the Admiral was pissed off. Well tough. That went with the territory. His eyes were two narrow, deep blue slits. They sat in a spider's web of red lines and ridges.

Hoffman terminated the email he had been composing and closed the laptop, and looked up at the Admiral, with his folded arms and severe face. He needed to give the commander of the JSOC his full attention. He said, 'Admiral. Have you finalized the list of options for the President?'

Edward frowned. 'It's in the final stages. Why?'

'Scrap it. We won't give the President any bad options. They won't give us the results we need. There is only one good option. These are dangerous times, Admiral.'

'What are you proposing?'

'A single fighter-bomber piloted by someone experienced. Someone with the right mix of skills. The aircraft would need to fly way above supersonic if its to have the slightest chance to intercept the SU-30. The SU-30 just took off from Vnukovo. The aircraft we send would need to take it out before it reaches the area of transmission. Then it would have to locate and extract Kamenskaya. In other words, it would need VTOL as well. A complex mission. Only suited to someone with a unique set of skills.'

Admiral Edward said, 'I was thinking along similar lines, and I agree. Only a supersonic fighter with VTOL capability could have any chance of success. It would need to be able to super-cruise sustainably and do VTOL. It would also need to be stealthy. And, of course, it has to be a two-seater. Anything in mind?'

'There's the modified F35. As you know, we had scaled it up and modified it so that could succeed in such catch and extract missions. It is a VTOL 3-seater. Scaled up, with huge scramjets. Even then, it would come down to the pilot.'

'Could you have a worse poker face, Hoffman?! I know very well who you are going to recommend! Colonel Lee Ross, right?'

'Right. He's still the best we have.'

'Current status?'

'On active duty in Barcelona. He just executed a high-speed chase across the North Atlantic. A SU had entered US airspace at the time of the election. Could you arrange that aircraft?'

'If this is the only way, yes, Hoffman. I'm on it! We have to be together on this from the start. I'll get back to you in ten minutes.'

Admiral Edward returned to the Langley situation room eight minutes later, finding Hoffman on the same sofa. Hoffman looked intense and worried, just as before. Edward said, 'Contact Ross. He needs the location of Kamenskaya, the train, and the next steps for the mission. We have a VTOL capable F35Z in Aviano, and you are authorised. Get it prepared. Do whatever it takes to get an aircraft and a backup for a stealth mission to Siberia. We need to pick up Kamenskaya before the Russians do.'

Chapter 51

Barcelona, Spain

Lee Ross finished his double espresso and placed another one on order. He was on the terrace and it was 07.45 am at his favourite haunt when in Barcelona, the cafe on a corner of Placa De Catalunya. For operational reasons, he had stayed put in Barcelona following the dash across the North Atlantic.

Café Zurich was a good place for people watching. Pigeons filled the square, and crowds of young Spaniards and not so young tourists passed, heading to sales or bargains on the Rambler, or further down the slope to the port and beach. Ross had taken one of the small, circular steel tables directly to the right of the entrance. His back was to the wall. His eyes followed the waiter for a second as he walked, tray balanced on straight fingers, into the interior. He rechecked the perimeter. Then he continued scanning the morning's newspapers. They lay on the table's shiny surface. He was bringing himself up to speed on the day's main events.

The papers were variations on two themes. Israel post 7.10, and Ukraine. Ross had a view, on both but it was not that of the majority. On Ukraine, Russia's Special Military Operation had always been a legal action by a Great Power. One reacting to events on its borders giving rise to a security interest. To believe that Ukraine was one hundred percent sovereign was just plain naïve. Countries were only sovereign so far as they didn't exceed a neighbouring Great Power's red lines. For Russia, the red line was Ukraine's transition into the Western sphere of influence. It would lead to Ukraine joining NATO. Russia had already taken Crimea, of necessity to protect its Sevastopol naval base, under threat as soon as the Western installed ultra-nationalist government came to power. If Ukraine joined NATO, the conflict's outcome would be unknown after the change. Through the Special Military Operation, Russia pre-emptively stopped Ukraine from joining NATO. It was an act of solid, reasonable statecraft from a responsible international player.

Ross was halfway down the first page of the second article to spark his interest, in the second newspaper. He was enjoying himself. He was on his favourite terrace, in his favourite city, drinking no bottom expressos with a killer article to read. He didn't want any distractions, and he wasn't expecting any calls. But the feeling he could feel every now and then in his Captain Hilts jacket's inner pocket was his phone buzzing. He pulled it out just in time to answer it before the call went to voicemail. Hoffman.

'Cafe Zurich?'

'Where else?'

'What about a mission deep into Russia, you and Bando, as pilots of the F35Z?'

'Yes Sir! That's what we do! Who's this for and what's it all about?'

'It'll be a DEVGRU operation until you're in the air, and then as usual, command will transfer to the CIA, to me personally.'

'That's understood, Sir.'

'Good. 'A car will pick you up in10 minutes. Look out for a black Jeep Cherokee. It'll take you to operations in the military airport, and we'll talk again when you get there. Your F35 is ready for a high-speed dash to Aviano. There, you will transfer to another F35, which is faster and better for the mission into Russia.

Chapter 52

Not much could have woken Kamenskaya that night. Her and Zhenya Tsvigun's first and last night together had left her satisfied and fulfilled. They had listened to the storm outside, and then passion and sleep had enveloped them. Later in the night, when the wind picked up again after a brief lull in its battering of the cabin, Kamenskaya's utopia was penetrated from an unknown quarter, and she had awoken.

The penetration seemed a prism of her life. It focused her existence. It was made up of the flight from Kosvinsky, the waterfall, the brush with death, Zhenya, and the cabin. She had to decipher and sift the results for relevance and meaning. She prolonged it and analysed it, for there had to be a reason for it all. Then she was able to put her finger on it. Thousands of thoughts had become one, but not the sort she wanted to think about. Guilt hit her full force.

She released her arms from around Zhenya, succeeding not to wake him.

She threw on her jacket and rekindled the fire and the wood burner. She wasn't going to be part of any suicide pact. Her life was not over. She still had things to do. Being captured was inevitable, so why not put everything in play? She was not a traitor, but the guilt feeling sensitized her to issues she had not considered. What exactly was her end game? She reached inside her coat, extracted the transmitter receiver and switched it on.

There was a lot of interference so she switched to different modes and configurations. A tank commander was talking to a sergeant. They were near the Lybov River. There was talk of the fire at the plunge pool. They were on her tracks, and and it wouldn't be long until they would discover Zhenya and Patrizia's cabin. Patrizia would not be there, but it wouldn't be long till they got to her in the Sartov apartment.

She was about to wake Zhenya when she heard a faint voice on the transmitter, and her heart all but missed a beat. It was Bagrov, and he was calling her by name, 'Kira, Kira. Come in. It's me, Sasha. I can bring you in, and we can work this all out.'

Time to fill in her companion.

She put her hand on Zhenya's shoulder, shook him lightly, and he opened his eyes. She said, 'They're onto your cabin.'

He turned onto his back, stared above, stretched, and said, 'That doesn't surprise me. We always knew it would only be a matter of time. It doesn't mean that they know you'll have been there.'

'They will know. They found my fire at the waterfall plunge pool. It won't be long till they'll search your cabin. Plus, they're onto your phone anyway. They'll do forensics on your cabin. Your apartment in Sartov will be next. Could you get a message to Patrizia?'

'No. We have no connections here. You know that.'

'Guess I was thinking about moving out to get a message to her. We can't stay here.'

'Just to get a message to Patrizia? Chances are they're already onto her.'

'You're right. No way to get a message to her for hours, even if we leave now. And the pace they're going, it's almost certain they'll get to her before we do.'

'And if she tells them the truth, she should be okay because she had no role at all in your running. And trying to contact her might make things worse.'

'So it's just you and me now,' said Kamenskaya. 'You can't argue you didn't help me. And now that we're well and truly in this together, you should know some other things. Because we need to make some decisions.'

'What things?'

Kamenskaya took the transmitter receiver out of her jacket pocket. 'This is how I knew about the waterfall and plunge pool. If we want, we can talk to the Russian authorities. But, of course, that will bring them to us in minutes.'

'So? Nothing to do. We can't give up.'

'Not exactly. There's a couple of things. First thing. The person calling is a friend. Alexander Bagrov. He's a state prosecutor. So unless we decide to let this friend bring me in, that's out of the question.'

'And second?' said Zhenya.

'Second, if we're going to keep running, we need money.'

'So?'

'I will show you top secret information. We've nothing to lose now, and you need to know everything.'

'I'm all ears,' said Zhenya. 'Keep talking. I'm just going to put coffee on.'

'You see, I'm Defence Minister. When I was still in Moscow, I investigated the killing of Sergei Magnitsky. This led me to access files on the case held by the GRU. I had the required access. But someone had protected the files. The only way I could access them was by using a loophole they had taught me in training. Anyone in the Kosvinsky Mountain bunker with my access wouldn't need anything else. They could see and download the Magnitsky files. I was afraid the GRU would find out. So, I flew on a military jet to the nearest base. I got into the mountain and accessed the files. But the files were all paired with another file called RS-28. The RS-28 file carried critical top-secret info on Russia's new ICBM. When I saw that information, I knew it could provide a way to stop this war. If Ukraine or the US had the information, they could wage conventional war against Russia. The US could stop a global nuclear war before either side launched nukes.

'So there I was, in the bunker, and when I came across the RS-28 files, I knew I had the power to change the odds in the war. It could be a bargaining chip. And in return for it, the US could be forced to put pressure on Ukraine to accept terms of peace with Russia. That's why I downloaded the files and ran. That's why I am here.'

'And why I'm here too!' said Zhenya.

'Which brings me to something we need to discuss.'

'What is it?'

'We have options right now. We need to escape from this place, but we have no money or resources. But we do have the information in these files. And something else in them gives us the power to blackmail one individual.'

The coffee hissed, and Zhenya poured it and returned to Kamenskaya's side. He handed her an espresso and said, 'Who is that?'

'I know him only as the 'mastermind' because he is the mastermind behind the death of Magnitsky. But the video files I downloaded are confessions. They are from eight OMON riot police officers who carried out the murder. I have the ID details of those officers. That means I have the power to find the mastermind's identity. It would be easy if I pulled in some favours;

it would happen quickly. No need for me to be back in Moscow. I could do that right now, from here.'

Zhenya said, 'So, you don't have the mastermind's identity yet. But, if the mastermind wasn't cooperating, you could find out their identity and make it public.'

'Yes!' yelled Kamenskaya. Zhenya was coming up to speed. 'So the blackmail should be effective even without the mastermind's identity.'

Kamenskaya took out her laptop, power packs, and the USB. She switched on the computer and plugged in one of the power packs. She inserted the USB and navigated to the files. One file was named "mastermind." She clicked it and brought it up.

It showed a sub-file entitled 'connection.' She brought up the properties of the file. GRU had created it, which fitted. GRU wanted the file as a failsafe for the stolen Magnitsky files. Whoever stole them might reach out to the mastermind for funds. Only she was one step ahead in the game. If she could cut a deal with GRU, everyone could walk away from this, even her and Zhenya. She clicked on 'connection.'

The file loaded, and the name Alison Kennedy flashed onto the screen. She was a CIA agent active in Moscow and Kazakhstan. Russia knew all about her but had decided not to go public. *That's going to change pretty quickly,* she thought. It'll force them to do it—to show the world that the US was to blame for Magnitsky's murder. She didn't know why the Russians had not made the information public. She didn't care. All she cared about was getting the information out, putting Russia in a better light and the US in a worse one. The correct state of affairs, considering where the truth in the case lay. A zero-sum game in which she was a player and a winner. She needed Zhenya's freedom too. That was not negotiable. And she would also need safe passage to the West. No way she was going to stay in Russia after this. But how could she guarantee all those things? What guarantees would she have? The Russians reneging on the deal once they had the USB and she was in custody. She needed a guarantor. The bones of a plan materialized. She said, 'How good are your survival skills?'

'Average to above average, I guess. Why?'

'Could you survive in the wilderness?'

'It depends on how long? But yes.'

'A few days. Three at the most.'

'I could do that. What exactly would I be doing?'

'I'll give you the USB, then I'll cut a deal with the GRU. Your freedom and mine, and passage to the West for the return of the USB and the confession of the mastermind.'

'Confession of the mastermind? The Kennedy agent?'

'Yes.'

'Couldn't the Russians get that already? It seems to me they already know who she is.'

'It seems they can't. For whatever reason. That doesn't concern me. It's something extra we can give them in return for the USB. It's also something that the guarantor would be aware of.'

'Guarantor?'

'Yes. Without a guarantor, there's no way I will risk giving up the USB. You are far from me and in a place only I will know. If they don't allow a guarantor, they'll never see those files again. They can't control what happens to them. I'll give you instructions to upload them to the Western Press. You'll do this if I'm arrested and miss our meeting.'

'And who is the guarantor?'

'A friend. Lee Ross. A former US Air Force pilot who is CIA.'

'So how will this all pan out?'

Kamenskaya unplugged the USB and handed it to Zhenya. 'First of all, here is the USB. I've copied the files to my laptop in case our plan goes sideways, and I need them myself. The deal depends on you being able to upload them within seconds to the guarantor. You must also send them to Western news agencies if they try to take you. If they don't guarantee our passage to the West, that's what they will get.'

'And if they do guarantee our demands?'

'Ross will get the files, and the war in Ukraine would get easier for the US to end. Russia would have no ability to use nuclear blackmail anymore. Then, we need to decide on the rendezvous point and timeframes. You'll need to get well clear of this place before I make contact. They'll be here within an hour.'

'They'll torture you to get the location, Darling.'

'I thought of that. You will be in a location with internet access. If you see anyone but me and Ross in an F35, send the files to these news websites and this address.' Kamenskaya passed Ross's email and a CIA email. 'Ross and the CIA will receive the files if GRU tries anything. But if Ross and I come in an F35, you'll leave the USB there, and you, Ross and I will fly out of Russia.'

'That means that the F35 must be capable of carrying three persons.'

'Believe me, the US has developed such a fighter. A larger, modified F35 with a capacity for three. The F35Z.'

'Okay. I'm in.'

'Okay. There are two layers of security for us both. First, only I will know your location with the USB. They would have to torture me, which is unlikely.'

'Why?'

'It would mean that I wouldn't help them get the confession of the mastermind. Also, even if they knew your location, they couldn't approach you. You would upload those files.'

'But what's to prevent Russia ordering a missile strike on my location and taking out the USB that way?'

'Too risky. You might be anywhere near the location. If the Russians go in with missiles, you'd upload the files to those email addresses.

'I'd need satellite communications.'

'You'll have it. Look. I have it right here.' Kamenskaya took out her rucksack. She put it on the deck, rummaged inside it, and pulled out the device. She said, 'Do you know how to use it?'

'Sure. But how long will it remain charged?'

'Military grade battery pack built-in. You won't switch it on until you get near the rendezvous point. Then, when you switch it on, you'll have internet through satellite. You can use this laptop to upload the files if you have to.'

'Which is where exactly?'

'Kosvinsky Kamen itself, on the summit.'

'Why? The summit is over 1,500m in altitude. Why make it more difficult for me?'

'Several reasons. The mountain has a rounded summit. They could not take you out in a single strike because you could be anywhere near the summit. You need to be at the summit in a matter of, say, 20 minutes from the moment when we contact you. Then we can pick you up. There are rocks and bushes dotted all over the summit cone, so it'll be difficult for them to take you out. It'll be tough for them to target you with missiles. They'll realize it's too risky to renege on the deal.'

'Yes, but I'm risking my life here!'

'So am I. Look. We're in this together. Right now, I see this as our only move. We can still make this turn out right. The only sure way for them to get all the files is to finish their side of the deal. This includes both the Magnitsky files and the RS-28 ones. The files for our freedom and the confession of the mastermind. They will go for it.'

'We're all out of options. We can't stay here long; without resources, we can't reach Ukraine as per your original plan. We could contact the mastermind. But, when we do, they will be here in minutes. And, we will have no bargaining power. It sounds like you got it all figured out!'

Chapter 53

Storm-force winds mixed with thin rain from the southwest. They swept straight down the main 07 heading runway at Barcelona Airport. No need to fly to Aviano. The Chairman of the Joint Chiefs had seen to it personally that the F35Z was flown from Aviano to Barcelona. It was necessary for Ross to succeed in taking out Bagrov, and the action would provide a reduction in his workload during the mission.

Ross stood in front of the modified F35Z fighter bomber. It was massive. A prototype. Much larger than the original F35. Its designers had scaled it up 2.3 times. It still had stealth, but its flight characteristics were different due to the increase in the power to weight characteristics. The original F35 could reach at most Mach 2.1. But, the aircraft in front of Ross could reach Mach 7 at altitude with full scramjets.

Ross climbed the ladder and strapped in. There were two extra seats behind him for two other passengers. CIA specifications. The configuration allowed for a navigator and weapons officer, additions which provided for the defeat of multiple targets. The aircraft could not be outrun by any known aircraft.

The double hybrid engines were located underneath and behind him. Below Mach 1.0 and up to Mach 2.0 engaged, with the scramjet kicking in progressively between those speeds. At Mach 2.0, the scramjet was the only source of power, which was not limited by the thin air of high altitude.

Akemi Bando was not aboard. He needed all available space for unforeseen events, and there could be many of those. It was a solo mission deep inside Russia without backup. He would have to pick up Kamenskaya, and possibly Zhenya Tsvigun also.

He pushed forward the throttle lever on the left of him, and taxied toward the holding point. He checked the mission parameters. Take off in 5 minutes to have any chance of completing the mission. And even then, there was no room for error. There would be risk from the get-go. Not close to the envelope. At it. Mach 7 and 60 km altitude over Ukraine. The lack of air would cool the airframe. It would let Ross reach Bagrov's SU30 somewhere over the Urals. He would do this before he made contact with Kamenskaya.

He checked the fuel and the weather in European Russia up to the point of engagement with Bagrov's SU-30.

The aircraft reached the holding point. He rolled across it without stopping, then straightened up. He got take-off clearance from the fighter controller, throttled up and took the giant fighter bomber airborne. He turned left onto the initial bearing—48.3 degrees, northeast.

Acceleration into the climb. Within a minute, he was supersonic. In another 35 seconds, the aircraft passed Mach 2, using only 55 percent of its power. Ross glanced at the double split screen in front and tapped to reveal the data link and flight information. The on-board computer was up and running. It was right there with him. His constant companion. It said, 'Time to destination at 55 percent power—3 hours 45 minutes.'

Time to put everything on his side, Ross thought. He throttled the engine to max and asked for an update.

'Re-computing. Time to destination at 100% power—48 minutes. Bearing now 48.2 degrees. Autopilot engaged.'

It was a moving target, but Bagrov didn't know he was coming.

Chapter 54

Ross was at 60 km altitude and Mach 6.9 and had a feeling that everything would work out. He felt in control. Nothing now could stop him from engaging Bagrov's SU-30. All checks had been finished and confirmed. There was enough fuel for sustained combat manoeuvres. More than enough to leave Russian airspace. The day had progressed. The sun would have already set on the ground, but, at 60,000ft, it still hung over the curved northwest horizon off Ross's left shoulder. He turned in his pressure suit to admire the view, the only bit of in-flight entertainment on offer, but welcomed to keep his mind focussed. Time to engagement was below three minutes, and he needed all the focus he could muster.

The final confirmation of Bagrov's position came loud and clear on the radio. 'Control to Ross. Target confirmed—contact bearing 085 at 60 miles and 24,000 feet. Reduce your speed and engage, over.'

'Copy Control. He's turning toward. I'm coming into him on his nine o'clock.'

Ross saw the SU. It was way below him, flying at a relatively pedestrian Mach 1.2. Ross cut his speed, braked hard, and dived.

'Roger. Stay on your heading, 89 degrees.'

'Copy.'

In seconds he was above and to the rear of the SU—still invisible to it. Stealth technology. The best in the world. Bagrov or the Russian pilot would only know about the US jet when the missile lock painted it. But then everything changed fast because the satellite's contact with control came alive.

'Control to Mission. Put your weapons on hold, I repeat, Control to Mission, put your weapons on hold.'

'Mission to Control. Copy. Weapons on hold. What's happening?'

'Bagrov is contacting Kamenskaya. Standby.'

'Copy.'

'Control to Mission. We got it. We have Kamenskaya's location.'

'Copy that. Awaiting confirmation of location and instructions.'

'Control to mission. Take out the SU and continue to coordinate 023.44N, 766.32E. That's the location of Kamenskaya.'

'Mission to Control. Take out the SU and continue to coordinate 023.44N, 766.32E. Copy. Is it necessary to take out the SU?'

With Kamenskaya located, Bagrov's role was redundant. There was no way for the SU to lock onto the F35Z. No risk to the mission. So why were they instructing him to take out the SU, and with it, his friend Alexander Bagrov?

'Control to Mission. Affirmative. The SU will be close enough behind you on the inbound run to be a threat. Your window to get Kamenskaya out will be longer if you take out the SU.'

Which seemed reasonable, thought Ross. Even at Mach 7, he would only have minutes ahead of the SU to pick up Kamenskaya. And while on the ground, the F35 would be vulnerable. The best bet was to take out his friend.

Ross vectored towards the SU. He painted it, locked it, heard a good tone, fired and saw the missile streak away. He said a silent prayer for his friend. War is tricky, with only two sides when things get serious. The SU disappeared from the radar.

Although Bagrov was dead, Kamenskaya was still alive, but she would be dead soon unless he succeeded. She was dead ahead.

He heard from the on-board computer again, updating him. It said there were three minutes to Kamenskaya. He hit the brakes, coming in straight and fast onto the locator. A half kilometre out, he saw the roof of the cabin, and the infra-red showed that there were fires lit inside of it.

The open area to one side of the cabin was clear of trees. There were boulders. But, the F35 had a strong undercarriage. It could withstand rough landings.

He put the aircraft down, released the bubble canopy, climbed out, and jumped to the snow. He had ten minutes at most until the Russians would be all over the location, so he raced around the corner from the cabin's rear, wading and stumbling through the deep snow. And then he saw Kamenskaya, standing in the doorway.

'Of all the gin joints in the world!' he said.

'I've heard you say that before,' said Kamenskaya, finally releasing him from her tight embrace, pushing him to arm's length so she could focus on his face. 'It was somewhere in Spain. Ibiza. You said those words to Maite Juan the first time we were engaged in stopping World War Three.'

'Here we go again!' said Ross. 'We have ten minutes before all hell breaks loose here. Get your things. Everything you need for a flight, but most of all, get the USB.'

'That, I don't have.'

'Where is it?'

'The guy I was with last night has it. I gave it to him so it would be safe.'

'Zhenya.'

'Yes.'

'Okay. We have to factor in that as well, but it shouldn't be too much of a problem, We leave right now!'

'But you said I can get my things?'

'That was before we wasted time talking. Now we have no time left if you want to have a chance to escape.'

Kamenskaya said, 'We're wasting time!'

They scrambled to the fighter bomber, and Ross activated the access ladder, and they clambered aboard. Ross helped Kamenskaya strap into one of the rear seats and then he went for the start sequence. The cockpit was warm. Kamenskaya shouted over the loud noise of the jet, 'How will we find him?'

'Leave that to me. All I need is your best guess for the direction.'

'North,' said Kamenskaya. 'Towards Kosvinsky Kamen.'

The F35Z rose vertically clearing the tops of the fir trees, rotated, and accelerated north. Ross calculated that 30 minutes in the deep snow would put Zhenya around a mile from the cabin. He pinpointed the location, the on-board computer doing the rest, engaging infrared and enslaved his helmet's visualization. Nothing. Not a single heat source in a mile radius. So he called up Kamenskaya. He said, 'Any other possible route he could have taken?'

'The river!' exclaimed Kamenskaya. 'It flows north to the area of Kosvinsky Kamen, and Zhenya would have used it for wayfinding.'

Ross pinpointed a new objective. The cabin was 1 mile away. The site was less than half a mile away. The plane's computer engaged AI and dialled in the power and heading. The plane accelerated at 30 percent power and then braked to bring it dead over the location.

'Got him,' said Ross. 'He's below us. He's keeping to the river.'

'I can't see a thing,' replied Kamenskaya.

'There's a clearing upstream.'

The river meandered around it in a wide half-circle bend, whose center was devoid of trees. Ross landed, but there was no sign of Zhenya.

Kamenskaya said, 'He thinks we're hostile and has gone to ground. Or he broke the ice and went into the river.'

'Got him,' said Ross. 'Coming straight at us. The opposite side of the river, opposite bank. On the edge of the trees!'

'Got him,' replied Kamenskaya. 'Open the canopy, and let's get him on board.'

The canopy opened and Ross activated the ladder. The on-board computer had already ID'd him. He knew what was going on. He ran and jumped for the first rungs of the ladder.

Zhenya was wet with sweat. Kamenskaya greeted him with anxious words. She said, 'Where's the USB?'

'Right here,' said Zhenya patting his jacket. 'The laptop too.'

'Good to go!' said Ross. 'You strap in. Kamenskaya, help him, please. We're out of here!'

Chapter 55

The stealth fighter bomber climbed, afterburners lit. Ross let them burn for twenty seconds, and then he switched to scramjet, and turned onto heading 340 at 20,000 feet. He levelled out just above a layer of thin cirrus clouds, trading altitude for speed. His sixth sense sensed something was coming. Something was about to happen and it was better to get away. He soon understood why. There was a blinding white flash which lit the sky with its sinister, platinum white quality.

'Don't look at it!' shouted Ross, the shock wave hitting the fighter-bomber. The F35Z lost two thousand feet in three seconds, so Ross reacted putting it into a steep dive. He levelled out at 10,000 feet.

Kamenskaya said, 'What about the radiation?!'

'That's the least of our worries,' said Ross, with calm. 'This plane is hardened to a nuclear blast strength. It also protects against radiation from the bomb. There's no danger whatsoever.'

'Like a walk in the park,' choked Kamenskaya hardly feeling any better. She was thankful to Ross, she thought. But whatever, World War Three was now inevitable. Gaining composure, she said, 'Where are we headed?'

'To an altitude where they can't get to us. And then we'll talk.'

'About what?'

'Objectives.'

'What about them?'

'Look. We're in this together. It's not about what the US wants anymore. I'm through with them, and I'm sure you feel the same way about Russia. Am I wrong?'

'What are you saying?'

'That we need to figure out what's best for us and the world, not only for Russia and the US.'

Ross said, 'We're above the service ceiling of every known Russian missile system. We're at Mach 5 and increasing. Edge of space. 50 km altitude. We can talk.'

'And the fuel?' asked Zhenya.

'Forty-five percent. We can coast as far as Alaska at this height and speed.'

Kamenskaya said, 'So let's talk.'

Ross said, 'No. You first.'

'Okay. I have two objectives. First, to change the regime leadership of Russia. Not because of the war but how they responded to the Magnitsky situation. If Russia was not to blame, we had to fight to show the world what happened.'

'And second?' asked Zhenya.

'For what's left of Ukraine, its people, and those of the world. To stop this war.'

Ross turned the comms to a general frequency. The three heard all kinds of comms on their helmet intercoms. Which wasn't surprising. An event likely to cause World War Three had just happened. Pilots from different places sent angry, rushed messages over the radio. They were about emergencies. There were Russian voices, French and English. Ross switched frequency again and heard a familiar voice.

'Control to Mission. What is your status, over?'

'Status good, over.'

'Continue on your present heading and altitude. Over.'

'Copy that. Continuing on present heading and flight level. Out.'

Kamenskaya said, 'Look. We are here deciding the future of the entire planet but that doesn't mean I don't think about life once all this is over.'

'What do you mean?'

'This is the start of World War Three. One day, it'll be over. Then I'll be dead, or I won't.'

'And?' said Ross.

'And if I survive, I want a life. No more scraping around for a living.'

Ross laughed out loud.

Kamenskaya smiled and said, 'Hope for the best and plan for the worst. Isn't it?'

Ross became serious, 'So what is it that you're saying?'

'I'm talking about some of the files. The Magnitsky files. I want to blackmail that son-of-a-bitch mastermind of Magnitsky's murder.'

Ross said, 'So?'

'The USB. Think about it. The only proof anyone in the West will ever have. That's in my backpack.'

'You're assuming Russia will never give it up. They have copies, don't they?'

'Lee. They have copies. Yes. At least we have to presume the ones I took are not the only ones, but they won't publish them.'

'You're saying that you're the only risk to the mastermind.'

'Those files are with me, and I'm as good as out of Russia. The mastermind risks the whole Magnitsky affair unravelling. I mean. It's a big deal.'

'It's a big deal for the US, too,' said Ross.

'How's that?'

'The US has banked a lot of political currency on corrupt officials having killed Magnitsky. The US President signed the Magnitsky Act in 2012. Many powerful people in the US would prefer the true reason for Magnitsky's murder to stay secret.'

'Which is good because the mastermind could tap into that capital,' said Kamenskaya. 'I mean, all those with something to lose.'

'How much would you want in exchange for the files?'

'That depends.'

'On what?'

'On who is in on the deal.'

'Ok. Tell me what you're thinking.'

'That this should be about the three of us. You, me, and Zhenya. If you're with us, it can work.'

Ross twisted around to eyeball Kamenskaya. He said, 'Isn't that right Zhenya?'

Zhenya said, 'I agree that we should work together on this, but for me, it's not about money. There are two objectives. One, blackmail the mastermind. We need money, of course, and it's right he should pay us for what we've had to go through. Compensation, I mean.'

Ross said, Okay. Agreed. And two?'

'Two is ensure the war stops. The two have a connection.'

Ross said, 'Do you agree, Kira?'

'I do. The war has to stop before it's too late.'

Ross looked ahead. They were heading due north at 60 km altitude. The Earth curved in all directions. He said, 'I'm with you guys, and I know how all this works out.'

'How?' asked Kamenskaya.

'A deal between the three of us and the US. The Kosvinsky files for peace in Ukraine and a considerable payment in compensation.'

'Blackmail!' said Kamenskaya.

'No. An agreement. A contract.'

'And how would it all pan out exactly?' asked Zhenya.

'A meeting on territory we control between the three of us. There will be three parties, the three of us representing Russia, the mastermind of Magnitsky's murder, and US state representatives. They would have to assure us that they would pressure Ukraine. We would push for an end to the conflict on Russian terms. For that claim, we would hand over the RS-28 files. This would compromise Russian ICBMs.'

'And the Magnitsky files?'

'Given up in return for money.'

'And what's to prevent them from nuking us at the location?'

'What and destroy the RS-28 files, which could give them the edge in a nuclear war with Russia? I don't think so! They would want this too much.'

'And how would we ensure they put pressure on Ukraine?'

'Leave that to me,' said Ross. 'That's between us. You have to trust me on that one. Just get me to the mastermind and the US reps. I'll make sure you get a Russian settlement for this conflict.'

Kamenskaya said, 'Agreed.' She took out a notebook. She tapped Ross on his shoulder. 'These are the contact details for the mastermind.'

Ross set the fighter-bomber on autopilot. He selected fighter control on the radio. He said, 'I request contact with the following number—01-475 4367 2344. Over.'

Fighter command came up to speed. 'Copy that. What's this about?'

'Just do it!'

Silence reigned for what seemed like an eternity, and then the fighter controller's voice returned. 'You're connected.'

Ross said, 'Who is this?'

'This is William Burns. Who are you?'

Ross took his hand well away from the transmission button, and said, 'Does the name add up?'

'It does,' said Kamenskaya. 'Bill Burns was Magnitsky's client. Or the other way round.'

Ross pressed the transmit button and said, 'Bill Burns. This is Colonel Lee Ross. You don't need to know more about me at this stage. Just my name and that I have video evidence. It shows that you acted for the CIA in the murder of Sergei Magnitsky.'

There was a pause, and then Burns's voice returned. It boomed down the telephone connection like a foghorn, 'What do you want?'

'To make a deal,' said Ross. 'The video files for cash.'

'And if I don't agree?'

'That's fine. The files will end up with the world media. You will face shame. People will know what you did. As it is, the world believes Magnitsky died at the hands of corrupt officials. They and the Russian State are responsible for Magnitsky's murder. I'm allowing you to let this state of affairs continue.'

'And how do I know there aren't copies?'

'You have my word. Either you trust me, make the deal, your status intact, or you don't, and I upload the videos. It's up to you.'

'If I do agree, you will hand me the files?'

'You have my word. You will receive the USB files in exchange.'

'And how much do you want?'

'Ten million US dollars in cash. You will bring it to the meeting. As for the location, I will determine that.'

'And how will the meeting be set up?'

'Leave that to the fighter controller,' said Ross, addressing the controller. 'Fighter controller. Confirm that you will stay on the call to Burns. Give him your contact details and the location for the exchange.'

'Confirmed,' said the fighter controller.

'Then I'll be at the location,' said Burns.

'Now you can hang up.'

Ross waited, and then he pressed the transmitter button. He said, 'I need you to contact CIA director Zak Hoffman. I need to talk to him. I can give you the telephone contact.'

'Go ahead with the contact,' said the controller.

'It's 01-210 2365 8739.'

The airwaves went silent. Seconds ran into minutes, and then the fighter controller came back and se said, 'You're connected.'

Hoffman's rasping wolf-like tones rattled through the equipment. He seemed distracted, tired. He was identifying himself, but his voice had done that already. He seemed slow and tired. And then Ross remembered that the first use of nuclear weapons in anger in over 75 years had occurred. Hoffman was in the thick of it. He said, 'This is you?'

Ross smiled. It was typical Hoffman. He was keeping names off the airwaves. He said, 'Sir. I need something.'

'Shoot!'

'I've come up against a brick wall. I can confirm that Russia and the US can make a deal to end the war.'

'Go ahead, Soldier,' said Hoffman.

'I have information on Russia, but I need your collaboration.'

'What are we talking about here?'

'In exchange for the critical information, I need William Burns to meet me, at North Cape, Norway. The security info can stop or cut Russian ICBM capabilities. That done, we can negotiate an exchange, if the US pressures Ukraine. But to hand it over, I need a US representative to deal with the Russians. I also need William Burns to meet at the same location. I have already spoken to him, and he agrees to deal with me. The location of the agreement will be North Cape.'

'That's a lot to take in, Soldier. Let me get this straight. You will give the US critical info on Russia. But, William Burns must be at the meeting.'

'Exactly that.'

'What, have you gone rogue now?'

'Zak, I remind you: The Russians have exploded a nuclear weapon in anger over their territory. Do you copy that? Have you seen where it occurred?'

'Sure I have, Ross. So what?'

'Then you'll know that it was an attempt by the Russians to take out myself and Kamenskaya.'

'I got that too. So what?'

'Well then, Zak, I'll leave it to you to figure out how serious the Russians are about protecting the Kosvinsky files.'

'Which is why we sent you to Russia. And now that you have Kamenskaya and the files, why this deal? You've gone rogue? Do you want to spend the rest of your life in jail?'

'You see, Zak. That's what separates us. You're sitting in an office in Washington. I'm in a fighter 60 km above Russia with files that can prevent this war from going nuclear. So excuse me if I see things different. The first nuclear detonation in anger since 1945 nearly took me out, so my perspectives have shifted. Do you copy that?'

'So what do you want?'

'The Kosvinsky files for US pressure on Ukraine to end the war on Russian terms. Because Russia is not going to back down, and you know it.'

'And what about Burns? How does he fit into this?'

'Enforceability of the thing. On the international plane, how can a state enforce an agreement? Only with detriment to each side creating penalties for reneging on the deal. Burns doesn't want the Magnitsky files to go viral, and neither does the US. Otherwise, the world would know it was the US, not Russia, who murdered Magnitsky.'

'Suppose I agree; getting agreement from President Budden will take time. Tell me about the next steps?'

'I will contact the fighter controller again when I have a meeting time. But, for now, get the other F35Z 3 seater prototype ready for a return flight from Washington to North Cape. Three seats on the flight. They are for the pilot, the US representative with presidential authority to negotiate, and Mr. William Burns. Out.'

Chapter 56

Potanin was well-dressed in a black suit and black tie. He sat alone at the head of a long, white table inlaid with gold designs. There was a mass of papers spread before him. He had a large black Lenovo laptop with the headset plugged in. The Kremlin Great Hall meeting room had a gigantic screen on the far wall, split into squares, each with a member of Potanin's political elite, the *Siloviki.*

He leaned forward, hunched, and cleared his throat. He pushed the laptop into the mass of papers. His hands formed a pointed gesture that showed his resolve. He looked up towards the video screen, his eyes narrowing, and he began to talk. 'Gentlemen. I have called this extraordinary meeting with one aim and objective—to give you a 10 hours heads-up. The reasons are clear. At the NATO summit in Bucharest in April 2008, we signalled to the West that adding Ukraine and Georgia to NATO would threaten Russia's security. You all know this. They did not listen to us or try to understand us. Instead, they doubled down on their promises to Ukraine. Since then, they have increased pressure on us. They escalate the New Cold War whenever they can. As you know, we do not do the incremental thing. We take control. And we invaded Ukraine to do just that—remove any danger of Ukraine becoming NATO. As you all know, since February 2022, Americans have continued to double down. They seem intent on using Ukraine as a tool, a battering ram to weaken Russia with. I cannot let that happen. I will not. We cannot allow the West to defeat Russia in Ukraine. Defeat in Ukraine is an existential threat to Russia. For these reasons alone I have decided to escalate the war against the West.

'Due to the West's actions, this is our only option. First came the first offensive weapons. These were the GMLRS, the HIMARS, the Javelins, and the Stingers. Then came the latest generation tanks, the Leopard 2s, the Challenger 2s, and the Abrams. Then came the aircraft, the F16s. Then came the ATACMs. Gentlemen, the war is entering a new phase. Western supplies are offensive weapons. We cannot win a conventional war against NATO in Ukraine. So Russia will launch a nuclear strike on Ukraine at 6 pm this evening.'

A chorus of noise arose from the video conference, but Potanin was undeterred. He continued his speech, saying, 'The Americans will reap what they have sowed. After we nuke Ukraine with one strategic nuclear device, they, not Russia, will pick their Major Attack Plan 1. It's their SIOP. We're escalating to de-escalate, Gentlemen, and the Americans must choose to de-escalate. Faced with the binomial choice of escalation, and risking a full scale nuclear war, or de-escalation, they will choose the latter. They will realize it is not the right time to use Ukraine to weaken Russia.'

One square of the wall-wide video screen flickered and came alive. It was Defense Minister Shoigu, who could not remain silent. He said, 'Vladimir Vladimirovich, in heaven's name, why now? What has changed in the last 24 hours for you to decide that there is no option but to explode a strategic nuclear device over Ukraine?'

'Two things, Defense Minister Shoigu. One, the nuking of Ukraine will bring what they're doing home to the Americans. They must choose between millions of citizens dying. Or, they must accept the failure of their attempt. They tried to use Ukraine and the Ukrainian people as a battering ram to break down Russia. To use Ukraine as a bulwark against Russia for the expansion of their liberal-democratic world order. When faced with this binomial, they will back down. President Budden's only other option would be to choose their latest SIOP, their nuclear war battle plan, the counterforce part of their Major Attack Plan One. That would use just over 1000 of their strategic nuclear missiles to target our nuclear forces, and it would mean the incineration of millions of Americans when we retaliate. I can tell you that President Budden is not the man who would have the guts to decide on such an option.'

'And two?' asked Shoigu.

'Two, comes down to a historical reason. This is only the second time in history when we have seen tanks marked with the German Military Cross coming across our western borders. They are in battles with our forces on the borderlands of our homeland. The last time this happened was in 1941, and the political ideology of the German leaders was Nazism. It was a threat to Russia. Russia responded to defeat the enemy. Millions of Russians died. Then came Stephan Bandera's army, attempting to form a Nazi Ukrainian puppet state of Germany. Then came the 2014 coup and the rise of Zelensky's politics. They increased discrimination against Russian speakers in Ukraine. In 2024, we face German tanks from the third generation. They have the German Military Cross. They are pushing us again in our borderlands. We risk losing the four newly conquered territories. Crimea is at risk, with Sevastopol. Gentleman, the very existence of Russia as we know her is at risk. I and we will, as in 1943, not let the enemy defeat us.'

Chapter 57

A presidential aide rapped his knuckles on the white door to the Oval Office. He entered without waiting, which was against White House protocol. He knew President Joe Budden would agree to the breach, because he was on the inside of the door, and because of the nature of the news he was carrying. The news came through from the high-security channels. It came from CIA headquarters at Langley, Virginia. It was about Russia—more than that the aide was not allowed to know.

President Budden looked up from his desk. He looked old and confused. He said 'What happened?'

'Mr. President, we have a situation in Russia. I must escort you immediately to the Sit Room.'

'In that case, lead the way.'

A large, multi-sectioned video screen covered the Sit Room's west wall. As President Budden stepped in, it was coming to life. There were various people flashing onto the screen squares. There was the National Security Adviser, the Vice President, the Chairman of the Joint Chiefs of Staff, the Secretary of State, CIA Director Hoffman, and the Secretary of Defense. The President sat opposite the video wall and signalled his presence. He said, 'Gentlemen. What's this about?'

The Secretary of Defence opened proceedings. He was fumbling with papers, trying to gather his thoughts. He said, 'Mr. President, we have confirmed military intel showing Russia is preparing for a strategic nuclear strike against Ukraine.'

'My God!' thundered President Budden. 'That son-of-a-bitch Potanin! I want to know everything about what we know, Hoffman. Right now. Why Ukraine? Why not Poland, Germany, or the UK?'

Hoffman was quick. He answered before the others could even consider butting in. He said, 'Because Ukraine, Mr President, cannot reply. Mr President. It's because they do not have nuclear weapons. Just like when we last bombed Japan—it's an ultimatum directed at you Sir. Stop this now while you can, while we have not hit NATO targets.'

President Budden said, 'I've read the brief. Escalation to de-escalate.'

'Precisely that, Mr President.'

The Secretary of Defence butted in, unable to restrain himself a second longer. 'Mr. President, our intel comes from satellites and an asset inside Potanin's circle. It looks like they will do it, Mr. President.'

'Then what do you recommend?'

'We take our forces to Defcon 2.'

'If nuclear war is so imminent, why not Defcon 1?'

'Mr. President, the Russians will know either way. Our war planners have war-planned going to DEFCON 1. They know the likely response, which would be to tip the Russians into launching strategic strike against the US. Going to DEFCON 2 is a safer option, Sir.'

'I understand that argument. But, if the Russians are ready to launch nuclear weapons at a NATO target, we need time to prepare our response. DEFCON 2 readies us for launch within 6 hours. That's no good to me if the Russians attack immediately. Their ICBMs could be airborne in fifteen minutes. That would give us 45 minutes before warheads hit the mid-west plains. We need our nuclear forces to be ready within the hour. So tell me, Gentlemen, whether by ordering DEFCON 2, we could have such readiness.'

The General of the Joint Chiefs said, 'No, Mr President. To have close to immediate response capacity, you need to order DEFCON 1.'

President Budden said, 'Very well, gentlemen, set DEFCON 1.'

Chapter 58

Buyan-class corvette in the Black Sea

'Spin up one 3M-54 Kalibr Cruise Missile. The target package is 5M2589. The target is the Starokostyantyniv Air Base. It's at 49°44'51"N, 27°16'19"E. Check. Airburst at 500m. Check—estimated yield 50 kilotons. The President has ordered the use of nuclear weapons. This is not an exercise.'

Lieutenant Yuri Popov was the last person in the line. Second use of nuclear weapons in anger since World War II. Popov was the weapons release officer. Before him, the Black Sea Fleet's corvette got the order to release nukes. They also got the release codes. Before the captain, the order had gone through three stages. The Russian President issued it. Now, only his finger on the missile launch panel stopped the 3M-54 Kalibr cruise missile. If fired, it could not be recalled.

Popov repeated the Captain's words. The Captain had reached him through the internal link. He said, 'Spinning up one 3M-54 Kalibr Cruise Missile. Target package 5M2589 confirmed. Starokostyantyniv Air Base at 49 degrees 44 minutes 51 seconds north, 27 degrees 16 minutes 19 seconds east. Check. Airburst at 500m, check—estimated yield 50 kilotons. The President has ordered the use of nuclear weapons. This is not an exercise.'

Lieutenant Popov removed the firing pin. He plugged in the release code, flicked off the metal protector, and fired the weapon, and a single Kalibr cruise missile cruised into the sky.

Chapter 59

Starokostyantyniv Air Base, Ukraine

The nuke detonated 500m above Starokostyantyniv at 18.15 Moscow time.

***

President Budden strode to the Sit Room. A broad smile graced his pink, aging face. He felt a surge of pride deep in his chest. The US three-pronged triad of nuclear forces was at the highest alert level. The silo fields holding the Minuteman ICBMs on the plains of the mid-west were ready. Each hardened silo contained a Minuteman ICBM targeting a single ICBM of Russia's strategic missile forces. Each could be launched within fifteen minutes. They would need 30 minutes to reach their targets in Russia. The majority of the US's fleet of B52 bombers were in the air. They were flying to positions outside Russian airspace. Each was armed with 12 AGM-129 advanced cruise missiles (ACMS) and 20 AGM-86A missiles. All US ballistic missile submarines were at sea. They were headed for their launch positions.

The Situation Room was empty, but there was a large screen on the far wall, and, there were the National Security Advisor, the Secretary of Defense, the Chairman of the Joint Chiefs, and the Secretary of State. They were all staring out at him. There was NORAD. There was Defense Military Intelligence Intel. There were CIA Intel comms. They all gave their latest information to the politics machine in the Situation Room.

The only person missing was CIA Director Hoffman and nobody knew where Hoffman was or why he wasn't present.

***

President Budden was discussing the latest Intel, and the latest on the scenarios. The others were familiarizing themselves with the options should a response become inevitable.

The NORAD comms representative stormed in and shouted above the chatter with astonishing calm, 'Mr. President, reports are coming in of an airburst nuclear blast in the west of Ukraine. It appears the missile delivery was a Kalibr fired from the Black Sea. Looks like the yield is in the 10-100 kilotons range.'

'Son-of-a-bitch!' cursed President Budden. 'He did it!'

'He did, Mr President,' said the Chairman of the Joint Chiefs, with an air of calm which surprised him. 'Question is, how do we respond, Mr President? The Single Integrated Operational Plan, the SIOP?'

'Is that your final advice?'

'It is, Mr President.'

One square of the screen flickered and turned yellow. It was the National Security Adviser. He cleared his throat and said, 'Or we could do nothing?'

'Do nothing?' said the President. 'No. After the first use of nuclear weapons since World War Two, we're not going to do nothing. Not on my watch!'

Confused chatter dominated the screens. Then the National Security Adviser's words reverberated through the room, drowning out everyone else. He said, 'Technically, Mr. President, this is the second use in anger, not the first. The first since 1945 was earlier today in Siberia. We are still evaluating that. As for doing nothing, that might be the smart option.'

'I agree,' cut in the Secretary of State. 'Mr. President, the only escalation left is the top rung of the escalation ladder, a nuclear strike on Russia. The SIOP. Such an action would have only one assured consequence. Russia would fire their surviving strategic nuclear weapons at us. It would likely be a strike on our cities. Which we would not be able to completely shoot down. So the option of doing nothing might be the smart option. Instead of starting a nuclear war between Russia and the US, we would signal de-escalation to the Russians. We would tell them that we are calming things down.'

President Budden scratched his balding head. He had wispy, silver-coloured hair. Then he said, 'You're all forgetting one thing. By de-escalation at that point, we would be handing the ultimate victory in Ukraine to Russia. Russia would have come out ahead at this inflection point; this turning point of history. This was in the conflict between the democratic West and the authoritarian East. That's not an option on my watch.'

President Budden turned to the Chairman of the Joint Chiefs and said, 'General. If we respond in kind to this Russian escalation, what are my options?'

'Mr. President, we have planned for this. The plan is Major Attack Plan One. It has two parts: the counterforce response and the countervalue response. The countervalue option is incontrovertibly illegal under International Law. Sir. Even now, it's not advisable. It targets their large cities and economy, which Russia greatly values. Russia would target our major cities. They would do this in response to what is left of Russia's nuclear weapons. Things that we value. In other words, a countervalue strike would encourage a retaliatory one by Russia on the US. They would also strike our Western allies in Europe. In summary, Russia would target every large city in Europe and continental North America. In minutes, millions would die, incinerated. We would seal our fate and cause the deaths of millions of Americans.'

'And what of the counterforce response?'

'If you select the counterforce version of Major Attack Plan One, we would hit all of their nuclear sites. We would use a coordinated attack with just over 1000 of our missiles. Our forces are at DEFCON 1. Within fifteen minutes of giving the order, our SLBMs would be airborne. They have a flight time of fifteen minutes. That strike would target their four fields of missile silos. Two warheads would target each of their 123 missile silos. They would hit them with ground bursts, with a 99.5 percent chance of taking them all out. Our Minuteman ICBMs would target Russia's seven Arctic and three Pacific nuclear submarine bases. They would have a 99.9 percent chance of success. Then Russia's third strategic leg is their strategic bombers. We would remove it with a 99% kill chance. We would do this by assigning other Minuteman missiles and SLBMs. We would keep enough ICBMs, SLBMs, and B52-launched weapons in reserve for dealing with any surviving Russian capability.'

President Budden said, 'Launch the counterforce version of Major Attack Plan One.'

'Yes, Sir.' It was all the general needed. He saluted, turned, and strode out of the room.

A minute passed, and then, there were more worried looks and quick discussions on procedure. An extra square appeared on the video screen. All those present recognized CIA Director Hoffman.

'Nice of you to join us, Mr. Hoffman,' said President Budden.

Hoffman said, 'Likewise, Mr President, I have received news from my team. You have ordered Major Attack Plan One. Is that correct?'

'That is correct, Mr Hoffman.'

'I must request that you rescind your order immediately.'

'But of course, Mr Hoffman. I can do that. But why should I? The Russians have nuked Ukraine, for Christ's sake!'

'Because I am on my way to a meeting with a representative of the Russian Federation at North Cape, Norway.'

'And what good could that possibly achieve?' asked the President. 'Tell me that!'

'Hear me out, Sir. Nothing less than a deal to end the Russo-Ukrainian War is what I propose. The other option is a thermonuclear war between the US and Russia, which would destroy America as we know it. I'm saying there is another way. It lets cooler heads win. The Russians' deal would ensure a return to peace between Russia and the US. The document on the table says Russia would compromise their main ICBM, the RS-28. They would do this if the US stops sending arms to Ukraine. The US must also pressure Ukraine to accept Russia's terms to end the war. The US would gain a strategic nuclear edge over Russia. This would weaken Russia's economy and military. Russia would have gained the four annexed territories plus Crimea. Both sides could declare victory. The only loser would be Ukraine. We would have sacrificed it like a lamb to slaughter to de-escalate the crisis. Not a good case scenario, but not the worst imaginable.'

President Budden was thinking about the plan, that much was obvious. His forehead was creased by frowns. Days of worry had taken its toll. Seconds passed, and finally, he said, 'Hoffman, Gentlemen, we need to think this through. If the scenario allows us to avoid escalation, we must try.' Then, he turned to the Secretary of Defence and said, 'Get that general back in here now, and put my last order on hold!'

Chapter 60

Northern Russia

The F35Z continued heading north, toward North Cape. The bleak northernmost tip of Europe. Below, an outline of a frozen lake spread out like a map. Ross surveyed the on-board computer which controlled their fate. A familiar voice came through on the radio. It was the fighter controller. He advised a change to another frequency, so Ross turned the dial and checked in. The voice said, 'Here's an associate to talk to you. Stand by.'

There was a pause punctuated by crackling. Ross and Kamenskaya exchanged glances. The 'associate' could be CIA, from Langley. They could pull strings if it were the case. A deal could be possible. Kamenskaya nodded.

Ross pressed the transmitter and said, 'Put them on.'

The channel crackled and Ross identified a familiar voice and high-pitched, jet-engine whine. It was Hoffman.

Hoffman said, 'Soldier! I am en-route to the North Cape meeting and have here with me the one you call the "Mastermind." I have full authority to deal, but with one further condition.'

'Hoffman?' said Ross, his words wrapped in incredulity. 'They sent you!?'

'I'm asking the questions here, Soldier. We need the deal to be enforceable.'

'And?' said Ross. 'You'll have files on the RS-28 for Christ's sake!'

'Ross! The files will not be verifiable until we analyse them. We will not be able to analyse them right away. No instant verification is possible at North Cape. You know that, Soldier. I'll need more than a bunch of files on a USB device. After the nuking of Ukraine, everyone wants de-escalation. The President, the Russians. Putting pressure on Ukraine to accept a settlement will not be a problem.'

'And the money? You have it?'

'All present and counted. And the Mastermind is on this flight.'

The "mastermind" jogged an image of North Cape in Ross's memory. The future meeting. The US should give up its goal of spreading the liberal-democratic world order. They would have to accept an agreement with him and Kamenskaya to prevent World War Three. But, to do that, they would have to get to North Cape. Neither side could cope with further escalation.

Ross considered his options. He took his hand from the transmitter button, attentive to "live mike" errors. He turned in his pressure suit and eyeballed his de facto co-pilot Kira Kamenskaya. He said, 'If we're going to make this deal, it must be to prevent escalation. You heard it. The US representatives are coming to North Cape to make a deal. But here's the problem. You represent Russia no more than any other Russian civilian. So any deal made will not bind Russia. What we need is for you to represent Russia. Your thoughts on that?'

Finally! thought Kamenskaya. *The Americans came to their senses after all, and I am exactly where I need to be.* She said, 'Not sure, but I can try. It's 9 pm in Moscow. I'll email my associates!'

'Don't try to send an email! For Christ sake! Call them! Now!'

'Okay Ross! Fly the plane will you!'

Which Ross did. They were at the limit of the atmosphere, Russia still below them. He pressed transmit. He said, 'Okay Hoffman! Rendez-vous point is the F35 crash site. You know it.'

Hoffman said, 'Rafjord. The end of the flat area. The place with large boulders, where wolves howl at night.'

'I knew you would remember it! 12 pm tomorrow. Ross out.'

Kamenskaya dialled and heard a ringtone, and then she got to the one person she needed. Anella Moskva.

With a throaty voice and considered calm, Moskva said, 'Kira. I was beginning to wonder if I would ever get this call. Quite a mess you've got us all into.'

'Me? No! No! No! I didn't do this. This was not what I signed up for. And yes, it's quite a mess for all Russia, not only Potanin and you! You should have called off the attack dogs when I was in Kosvinsky Mountain!'

'Nothing I could do about that.'

'Bull shit!'

'Be that as it may, my conscience is clear. I tried my best, but you ran towards Ukraine. What were we supposed to think?'

'Whatever!' Kamenskaya said, 'Things have escalated…'

'No kidding!'

Kamenskaya composed herself. She took a deep breath. It was a sensitive moment. She could feel Ross's eyes drilling into her. She said, 'You might not see it, but we can both walk away from this.'

'How in Hell's name can we both walk away?'

'Shut up and listen.' There was crackling on the connection. Kamenskaya hoped that technical issues were not going to torpedo the whole thing. 'The Americans are meeting with me at North Cape tomorrow at midday. The director of the CIA, Zak Hoffman, will be there. They want to negotiate a deal. The war will end, with Ukraine giving up on joining NATO. If I represent Russia, we can make a deal. This is our chance. The last chance. Everything we had hoped for in Park Parbedy. Warp power in the negotiations? I have it!'

'Amazing, Kira. This is fantastic. You've come good! What are the parameters?'

'Assurances. I have assurances. The US won't escalate if we give them the information I stole from Kosvinsky Mountain.'

'Being?'

'The Magnitsky files and those on the RS-28.'

'And Ukraine?' said Moskva.

'Ukraine will remain as it is now. The US will assure the Ukrainians will accept a settlement based on Russian terms. It would mean that Russia has won the war. The US will not stomach any further risk of nuclear war with Russia over Ukraine. In effect, they're backing down. A humiliating defeat for the US, but one they brought on themselves. Things are getting too risky. They've realised that a nuclear superpower must never have to choose between a humiliating defeat and use of tactical nuclear weapons.'

Moskva said, 'Well, the US is the one facing the humiliating defeat. Fine. I have Potanin's authority to make the deal.'

'How's that? How can you say he agrees?'

'Because he is standing right next to me.'

'Then put him on!'

Potanin's voice came through Kamenskaya's headset, saying. 'This is me, Kira. I agree. If the US will end their support for

Ukraine, and end the war on our terms, we will accommodate them. We will give up the coding to the new ICBMs. The US will have the frequencies used to control them after launch.'

Kamenskaya said, 'That's fine. Now, put Anella back on the call.'

'It's me,' said Moskva.

'Send me an email with these written terms. You have my email address. Copy Vladimir Vladimirovich into the email. We await your email.'

'And when will you be meeting the US delegation at North Cape?'

'Tomorrow, at 12.pm.'

Ross said, 'Is the call ended?'

'Yes.'

Ross pressed the transmitter. It was set to the frequency of the last talk with Hoffman. He said, 'This is Ross.'

'Go ahead, Soldier!' said Hoffman.

'We confirm that Kira Kamenskaya has full authority. The authority is from the Russian President to represent Russia.'

'Copy that. Good work. We'll be in touch again from North Cape. Crash site. Tomorrow, 12.p.m. Hoffman out.'

Chapter 61

The three MIG 31s picked up the trace 3 km from Rafjord. A small blip on the screen, tracing towards North Cape. Major Klimov told his two wingmen to close in and increase speed to Mach 2.5.

They came up on the F35's tail. Ross was unaware. The only danger lay ahead. NATO. Russia knew all about him. Anella Moskva had taken care of that.

The first he knew about the danger was when the MiGs released three missiles, and the radar came alive. The computer told him he had 1minute and 30 seconds to impact.

He executed an emergency dive. If any of them were going to survive, he needed to be close to the deck. The F35 dived.

Priorities. The best indicator of next steps. Priority number one was get to the meeting with Hoffman. He looked at his watch. *No, stupid*, he thought. The meeting was the next day at 12pm. More than 12 hours in the future. Priority number two, make sure the USB was with him at the meeting. He felt it in his fatigues. Which led to Priority three. Sidearm. His Glock was in his webbing, along with five magazines. Priority number four. Get out of the aircraft before impact. He looked down.

The coast of Rafjord was ahead. He pulled out of the dive, and the on-board computer advised him there was ten seconds to impact. He hit autopilot and ejected.

He watched as the stricken plane headed straight over the low hills in the middle of the biggest storm to affect Norway. The missile was on its tail. Both disappeared.

He looked down through the maelstrom. The storm was terrible. But he was over land. Finnmark. North Cape. One last, long look in the direction the F35 had taken, and he said a silent prayer for Kamenskaya and Tsvigun. The rasping of the jet was gone, and in its place the whistling of the wind through his fatigues.

The ground, white and frozen, rushed up, and he steered towards the lee of a ridge, where he figured the snow would be deep and soft. Which it was. He landed heavily all the same; it jolted him to his core. The wind filled the canopy, dragging him with it headlong towards the coast. Dizzy, he remembered how close he was to the edge of the plateau. Not further than a hundred meters, he thought. With the stark reality staring him in the face, he knew he had to stop his headlong rush. The plateau was bordered by cliffs which fell away in steep slabs and rock walls to the wave swept headlands of Rafjord.

The wind in the parachute was bowling him along, and he saw a ridge up ahead. There would be more deep snow on the lee side. It came up fast, and he launched over it, feet first, guided as much by luck as by judgement. He thrust his weight into the snow drift. For a brief second, he was stationary. He struck the release with his right palm, and the chute flew on the wind.

Ross cursed. Without the silk of the chute, he knew it would be more difficult to sleep, even if he did find shelter. *At least he was alive*, he thought, as he lay there between, rock, snow and ice.

He was stationary, and saw the chute snagged on a large boulder, up ahead.

He had escaped the death trap of the F35. Slowly but steadily, he crawled forward, leaving a trench in the snow. If he stood, he would get blown again.

The rocky outcrop was high and made up of jagged granite. He pulled in the white chute, stuffing it in his pressure suit; his movements restricted. Then he reached inside his fatigues and took out the survival knife. The end of it was a miniature compass, which was going to help. There was a map in his head, but he needed to put all on his side. The blizzard was increasing. It was fast making North Cape a whiteout. Without constant checking he could move in circles. Safety lay at the cave above Rafjord, where the freezing winds would eddy. Due south. Around a kilometre if memory served.

After an hour, he reached the summit of a hill from where a break in the clouds allowed a view. Ahead stretched a landscape he knew years ago, and he breathed a sigh of relief. He was right on course. There was half an hour of light left, but the descent was simple. He checked the compass for a final bearing, and set off down the slope to the cliff's edge.

The place was just as he left it all those years earlier. The cave looked as if nobody had spent a night there since he used it. He even thought the dry heather at the cave entrance was the same as he had placed there. In front of it, there was charcoal sticks and a circular area clear of snow. The fire pit.

The path to the beach was as he remembered it too. The blizzard was still strengthening, so he needed fire, and the beach was the best bet for fuel, so he cut down to it. There was plenty of it, so for the next hour he accumulated a stack next to the fire pit. Next, he unscrewed the top of the knife, extracted the magnesium block, and sheared off a pile of magnesium shavings. The wind took some of them, so he scraped deeper so that they were bigger, and more immune to the gusty wind which eddied around him.

He pushed the shavings into a pile, and placed dry wood over and above. Then he drew the blade over the flint side of the magnesium block, and hot white sparks flew into the magnesium which burst into flame. He placed bigger and thicker pieces of driftwood until he thought the fire was safe. He reclined into the folds of the chute, bathed in the heat of the fire, and warmed himself to the core.

During the latter part of the night, the storm reached its crescendo. When the first rays began to lighten the sky, Ross was fast asleep, enveloped in the warm folds of the chute. He woke with a start and a feeling that he had missed the rendezvous. He checked his watch. 8 am. Another four hours till the meeting. He built up the fire, throwing on the last of the drift wood into the burning embers.

Chapter 62

Rafjord, Finnmark, Norway

Ross thought that the storm meant that no plane would be able to land. The US weather service had given him the latest data on the storm coming into Finnmark from the south. They told him the storm had originated in the Gulf of Mexico. It became a Category 4 storm, dumping a lot of snow on the eastern United States, and then it crossed the North Atlantic, gaining strength from the jet stream and the big temperature differences. It picked up a lot of humidity and energy and then it headed to Europe.

It wasn't an issue for either Hoffman or his pilot. The second of the vast prototypes got the delay heads-up. They were cruising at Mach 6, 50,000 meters above Baffin Island. They could coast for hours at that speed and altitude with minimal fuel consumption.

No more messages had come from Ross, so, the pilot of Hoffman's F35Z landed on the desolate airstrip. An F35 had crashed into boulders there years before.

All three on-board Hoffman's F35 knew why Ross had chosen that spot for the meeting. The crash site. Ross had crash-landed at the site in the events following the outbreak of the last war. It was part of US folklore. Ross himself known for his actions during the crash landing. He was known too for his liberation of Anna Kuznetsova.

The pilot raised the canopy, and the descent ladder extended. He climbed down, and so did his two passengers, the blizzard tearing at their clothes. The snow was falling. The wreckage was visible in the boulders. They were at the edge of a smooth area which sloped down to Rafjord.

Hoffman and Burns wanted to touch the wreckage, and the pilot watched them closely as they walked over to it. A strange place for tourism, he thought, but history weighs on the shoulders of key players. He stayed close to his aircraft.

The snow was drifting. The worst storm he had ever experienced. There was hurricane force winds and freezing temperatures. He and Hoffman struggled in its icy blasts to tie down the plane. When they got back to the tent, they heard the crackling of the radio. Ross was communicating again, and so Hoffman shouted to Burns and the pilot. Burns remained close to the wreck, crouching behind it in the lee of the winds.

Ross said, 'What is your location? Over.'

Hoffman said, 'Rafjord, as per your request. The wreck. Where are you?'

'Where I stayed last time around, with Kira and Lena and the Russian patrols.'

'Then you'll know all about the current conditions, and that it's about to get real bad. The storm's centre is still out in the Norwegian Sea—no chance to meet in this.'

Ross said, 'Agreed. Which is why I requested the meeting today midday. You have submarine units in the area in case you need backup. No danger. There's no reason to postpone the meeting.'

Hoffman said, 'Not yet, anyway. We'll ride out the storm. We'll stay put until further notice. The US will not launch any imminent attack.'

Ross said, 'Agreed. Tie down the F35. We're in for a stormy night. Hurricane force winds are due to hit from midnight to 2 am. And snowfall will be severe till the morning. Hurricane-force winds and freezing temperatures. It's not due to ease until 10 a.m. tomorrow.'

'Copy that. We'll communicate tomorrow at 10 a.m.'

Chapter 63

Lee Ross was closing on the location of the meeting between the US and Russia, the airstrip, if it could be called that, with boulders at the end of it. The airstrip was around the headland. A flattened area at the base of the valley of Rafjord. Decades earlier, he had crash-landed an F35 there when it had been caught in a hail of bullets from a MiG 25. Now it was a twisted wreck in the boulder field at the end of the strip, the end furthest from Rafjord, the arm of the Barents Sea around whose headland he was now turning.

Ross reckoned it would take him an hour to get there. The snow. The storm. The hurricane force wind. The biting blizzard and the deep drifts were all going to slow him down.

But despite the conditions, he made quick progress. The snow was deep, but the strong wind had drifted it, sweeping areas clear to leave the hard, frozen tundra.

He rounded the headland, and the winds increased further. They pulled at his flight suit, causing any loose straps to flap incessantly. He pulled the flight suit close, and struggled on. The wind chill was severe. It felt like his face wood freeze before he got to the landing strip. Slowly, the valley opened out ahead, but the wind didn't ease.

He came to a large boulder, and took a breather on its lee side. He saw the hulk of a US submarine in the fjord. Backup, he thought, in case Hoffman needed it.

There was a lull in the wind, and he squinted into the teeth of the gale and the stinging spindrift. Up ahead, the landing strip was visible. He made out a tent and the US aircraft—the other prototype F35, scaled up and three seater.

Ross didn't want to approach the US encampment direct, along the landing strip from Rafjord. Too obvious. No surprise. Instead, he cut inland, fighting his way through the blizzard up to the ridge. Years ago, Lena Bernstein had told him it was an ancient path made by reindeer herders. The path was swept clear of snow as its direction corresponded to that of the wind. Now it served another purpose; preventing World War Three.

He reached the end of the ridge, where the ridge path forked. One branch continued straight, towards Mehamn, while the other switched left towards the end of the airstrip. Below him, he could see the American camp, with the delegation's F35Z. A campfire was burning near the boulders at the edge of the airstrip, where the old F35 wreck lay twisted and bent. He wondered how Hoffman and his associates had kept such a big fire going, but then he remembered he had kept a similar one going all night.

The tent faced the fire and the F35Z, and he kept the tent in view as he continued his approach. The path was no longer clear of snow which lay deep and untouched. Not total surprise, but better than nothing. The light helped. It was later than arranged. Not a deal breaker, not now that the US and Russia seemed all out of ideas.

Ross swung above and behind the tent in a half circle, coming into it from the high ground to the north. He rounded the corner of the tent, between the tent and the F35, and stopped at the sight of Hoffman. He was standing there in front of the large fire, cigarette in hand. Ross sensed the burnt tobacco smell despite the wind.

Ross noted that Hoffman looked flushed and warm in his parker and the heat of the fire. Ross said, 'Did you check your email?'

There wasn't a glimmer of surprise from Hoffman, which wasn't really surprising. He drew deeply on the cigarette and flicked it with one finger towards the snow, but the wind caught it and it ended up in the fire.

Hoffman said, 'Your email about the Agreement you mean? Come into the tent, and I'll show you.'

'No. We'll discuss in the open, next to the fire.'

'Why's that? Worried about something? Anyway, not a problem. We can discuss it here!'

Ross said, 'Its terms are clear?'

Hoffman took a couple of steps toward the fire.

He selected a couple of large pieces of driftwood from the pile, and threw them one by one onto the fire. Then he stood in the fire's heat, with his back to the wind, and said, 'Here's the deal. You give us the USB with the RS-28 ICBM files and the Magnitsky videos. We'll give something in return.'

'That's a pretty big quid. How about the quo?'

'We put pressure on Zelensky to end the war on Russia's terms.'

'That's part of it.'

There was a flicker of disappointment on Hoffman's face. He said 'No. That was the whole agreement.'

'Things change. Let's call that Agreement One; the basis for Agreement Two, which will flesh out the agreement.'

'Why?'

'Hoffman. Agreement One is one-sided. With the USB, you'll be able to neutralize Russia's ICBMs. Russia will not give up that for some pithy promise to put pressure on Zelensky. Russia needs guarantees.'

'I expected as much,' said Hoffman.

They heard the hiss of a zip from the tent on the other side of the fire. Burns and the DEVGRU pilot came out to join them.

Ross pointed to them, saying, 'They stay on that side of the fire. Far from you and me.'

Hoffman motioned to Burns and the DEVGRU pilot to stay on the other side of the fire.

Ross said, 'I'm glad. Better that we're all here in one place, with some witnesses to what we say here.'

Hoffman said, 'So, Ross. What guarantees?'

'You take the USB. We would need to take something too. Each has a guarantee.'

'You want to take what exactly?'

'We would need to remove someone or something, so that the US cannot renege.'

'Name it!'

'The Mastermind behind the murder of Sergei Magnitsky of course.'

Hoffman laughed out loud. Then his look turned serious, and he said, 'And why? If such a person exists, how exactly would the Mastermind guarantee anything?'

'Because the US political establishment has put much faith and much political capital in this idea. They believe Russia murdered Magnitsky. The truth lies, of course, in a different place and you know it. And the truth must not come out. The US President signed the Magnitsky Act into law. 2012. All that legitimacy for the liberal democratic international order would come crashing down.'

'Fine,' said Hoffman. 'As you know, William Burns is the mastermind behind Magnitsky's death.'

William Burns was on the fire's far side. Out of earshot. He saw Hoffman and Ross look in his direction, but with the howling of the wind, and the hissing of the snow, Burns could not hear what was said.

Ross said, 'No.'

'No? What are you talking about?'

'William Burns is a scapegoat. Nothing more than a patsy; always has been, and I have proof; I have the Magnitsky files. They're here in my pocket, and they include one between William Burns and a third person.'

Hoffman knew what was coming. He hadn't been born yesterday. The writing was bold and black on the wall, but he asked anyway.

'News to me. If William Burns isn't the mastermind? Then who is?'

'That would be you, Zak, and don't give me any surprised look! We have a video to prove it.'

Hoffman said, 'Ah. A video. Two people appear right, both identifiable?'

'You got it. One is William Burns, and the other is you, Zak. There's sound and footing. If it went to court, it would be an open and shut case.'

Hoffman said, 'And this file, this USB with the video, is where? I'm guessing it's here with you and there are copies.'

Ross tapped his thigh; a pocket of his flight suit. 'Right here, Zak, along with the Magnitsky and ICBM files.'

'Hmm. So you're coming with some digital so called "evidence." True even. But without you, or that USB, how can the US prove it?'

'For one reason, Zak—it's written all over your face. The only question on my mind is, why you aren't playing ball already. You're all out of moves. You being here is proof in itself. Worried, were you? About what William Burns might say to us should he come here alone and come clean? I guess you thought you needed to be on the front foot. You needed control of the situation, and you sure as hell couldn't do that from an office at Langley.'

Hoffman just stood there. Ross thought that he looked comfortable even. Confident and at ease. Which made sense. Hoffman hadn't come 6,000 miles without a plan B.

Ross said, 'You had to protect the CIA and America's dirty secret. You wanted to protect yourself too, and the rest of the American political elites who have so much to lose. You couldn't do that from your office in Langley. So you had to be here. Close. In case things went south, and you needed to fine tune things; to take me out. That's why the exchange. Russia gets you and America's promise to put pressure on Zelensky. America gets the USB.'

'All plausible. Probable even,' said Hoffman.

'You're finished, Zak! Your career is over.'

'Not quite so fast, Ross. The fact is, you're overlooking something.'

'Your pilot? Don't insult me. He can't turn this around. Three against one, and your pilot has a Glock. Maybe William Burns has one too. But didn't you learn anything about me over the years? Your pilot could shoot me, yes. But he does, and the planet will die. And, both he and you will die.'

'How's that?'

'Because out there in the snow and the boulders, there's a sniper. He has an M60 rifle. He has a good telescopic sight. Top of the range. US Special Forces standard kit, and your eyes in the crosshairs. Of course, his orders are to shoot both you and the DEVGRU pilot should you kill me. A hail of shots within three seconds. Your DEVGRU pilot could decide to kill me. But, that'll be the last thing to go through his mind, apart from twenty or so

7.62mm rounds. My guy has the bodycam receiver, which means he has recorded this conversation. So go ahead, kill me, and you'll see. Or make this deal and all go home. Or you, William Burns, the DEVGRU pilot, and I all die here.'

Ross's bluff was a good one. It was well thought out, and executed. Hoffman's look was a sight to behold. A realisation that he really had no more moves. Checkmate. His eyes twitched, a tell-tale sign that his confidence had taken a hike. He said, 'Tell me about the deal.'

Ross said, 'That, my friend, is an agreement to end the Russo-Ukrainian war. A treaty. An international agreement. Binding under International Law.'

Hoffman straightened up. His body language was talking, and it was saying more than a thousand words. He folded his arms.

Ross said, 'Okay. You, that is, the US, will put pressure on Ukraine to end the war on Russia's terms. When Ukraine, the US and Russia have signed the treaty, we will give you the USB, but will keep a copy of all the files on it. The Kosvinsky files. With the USB the US can stop Russia's new ICBMs. The USB has the frequencies Russia uses to control them in flight. We keep copies of the Magnitsky files and will take you hostage to the deal.'

Hoffman said, 'The US would need a guarantee.'

'Unfortunately for you, the only guarantee is my word.'

'And you have complete authority to make this deal?'

'From Potanin himself.'

Ross reached into his pressure suit, and pulled out his satellite phone.

'There's an agent of the GRU on the other side of this call. Her name is Anella Moskva, and she is currently with Potanin. I can put them on loudspeakers.'

'I have a better idea. Quicker. Faster.'

'What?'

'The Washington-Kremlin hotline.'

Hoffman reached into the left hand side pocket of his thick parker. He extracted a block of technology which looked more like a block of metal and plastic than a communication device. And yet, it had the desired effect on Ross, because of what Hoffman knew about Ross's obsession with it.

Seeing the hotline froze Ross. His mind jumped back to the last case—Victoria Feodor. The inner workings of his mind left him stupefied. Among all the intervening thoughts and actions, his mind had retained the unsolved case linked to the hotline.

In an instant, Ross was back in his apartment, remembering his drunkenness, and the hotline. He remembered the fact that he had asked Anella Moskva about Victoria Feodor. But then he saw a Glock in Hoffman's hand, and said, 'What's going on?'

'Ross. You have never lied to me, and I see no reason to suspect you are lying now.'

'So why the gun?'

'Because there'll be no deal. We will, however, take your files. And you die here for betraying your country.'

Ross saw his life flash before his eyes. The feelings every dying man has, but can never tell about because they don't survive. Only it wasn't an effect of his mind or one of Hoffman's moves, because Kirilenka appeared. It was her presence that was playing tricks with Ross.

Alexandra Kirilenka succeeded in approaching the fire. She stopped next to Burns, and Ross saw her. She noticed the look of recognition on Ross's face and knew that he must after all have seen her at Cafe Zurich, Barcelona. He must have noticed she was acting suspicious before the shooting.

'Put down the gun, Hoffman,' she said calmly and deliberately.

'Who the hell are you?' asked Hoffman.

Kirilenka said, 'Right now, I'm your biggest nightmare, because this is where you really get checkmated.'

Hoffman felt exposed; disadvantaged. Ross needed no help. He saw his chance and acted with a high kick; a jiu-Jitsu move well placed, straight into Hoffman's chest. Full power. Full weight. Hoffman had nothing to counter it, and he was rammed onto the ground.

Ross turned, and saw that Kirilenka had the initiative and wasn't about to let it slip.

Hoffman tried to get to his feet. Tried, not succeeded, because Kirilenka beat him to it. She kicked his Glock into the snow drift, and then she aimed hers at his hand, and fired. No prisoners. Hoffman squirmed, doubling up, his hands held to his front. Kirilenka picked up the hotline.

'See to his hand,' shouted Kirilenka. She held the Glock to Hoffman's head. She reached inside his jacket, and pulled the Washington-Kremlin hotline, and handed it to Ross.

Kirilenka stood behind the fire, with a Glock trained on the DEVGRU pilot. No mistake. No prisoners.

'That is the Kremlin-Washington hotline,' said Ross. It was more of a statement than a question.

'Which has only one purpose,' said Kirilenka. 'To prevent nuclear Armageddon.'

Now that Ross had it, and it didn't matter anymore what status he had; what agency. He was the one on the end of it. There was a red button, and he pressed it.

Kirilenka watched the pilot approach. His eyes never left her. He had seen everything and had no plans to intervene on his own. No orders from above. He said, 'We need to end this.'

Ross heard a ringtone and a female voice, strangely familiar.

'Anella?' said Ross.

'Ross? You sure took your time, but came good after all. Hoffman's dead?'

'Not bad. You have a good memory.'

'It's not difficult. You're one of three men I know to be at your location. North Cape right?'

'Right.'

'Hoffman is dead?'

'No, he's alive.'

'What now?'

Ross said, 'First, I have a question. You answer it and we can get down to negotiations to end this.'

Moskva said, 'You got that right. We end this thing right now. You and me. Potanin is here with me. We can do that. So shoot!'

'Do you remember how we left it last time?'

'Outside your base? Sure. You wanted information on the victim. Victoria Feodor. Why?'

'Well. Now I need that information.'

'I thought we're here negotiating a deal to stop World War Three, and all you want to do is talk about Victoria Feodor?'

'I want to clear up the case. Nothing wrong with that. We're saving the world here.'

'Get real, Ross! This isn't about saving the world. This is about you. You want the glory. You're greedy.'

'No. I am just curious, and want to tie up a loose end.'

'Ok. I guess. Shoot!'

'Feodor's client. Anything you know? The reason I ask, is that I have a hunch.'

'You mean the President,' said Moskva.

'The President? Of...?'

'The United States.'

'Do you know why she was killed?'

'Affirmative. She had dirt on the President. No prejudice coloured the President in his relations with Russia right? At least, that's the narrative.'

'Right.'

'Wrong!'

'How?'

Moskva said, 'Victoria Feodor had evidence to prove it. The President was her client.'

'But her clientele was Russian oligarchs,' said Ross.

'No,' said Moskva. 'True, most were Russian. The President was an exception to the rule. She got him as a client because she was good at what she did.'

'Which was?'

'You know it,' said Moskva.

'I want to hear it from you.'

'Gross negligence manslaughter. The President knew he would be accountable for a general thermonuclear war between the US and Russia. The deaths of millions on his hands. He wanted to know definitively if he would be liable legally, from a lawyer an expert in the field.'

'So what did she find?'

'As with all her clients, she drilled down into every aspect of the case. She found that the President had travelled to Ukraine. He was a young man in what was then the Soviet Union. In a bar in Kiev, something happened. An incident which would colour his whole life and turn him into a perpetual Russia hater.'

'What exactly?'

Kirilenka stepped away from the DEVGRU pilot, as the time had come. She said to Ross, 'This isn't libellous. Put the phone on loudspeaker. I need to talk to Anella and you. I need to join the conversation. Anella doesn't know who I am.'

Moskva heard it. Kirilenka said to Ross. 'Tell her to let me handle this.'

Ross said, 'Who are you?'

Kirilenka said, 'I know there's difficulty here. It's difficult to grasp how I would know. And why. But it's a fact. Anella knows everything, except the reason why Budden hates Russia. Say it Lena.'

There was a pause, and then Anella's voice. She said 'Kirilenka says the truth. Victoria Feodor told me everything, except why Budden hates Russia. Because of that night in the cocktail bar. More than that, I don't know. But is this a deal breaker? We all want to end World War Three. We're really going to do this?'

Kirilenka said, 'We are. Because Ross want's this. And besides, it's important. We need to know the reason the planet came within a hair's breadth of destruction. And how do you know?'

There was a long pause, which Ross thought was normal. He could well imagine the reasons for it. Moskva would have put her finger over the microphone while she explained to Potanin what was going on. Then he heard clicks and thuds, and Potanin's voice.

Ross said, 'We want to end this. We know why the US have been doubling down all these years. It's all in the past and we will solve it. There is scapegoat here. The US President himself. We, the CIA, will deal it; with him. Because I am and always will be CIA and a patriot. I will see to it. I have the hotline, and you can deal with me.'

Potanin's comeback was immediate, 'I can deal with you, Ross. Accepted. You have the hotline, and I have confirmed your location, and your company. But can I trust you?'

'Yes, you can, Vladimir, Vladimirovich!'

'I have no confidence. The whole reason Russia got into this war is because we believed you in 1991. Since that time, you have proved again and again that you are not to be trusted. Why should I believe you now?'

'Because you are not talking to one of the neo-cons sitting in the gilded Oval Office of the White House. You're talking to a soldier who has fought on the front lines. Someone who understands you. Understands Russia.'

'You are with Hoffman?'

'Yes. You know it.'

'Put him on.'

Ross thought for a second Potanin had got it. He understood that Hoffman was the key. He knew the reasons for the US doubling down since 2020. He walked over to the tent. Hoffman was inside, still doubled up in pain. His hand was bandaged.

Ross said to Kirilenka, 'Is he able to talk?'

'Ask him for yourself,' said Kirilenka.

Ross pointed his Glock at Hoffman, and handed him the phone, saying, 'Confirm to this person who you are.'

Hoffman groaned, 'This is Zak Hoffman. What do you need to know?'

Potanin said, 'Your position in the US government, and your date of birth.'

Through more agony a few more words came from Hoffman's throat. 'Director of the Central Intelligence Agency, and 17 December 1969.'

Potanin said, 'Very well. Hand me back to Ross.'

Ross said, 'Is that good enough for you.'

'Yes. With Hoffman we will have complete control of the situation. As for you. You have confirmed that you will deal with him. But do you also say that you will publicise the whole sordid affair?'

'You have my word. And you will have Hoffman to make sure of it.'

'Then I agree. If you send me the draft Treaty to end the war, I will consider it. Send it to Anella. Her email address is Anella. Moskva@gov.ru.'

'Goodbye Vladimir Vladimirovich!'

The following text pinged to Lena thirty minutes later. It had been written by AI, but the input was perfect, and the results checked and rechecked:

Draft TREATY

Treaty of the North Cape: Framework for Peace in Ukraine

Preamble

The United States of America and the Russian Federation, hereinafter referred to as the Parties, recognizing the need to restore peace, stability, and security in the region, and in the interest of ending the conflict in Ukraine, hereby agree to the following terms:

Article 1: Neutrality of Ukraine

Ukraine shall adopt a status of permanent neutrality. It shall not join any military alliances, including but not limited to the North Atlantic Treaty Organization (NATO).

Ukraine shall refrain from permitting foreign military bases or troops to be stationed on its territory, except under a United Nations mandate approved by both Parties.

Article 2: Termination of Security Ties with the West

Ukraine shall sever all security agreements and military cooperation with the United States, NATO, and other Western countries.

Ukraine shall withdraw from any defense pacts, security arrangements, or other military collaborations with Western states or entities.

Article 3: Outlawing the Bandera Movement

Ukraine shall outlaw the Bandera movement and any affiliated groups or organizations that promote extremist ideologies or actions.

Ukraine shall ensure that any individuals or groups associated with the Bandera movement are disbanded and prosecuted in accordance with its domestic laws.

Article 4: Territorial Adjustments

The Russian Federation shall retain sovereignty over the four annexed oblasts of Donetsk, Luhansk, Zaporizhzhia, and Kherson, which are predominantly Russian-speaking regions.

The borders of these oblasts shall be recognized by all Parties as final and inviolable.

Article 5: Security Guarantees

Both Parties commit to respecting Ukraine's sovereignty and territorial integrity within the new borders as defined by this treaty.

The Parties agree to refrain from any military actions, subversion, or interference in Ukraine's internal affairs.

Article 6: Economic and Humanitarian Cooperation

The Parties agree to work together to ensure the safe return of refugees and internally displaced persons to their homes in Ukraine or the annexed territories.

Economic sanctions related to the conflict shall be lifted by the Parties within a mutually agreed timeframe following the full implementation of this treaty.

Article 7: Monitoring and Verification

A joint commission, with representatives from neutral countries and international organizations, shall be established to monitor and verify the implementation of this treaty.

The commission shall report to the United Nations Security Council on the progress of the treaty's implementation.

Article 8: Dispute Resolution

Any disputes arising from the interpretation or implementation of this treaty shall be resolved through diplomatic channels or, if necessary, arbitration by a mutually agreed third party.

Article 9: Final Provisions

This treaty shall enter into force upon signature by the authorized representatives of the Parties and ratification by their respective governments.

This treaty shall be deposited with the United Nations, and the Secretary-General shall serve as the depositary of the treaty.

Signatories

In witness whereof, the undersigned, being duly authorized by their respective governments, have signed this treaty.

For the United States of America: [Signature]

For the Russian Federation: [Signature]

Date: [Day, Month, Year]

Location: Istanbul, Turkey

***

On Archaia 9, Colonel Richard Kemp came across the airwaves to the city rulers, saying, 'Yes. As far as we know, the wormhole has closed.'

The Minister for External Actions asked, 'So you confirm that no one on Earth is any the wiser? That Helen "Anella" Moskva has returned? '

'Affirmed. Because of the external action, Lee Ross would have died on 1 November 2024. A giant wave off Koh Tao capsized him and smashed him onto the granite rocks of Cape Ja Te Kang. Our action saved him. It also saved humanity because of his actions in the Russo-Ukrainian war. But as you know, his death was only postponed. The wormhole had to close. We decided the best location was North Cape, before the end of the negotiations.'

'And now?'

'The wormhole closed, Ross is dead, Moskva has returned and Earth is once again a closed deterministic system. We're out.'

THE END